HARLAN ELLISON

TROUBLEMAKERS

HARLAN ELLISON has been called "one of the great living American short story writers" by the *Washington Post*. The *Los Angeles Times* has said, "It's long past time for Harlan Ellison to be awarded the title: 20th century Lewis Carroll." In a career spanning fifty years, he has won more awards for the 74 books he has written or edited, the more than 1700 stories, essays, articles, and newspaper columns, the two dozen teleplays and a dozen motion pictures he has created, than any other living fantasist. He has won the Hugo award $8\frac{1}{2}$ times, the Nebula three times, the Bram Stoker Award, presented by the Horror Writers Association, five times (including the Lifetime Achievement Award in 1996), the Edgar Allan Poe Award of the Mystery Writers of America twice, the Georges Méliès fantasy film award twice, and the Silver Pen for Journalism by P.E.N., the international writers' union. He is also the only author in Hollywood ever to win the Writers Guild of America award for Most Outstanding Teleplay (solo work) four times, most recently for "Paladin of the Lost Hour," 1987, *The Twilight Zone.* In March, 1998, the National Women's Committee of Brandeis University honored him with their Words, Wit & Wisdom award. He recently completed the screenplay for Dimension Films, *Demon with a Glass Hand*, to be directed by David Twohy.

OTHER BOOKS BY HARLAN ELLISON

Novels:

Web of the City (1958); *The Sound of a Scythe* (1960); *Spider Kiss* (1961).

Short Novels:

Doomsman (1967); *All the Lies That Are My Life* (1980); *Run for the Stars* (1991); *Mefisto in Onyx* (1993).

Graphic Novels:

Demon with a Glass Hand (adapted with Marshall Rogers; 1986); *Night and the Enemy* (adapted with Ken Steacy, 1987); *Vic and Blood: The Chronicles of A Boy and His Dog* (adapted with Richard Corben, 1989); *Harlan Ellison's Dream Corridor* (1996).

Short Story Collections:

The Deadly Streets (1958); *A Touch of Infinity* (1960); *Children of the Streets* (1961); *Gentleman Junkie and Other Stories of the Hung-Up Generation* (1961); *Ellison Wonderland* (1962); *Paingod and Other Delusions* (1965); *I Have No Mouth & I Must Scream* (1967); *From the Land of Fear* (1967); *Love Ain't Nothing But Sex Misspelled* (1968); *The Beast That Shouted Love at the Heart of the World* (1969); *Over the Edge* (1970); *All the Sounds of Fear* (British publication only—1973); *The Time of the Eye* (British publication only—1974); *Approaching Oblivion* (1974); *Deathbird Stories* (1974); *No Doors, No Windows* (1975); *Strange Wine* (1978); *Shatterday* (1980); *Stalking the Nightmare* (1982); *Angry Candy* (1988); *Mind Fields* (with Jacek Yerka, 1994); Slippage (1997); *The Essential Ellison: A Fifty-Year Retrospective* (2001).

Non-Fiction and Essay Collections:

Memos from Purgatory (1961); *The Glass Teat, Essays of Opinion on Television* (1970); *The Other Glass Teat, Further Essays of Opinion on Television; The Book of Ellison* (1978); *Sleepless Nights in the Procrustean Bed,* (1984); *An Edge in My Voice* (1985); *Harlan Ellison's Watching* (1989); *The Harlan Ellison Hornbook* (1990).

TROUBLEMAKERS

Stories by

HARLAN ELLISON

an EDGEWORKS ABBEY offering

in association with

ibooks

new york

www.ibooksinc.com

DISTRIBUTED BY SIMON & SCHUSTER, INC

Distributed by Simon & Schuster, Inc.
1230 Avenue of the American, New York, NY 10020

ibooks, inc.
24 West 25th Street
New York, NY 10010

The ibooks World Wide Web Site Address is:
http://www.ibooksinc.com
Harlan Ellison website: www.Harlanellison.com

ISBN 0-7434-2398-4
First printing October 2001
10 9 8 7 6 5 4 3 2 1

Cover designed by Mike Rivilis and j.vita
Interior design by Westchester Book Composition

Printed in the U.S.A.

This one is for my
long-time partner in crime,
the great cinematic auteur,

JIM WYNORSKI

CONTENTS

CONTENTS

TROUBLEMAKERS:
Stories by
HARLAN ELLISON

INTRODUCTION:
"THAT KID'S GONNA WIND UP IN JAIL!"

No use pretending: too many of the "young people" (whatever *that* means, 4–6 year olds, 10–13, 15–20ish?) I'm thrown into contact with these days are, in the words of Daffy Duck, maroons . . . *ultra*maroons. Dumb, apathetic, surly, dumb, arrogant, semiliterate, dumb, disrespectful, oblivious to what's going on around them, ethically barren, dishonorable, crushed by peer pressure and tv advertising into consumer conformity, crude, dumb, slaves to the lowest manifestations of cheap crap popular culture (as, for instance, WWF wrestling; boy bands; idiot Image comics featuring prepubescent fanboy representations of women with the vacuous stares of cheerleaders, all legs and bare butts, with breasts like casaba melons grafted to their chests at neck level; horse-trank home-made mosh-pit Xtasy kitty-flippin' dope; and Old Navy rags that make everyone look like a bag lady or wetbrain bindlestiff with a sagging pants-load), inclined to respond to even minor inconveniences with anger or violence because they've been brainwashed into believing everything they want, they ought to have, and everything ought to be given to them free, and oh yeah . . . did I mention they're dumb? Did I mention, also, that they're ignorant as a sack of doorknobs? Which ain't *exactly* the same as dumb.

And isn't that *exactly* what you needed today, on a day that has already been as friendly as a paper cut? Smartmouth from some total stranger 'way older than you, some guy you never heard of before, comes on fronting you with his "young people suck" riff, tripping on you before you even know what you did wrong to get this geezer so on a mission. Very nice, very cool. Yeah, you say: I gotcher cool right here.

So okay, I'm not talking about *all* teenaged kids. Just the ones *you* have to deal with every day. The pinheads, the bullies, the mean little rats who laugh at you behind your back or right to your face because you're too fat or too scrawny or too tall or too short or you can't control the farts or you bump into things all the time or you got a helluva acne plague this week or your mommy dressed you weird or you speak with an accent, or you're good at sports but the other creeps think you're just a big dumb ox, or you really like to read and you get decent grades but the jocks and sosch skanks think you're the Prince of the Kingdom of Geek.

Not *all* "young people," just the lames who bust *your* chops. Yeah, all of 'em . . . they should itch forever with no scratch available. They should break a leg or two.

When I was your age, they were on me, too.

That's who this guy snarling at you claims to be. The kid who was there, same place as you, before you got here. And I've got this book of stories that definitely won't save your life, or get you off crystal-meth, or turn your academic slide into a climb back up, or even clear up your acne.

It's a book about some of the kinds of trouble we all get into. The stuff that seems to be a good idea at the time, but turns out to be six months in rehab or a beef in the juvie hall of your choice. Trouble has been my middle name since I was two—three years old. Yeah, that far back, I was the one they always swore was gonna wind up in jail or lying in a gutter with UPS trucks splashing garbage and mud on my wretched carcass. Well, it didn't happen. I've got fame and money, and skill and a great wife, and a boss home. And now they ask me to put together a book for youse guys.

Well, imagine my surprise. Not to mention my nervousness. I do a lot of high school and college lecturing, and it's not at all like what it was, hell, even *ten* years ago. Today, when I confront an audience of "young people" I get more mood 'n' tude than a serial killer trying to cop a plea. So, like a jerk, I get really honked at them and start insulting the audience.

And here's what *really* fries my frijoles . . .

They *take* it!

They don't learn from it, they don't get openly upset by it, they just sit there and pout like babies. And so, I've packed it in, pretty much. Not like it was when I did colleges in the '60s and '70s, when everyone was questioning and smart about what was happening in this country, when "young people" really had things to rebel against, instead of being upset that they're not allowed to play their Gameboy in class.

So here's this book of weird little stories, something like a modern-day version of Aesop's Fables, except not really. A book of warnings, what we call "gardyloos." With lessons to be learned that come out of my own corrupt and devilish adolescence.

Careful, though. Gardyloo! I am nobody's hero, and I am as fu-- well, you know what I mean, I'm as messed up as you. So read the stories for pleasure, and if they make you grin or scare you a little, and you turn out okay as an adult, and you get rich . . . send me some money.

Because I'm just a poor old guy trying to make a sparse

living in a world full of "young people" who are smarter than I, cleverer than I, faster than I; and I'm just about on the verge of becoming like y'know a "bag lady" kind of guy, gnawing the heads off rats, peeing in doorways, begging from door to door. So, when these stories make you rich and famous, and they've just completely like y'know *altered* your life, send me a couple of bucks.

Because I love you folks, you know that, doncha?

I just love ya.

(And while we're at it, I'd like to sell you some shares in the Panda Farm I've got growing in my butt. Very reasonable.)

Yr. pal, Harlan.

HARLAN ELLISON
Sherman Oaks, California

ON THE DOWNHILL SIDE

Here's one of the few Secret Truths I've learned for certain, having been "on the road" since I was thirteen and ran away. (Had nothing to do with my folks; they didn't beat me; I was a restless kid, wanted to see the world.) The Truth is this: most of the reasons we give for having done something or other, usually something that got us yelled at or grounded or busted, most of the reasons we dream up are horse-puckey. (I'd use the B-word, but libraries are going to be stocking this book.) All those reasons and excuses are just lame rationalizations, and they only tick off the people yelling at you. So shine 'em on. Forget them. The only reason that makes any sense is "It *seemed* like a good idea at the time." Lame though it may be, it's the Truth. "Why did you bust that window?" It *seemed* like a good idea at the time. "Why did you get hung up on that guy/girl when you knew it was a destructive hookup?" It *seemed* like a good idea at the time. "Why did you do that lump of crack?" It *seemed* . . . well, you get it. Too bad the guy in this first story didn't get it, because the True Answer to why you fell in love with someone who ranked & hurt you is . . . it *seemed* like . . .

In love, there is always one who kisses and one who offers the cheek.

—French proverb

I knew she was a virgin because she was able to ruffle the silken mane of my unicorn. Named Lizette, she was a Grecian temple in which no sacrifice had ever been made. Vestal virgin of New Orleans, found walking without shadow in the thankgod coolness of cockroach-crawling Louisiana night. My unicorn whinnied, inclined his head, and she stroked the ivory spiral of his horn.

Much of this took place in what is called the Irish Channel, a strip of street in old New Orleans where the lace curtain micks had settled decades before; now the Irish were gone and the Cubans had taken over the Channel. Now the Cubans were sleeping, recovering from the muggy today that held within its hours the *déjà vu* of muggy yesterday, the *déjà rêvé* of intolerable tomorrow. Now the crippled bricks of side streets off Magazine had given up their nightly ghosts, and one such phantom had come to me, calling my unicorn to her—thus, clearly, a virgin—and I stood waiting.

Had it been Sutton Place, had it been a Manhattan evening, and had we met, she would have kneeled to pet my dog. And I would have waited. Had it been Puerto Vallarta, had it been 20° 36' N, 105° 13' W, and had we met, she would have crouched to run her fingertips over the oil-slick hide of my iguana. And I would have waited. Meeting in streets requires ritual. One must wait and not breathe too loud, if one is to enjoy the congress of the nightly ghosts.

She looked across the fine head of my unicorn and smiled at me. Her eyes were a shade of gray between onyx and miscalculation. "Is it a bit chilly for you?" I asked.

"When I was thirteen," she said, linking my arm, taking a tentative two steps that led me with her, up the street, "or perhaps I was twelve, well no matter, when I was that approximate age, I had a marvelous shawl of Belgian lace. I could look through it and see the mysteries of the sun and the other stars unriddled. I'm sure someone important and very nice has purchased that shawl from an antique dealer, and paid handsomely for it."

It seemed not a terribly responsive reply to a simple question.

"A queen of the Mardi Gras Ball doesn't get chilly," she added, unasked. I walked along beside her, the cool evasiveness of her arm binding us, my mind a welter of answer choices, none satisfactory.

Behind us, my unicorn followed silently. Well, not entirely silently. His platinum hoofs clattered on the bricks. I'm afraid I felt a straight pin of jealousy. Perfection does that to me.

"When were you queen of the Ball?"

The date she gave me was one hundred and thirteen years before.

It must have been brutally cold down there in the stones.

There is a little book they sell, a guide to manners and dining in New Orleans: I've looked: nowhere in the book do they indicate the proper responses to a ghost. But then, it says nothing about the wonderful cemeteries of New Orleans' West Bank, or Metairie. Or the gourmet dining at such locations. One seeks, in vain, through the mutable, mercurial universe, for the compleat guide. To everything. And, failing in the search, one makes do the best one can. And suffers the frustration, suffers the ennui.

Perfection does that to me.

We walked for some time, and grew to know each other, as best we'd allow. These are some of the high points. They lack continuity. I don't apologize, I merely point it out, adding with some truth, I feel, that *most* liaisons lack continuity. We find ourselves in odd places at various times, and for a brief span we link our lives to others—even as Lizette had linked her arm with mine—and then, our time elapsed, we move apart. Through a haze of pain occasionally; usually through a veil of memory that clings, then passes; sometimes as though we have never touched.

"My name is Paul Ordahl," I told her. "And the most awful thing that ever happened to me was my first wife, Bernice. I don't know how else to put it—even if it sounds melodramatic, it's simply what happened—she went insane, and I divorced her, and her mother had her committed to a private mental home."

"When I was eighteen," Lizette said, "my family gave me my coming-out party. We were living in the Garden District, on Prytania Street. The house was a lovely white Plantation—they call them antebellum now—with Grecian pillars.

We had a persimmon-green gazebo in the rear gardens, directly beside a weeping willow. It was six-sided. Octagonal. Or is that hexagonal? It was the loveliest party. And while it was going on, I sneaked away with a boy . . . I don't remember his name . . . and we went into the gazebo, and I let him touch my breasts. I don't remember his name."

We were on Decatur Street, walking toward the French Quarter; the Mississippi was on our right, dark but making its presence known.

"Her mother was the one had her committed, you see. I only heard from them twice after the divorce. It had been four stinking years and I really didn't want any more of it. Once, after I'd started making some money, the mother called and said Bernice had to be put in the state asylum. There wasn't enough money to pay for the private home any more. I sent a little; not much. I suppose I could have sent more, but I was remarried, there was a child from her previous marriage. I didn't want to send any more. I told the mother not to call me again. There was only once after that . . . it was the most terrible thing that ever happened to me."

We walked around Jackson Square, looking in at the very black grass, reading the plaques bolted to the spear-topped fence, plaques telling how New Orleans had once belonged to the French. We sat on one of the benches in the street. The street had been closed to traffic, and we sat on one of the benches.

"Our name was Charbonnet. Can you say that?"

I said it, with a good accent.

"I married a very wealthy man. He was in real estate. At one time he owned the entire block where the *Vieux Carré* now stands, on Bourbon Street. He admired me greatly. He came and sought my hand, and my *maman* had to strike the bargain because my father was too weak to do it; he drank.

I can admit that now. But it didn't matter, I'd already found out how my suitor was set financially. He wasn't common, but he wasn't quality, either. But he was wealthy and I married him. He gave me presents. I did what I had to do. But I refused to let him make love to me after he became friends with that awful Jew who built the Metairie Cemetery over the race track because they wouldn't let him race his Jew horses. My husband's name was Dunbar. Claude Dunbar, you may have heard the name? Our parties were *de rigueur*."

"Would you like some coffee and *beignets* at du Monde?"

She stared at me for a moment, as though she wanted me to say something more, then she nodded and smiled.

We walked around the Square. My unicorn was waiting at the curb. I scratched his rainbow flank and he struck a spark off the cobblestones with his right front hoof. "I know," I said to him, "we'll soon start the downhill side. But not just yet. Be patient. I won't forget you."

Lizette and I went inside the Café du Monde and I ordered two coffees with warm milk and two orders of *beignets* from a waiter who was originally from New Jersey but had lived most of his life only a few miles from College Station, Texas.

There was a coolness coming off the levee.

"I was in New York," I said. "I was receiving an award at an architects' convention—did I mention I was an architect— yes, that's what I was at the time, an architect—and I did a television interview. The mother saw me on the program, and checked the newspapers to find out what hotel we were using for the convention, and she got my room number and called me. I had been out quite late after the banquet where I'd gotten my award, quite late. I was sitting on the side of the bed, taking off my shoes, my tuxedo tie hanging from my unbuttoned collar, getting ready just to throw clothes on the floor and sink away, when the phone rang. It was the mother. She was a terrible person, one of the worst I ever knew, a shrike, a terrible, just a terrible person. She started telling me about Bernice in the asylum. How they had her in this little room and how she stared out the window most of the time. She'd reverted to childhood, and most of the time she couldn't even recognize the mother; but when she did, she'd say something like, 'Don't let them hurt me, Mommy, don't let them hurt me.' So I asked her what she wanted me to do, did she want money for Bernice or what . . . did she want me to go see her since I was in New York . . . and she said God no. And then she did an awful thing to me. She said the last time she'd been to see Bernice, my ex-wife had turned around and put her finger to her lips and said, 'Shhh, we have to be very quiet. Paul is working.' And I swear, a snake uncoiled in my stomach. It was the most terrible thing I'd ever heard. No matter how secure you are that you honest to God had *not* sent someone to a madhouse, there's always that little core of doubt, and saying what she'd said just burned out my head. I couldn't even think about it, couldn't even really *hear* it, or it would have collapsed me. So down came these iron walls and I just kept on talking, and after a while she hung up.

"It wasn't till two years later that I allowed myself to think about it, and then I cried; it had been a long time since I'd cried. Oh, not because I believed that nonsense about a man isn't supposed to cry, but just because I guess there hadn't been anything that important to cry *about*. But when I let myself hear what she'd said, I started crying, and just went on and on till I finally went in and looked into the bathroom mirror and I asked myself, face-to-face, if I'd done that, if I'd ever made her be quiet so I could work on blueprints or drawings . . .

"And after a while I saw myself shaking my head no, and it was easier. That was perhaps three years before I died."

She licked the powdered sugar from the *beignets* off her fingers, and launched into a long story about a lover she had taken. She didn't remember his name.

It was sometime after midnight. I'd thought midnight would signal the start of the downhill side, but the hour had passed, and we were still together, and she didn't seem ready to vanish. We left the Café du Monde and walked into the Quarter.

I despise Bourbon Street. The strip joints, with the pasties over nipples, the smell of need, the dwarfed souls of men attuned only to flesh. The noise.

We walked through it like art connoisseurs at a showing of motel room paintings. She continued to talk about her life, about the men she had known, about the way they had loved her, the ways in which she had spurned them, and about the trivia of her past existence. I continued to talk about my loves, about all the women I had held dear in my heart for however long each had been linked with me. We talked across each other, our conversation at right angles, only meeting in the intersections of silence at story's end.

She wanted a julep and I took her to the Royal Orleans Hotel and we sat in silence as she drank. I watched her, studying that phantom face, seeking for even the smallest flicker of light off the ice in her eyes, hoping for an indication that glacial melting could be forthcoming. But there was nothing, and I burned to say correct words that might cause heat. She drank and reminisced about evenings with young men in similar hotels, a hundred years before.

We went to a night club where a flamenco dancer and his two-woman troupe performed on a stage of unpolished woods, their star-shining black shoes setting up resonances in me that I chose to ignore.

Then I realized there were only three couples in the club, and that the extremely pretty flamenco dancer was playing to Lizette. He gripped the lapels of his bolero jacket and clattered his heels against the stage like a man driving nails. She watched him, and her tongue made a wholly obvious flirtatious trip around the rim of her liquor glass. There was a two-drink minimum, and as I have never liked the taste of alcohol, she was more than willing to prevent waste by drinking mine as well as her own. Whether she was getting drunk or simply indulging herself, I do not know. It didn't matter. I became blind with jealousy, and dragons took possession of my eyes.

When the dancer was finished, when his half hour show was concluded, he came to our table. His suit was skintight and the color of Arctic lakes. His hair was curly and moist from his exertions, and his prettiness infuriated me. There was a scene. He asked her name, I interposed a comment, he tried to be polite, sensing my ugly mood, she overrode my comment, he tried again in Castilian, *th*-ing his *esses*, she answered, I rose and shoved him, there was a scuffle. We were asked to leave.

Once outside, she walked away from me.

My unicorn was at the curb, eating from a porcelain *Sèvres* soup plate filled with *flan*. I watched her walk unsteadily up the street toward Jackson Square. I scratched my unicorn's neck and he stopped eating the egg custard. He looked at me for a long moment. Ice crystals were sparkling in his mane.

We were on the downhill side.

"Soon, old friend," I said.

He dipped his elegant head toward the plate. "I see you've been to the Las Americas. When you return the plate, give my best to *Señor* Pena."

I followed her up the street. She was walking rapidly toward the Square. I called to her, but she wouldn't stop.

She began dragging her left hand along the steel bars of the fence enclosing the Square. Her fingertips thudded softly from bar to bar, and once I heard the chitinous *clak* of a manicured nail.

"Lizette!"

She walked faster, dragging her hand across the dark metal bars.

"Lizette! Damn it!"

I was reluctant to run after her; it was somehow terribly demeaning. But she was getting farther and farther away. There were bums in the Square, sitting slouched on the benches, their arms out along the backs. Itinerants, kids with beards and knapsacks. I was suddenly frightened for her. Impossible. She had been dead for a hundred years. There was no reason for it . . . I was afraid for her!

I started running, the sound of my footsteps echoing up and around the Square. I caught her at the corner and dragged her around. She tried to slap me, and I caught her hand. She kept trying to hit me, to scratch my face with the manicured nails. I held her and swung her away from me, swung her around, and around, dizzyingly, trying to keep her off-balance. She swung wildly, crying out and saying things inarticulately. Finally, she stumbled and I pulled her in to me and held her tight against my body.

"Stop it! Stop, Lizette! I . . . *stop it!*" She went limp against me and I felt her crying against my chest. I took her into the shadows and my unicorn came down Decatur Street and stood under a streetlamp, waiting.

The chimera winds rose. I heard them, and knew we were well on the downhill side, that time was growing short. I held her close and smelled the woodsmoke scent of her hair. "Listen to me," I said, softly, close to her. "Listen to me, Lizette. Our time's almost gone. This is our last chance.

You've lived in stone for a hundred years; I've heard you cry. I've come there, to that place, night after night, and I've heard you cry. You've paid enough, God knows. So have I. We can *do* it. We've got one more chance, and we can make it, if you'll try. That's all I ask. Try."

She pushed away from me, tossing her head so the auburn hair swirled away from her face. Her eyes were dry. Ghosts can do that. Cry without making tears. Tears are denied us. Other things; I won't talk of them here.

"I lied to you," she said.

I touched the side of her face. The high cheekbone just at the hairline. "I know. My unicorn would never have let you touch him if you weren't pure. I'm not, but he has no choice with me. He was assigned to me. He's my familiar and he puts up with me. We're friends."

"No. Other lies. My life was a lie. I've told them all to you. We can't make it. You have to let me go."

I didn't know exactly where, but I knew how it would happen. I argued with her, trying to convince her there was a way for us. But she couldn't believe it, hadn't the strength or the will or the faith. Finally, I let her go.

She put her arms around my neck, and drew my face down to hers, and she held me that way for a few moments. Then the winds rose, and there were sounds in the night, the sounds of calling, and she left me there, in the shadows.

I sat down on the curb and thought about the years since I'd died. Years without much music. Light leached out. Wandering. Nothing to pace me but memories and the unicorn. How sad I was for *him*; assigned to me till I got my chance. And now it had come and I'd taken my best go, and failed.

Lizette and I were the two sides of the same coin; devalued and impossible to spend. Legal tender of nations long since vanished, no longer even names on the cracked papyrus of cartographers' maps. We had been snatched away from final rest, had been set adrift to roam for our crimes, and only once between death and eternity would we receive a chance. This night ... this night ... this nothing-special night ... this was our chance.

My unicorn came to me, then, and brushed his muzzle against my shoulder. I reached up and scratched around the base of his spiral horn, his favorite place. He gave a long, silvery sigh, and in that sound I heard the sentence I was serving on him, as well as myself. We had been linked, too. Assigned to one another by the One who had ordained this night's chance. But if I lost out, so did my unicorn; he who had wandered with me through all the soundless, lightless years.

I stood up. I was by no means ready to do battle, but at least I could stay in for the full ride ... all the way on the downhill side. "Do you know where they are?"

My unicorn started off down the street.

I followed, hopelessness warring with frustration. Dusk to dawn is the full ride, the final chance. After midnight is the downhill side. Time was short, and when time ran out there would be nothing for Lizette or me or my unicorn *but* time. Forever.

When we passed the Royal Orleans Hotel I knew where we were going. The sound of the Quarter had already faded. It was getting on toward dawn. The human lice had finally crawled into their flesh-mounds to sleep off the night of revelry. Though I had never experienced directly the New Orleans in which Lizette had grown up, I longed for the power to blot out the cancerous blight that Bourbon Street and the Quarter had become, with its tourist filth and screaming neon, to restore it to the colorful yet healthy state in which it had thrived a hundred years before. But I was only a ghost, not one of the gods with such powers, and at that moment I was almost at the end of the line held by one of those gods.

My unicorn turned down dark streets, heading always in the same general direction, and when I saw the first black shapes of the tombstones against the night sky, the *lightening* night sky, I knew I'd been correct in my assumption of destination.

The Saint Louis Cemetery.

Oh, how I sorrow for anyone who has never seen the world-famous Saint Louis Cemetery in New Orleans. It is the perfect graveyard, the complete graveyard, the finest graveyard in the universe. (There is a perfection in some designs that informs the function totally. There are Danish chairs that could be nothing *but* chairs, are so totally and completely *chair* that if the world as we know it ended, and a billion years from now the New Orleans horsy cockroaches became the dominant species, and they dug down through the alluvial layers, and found one of those chairs, even if they themselves did not use chairs, were not constructed physically for the use of chairs, had never seen a chair, *still* they would know it for what it had been made to be: a chair. Because it would be the essence of *chairness*. And from it, they could reconstruct the human race in replica. *That* is the kind of graveyard one means when one refers to the world-famous Saint Louis Cemetery.)

The Saint Louis Cemetery is ancient. It sighs with shadows and the comfortable bones and their afterimages of deaths that became great merely because those who died went to be interred in the Saint Louis Cemetery. The water table lies just eighteen inches below New Orleans—there are no graves in the earth for that reason. Bodies are entombed aboveground in crypts, in sepulchers, vaults, mausoleums. The gravestones are all different, no two alike, each one a testament to the stonecutter's art. Only secondarily testaments to those who lie beneath the markers.

We had reached the moment of final nightness. That ultimate moment before day began. Dawn had yet to fill the eastern sky, yet there was a warming of tone to the night; it was the last of the downhill side of my chance. Of Lizette's chance.

We approached the cemetery, my unicorn and I. From deep in the center of the skyline of stones beyond the fence I could see the ice-chill glow of a pulsing blue light. The light one finds in a refrigerator, cold and flat and brittle.

I mounted my unicorn, leaned close along his neck, clinging to his mane with both hands, knees tight to his silken sides, now rippling with light and color, and I gave a little hiss of approval, a little sound of go.

My unicorn sailed over the fence, into the world-famous Saint Louis Cemetery.

I dismounted and thanked him. We began threading our way between the tombstones, the sepulchers, the crypts.

The blue glow grew more distinct. And now I could hear the chimera winds rising, whirling, coming in off alien seas. The pulsing of the light, the wail of the winds, the night dying. My unicorn stayed close. Even we of the spirit world know when to be afraid.

After all, I was only operating off a chance; I was under no god's protection. Naked, even in death.

There is no fog in New Orleans.

Mist began to form around us.

Except sometimes in the winter, there is no fog in New Orleans.

I remembered the daybreak of the night I'd died. There had been mist. I had been a suicide.

My third wife had left me. She had gone away during the night, while I'd been at a business meeting with a client;

I had been engaged to design a church in Baton Rouge. All that day I'd steamed the old wallpaper off the apartment we'd rented. It was to have been our first home together, paid for by the commission. I'd done the steaming myself, with a tall ladder and a steam condenser and two flat pans with steam holes. Up near the ceiling the heat had been so awful I'd almost fainted. She'd brought me lemonade, freshly squeezed. Then I'd showered and changed and gone to my meeting. When I'd returned, she was gone. No note.

Lizette and I were two sides of the same coin, cast off after death for the opposite extremes of the same crime. She had never loved. I had loved too much. Overindulgence in something as delicate as love is to be found monstrously offensive in the eyes of the God of Love. And some of us—who have never understood the salvation in the Golden Mean—some of us are cast adrift with but one chance. It can happen.

Mist formed around us, and my unicorn crept close to me, somehow smaller, almost timid. We were moving into realms he did not understand, where his limited magics were useless. These were realms of potency so utterly beyond even the limbo creatures—such as my unicorn—so completely alien to even the intermediary zone wanderers—Lizette and myself—that we were as helpless and without understanding as those who live. We had only one advantage over living, breathing, as yet undead humans: we *knew* for certain that the realms on the other side existed.

Above, beyond, deeper: where the gods live. Where the One who had given me my chance, had given Lizette *her* chance, where He lived. Undoubtedly watching.

The mist swirled up around us, as chill and final as the dust of pharaohs' tombs.

We moved through it, toward the pulsing heart of blue light. And as we came into the penultimate circle, we stopped. We were in the outer ring of potency, and we saw the claiming things that had come for Lizette. She lay out on an altar of crystal, naked and trembling. They stood around her, enormously tall and transparent. Man shapes without faces. Within their transparent forms a strange, silvery fog swirled, like smoke from holy censers. Where eyes should have been on a man or a ghost, there were only dull flickering firefly glowings, inside, hanging in the smoke, moving, changing shape and position. No eyes at all. And tall, very tall, towering over Lizette and the altar.

For me, overcommitted to love, when dawn came without salvation, there was only an eternity of wandering, with my unicorn as sole companion. Ghost forevermore. Incense chimera viewed as dust-devil on the horizon, chilling as I passed in city streets, forever gone, invisible, lost, empty, helpless, wandering.

But for her, empty vessel, the fate was something else entirely. The God of Love had allowed her the time of wandering, trapped by day in stones, freed at night to wander. He had allowed her the final chance. And having failed to take it, her fate was with these claiming creatures, gods themselves . . . of another order . . . higher or lower I had no idea. But terrible.

"Lagniappe!" I screamed the word. The old Creole word they use in New Orleans when they want a little extra; a bonus of *croissants*, a few additional carrots dumped into the shopping bag, a baker's dozen, a larger portion of clams or crabs or shrimp. *"Lagniappe!* Lizette, take a little more! Try for the extra! Try . . . demand it . . . there's time . . . you have it coming to you . . . you've paid . . . I've paid . . . it's ours . . . *try!"*

She sat up, her naked body lit by lambent fires of chill blue cold from the other side. She sat up and looked across the inner circle to me, and I stood there with my arms out, trying desperately to break through the outer circle to her. But it was solid and I could not pass. Only virgins could pass.

And they would not let her go. They had been promised a feed, and they were there to claim. I began to cry, as I had cried when I finally heard what the mother had said, when I finally came home to the empty apartment and knew I had spent my life loving too much, demanding too much, myself a feeder at a board that *could* be depleted and emptied and serve up no more. She wanted to come to me, I could *see* she wanted to come to me. But they would have their meal.

Then I felt the muzzle of my unicorn at my neck, and in a step he had moved through the barrier that was impenetrable to me, and he moved across the circle and stood waiting. Lizette leaped from the altar and ran to me.

It all happened at the same time. I felt Lizette's body anchor in to mine, and *we* saw my unicorn standing over there on the other side, and for a moment *we* could not summon up the necessary reactions, the correct sounds. *We* knew for the first time in either our lives or our deaths what it was to be paralyzed. Then reactions began washing over me, *we*, us in wave after wave: cascading joy that Lizette had come to . . . us; utter love for this Paul ghost creature; realization that instinctively part of us was falling into the same pattern again; fear that that part would love too much at this mystic juncture; resolve to temper our love; and then anguish at the sight of our unicorn standing there, waiting to be claimed . . .

We called to him . . . using his secret name, one *we* had never spoken aloud. *We* could barely speak. Weight pulled at his throat, our throats. "Old friend . . ." We took a step toward him but could not pass the barrier. Lizette clung to me, Paul held me tight as I trembled with terror and the cold of that inner circle still frosting my flesh.

The great transparent claimers stood silently, watching, waiting, as if content to allow us our moments of final decision. But their impatience could be felt in the air, a soft purring, like the death rattle always in the throat of a cat. "Come back! Not for me ... don't do it for me ... it's not fair!"

Paul's unicorn turned his head and looked at us.

My friend of starless nights, when we had gone sailing together through the darkness. My friend who had walked with me on endless tours of empty places. My friend of gentle nature and constant companionship. Until Lizette, my friend, my only friend, my familiar assigned to an onerous task, who had come to love me and to whom I had belonged, even as he had belonged to me.

I could not bear the hurt that grew in my chest, in my stomach; my head was on fire, my eyes burned with tears first for Paul, and now for the sweetest creature a God had ever sent to temper a man's anguish ... and for myself. I could not bear the thought of never knowing—as Paul had known it—the silent company of that gentle, magical beast.

But he turned back, and moved to them, and they took that as final decision, and the great transparent claimers moved in around him, and their quickglass hands reached down to touch him, and for an instant they seemed to hesitate, and I called out, "Don't be afraid ..." and my unicorn turned his head to look across the mist of potency for the last time, and I saw he *was* afraid, but not as much as he would have been if *we* had not been there.

Then the first of them touched his smooth, silvery flank and he gave a trembling sigh of pain. A ripple ran down his hide. Not the quick flesh movement of ridding himself of a fly, but a completely alien, unnatural tremor, containing in its swiftness all the agony and loss of eternities. A sigh went out from Paul's unicorn, though he had not uttered it.

We could feel the pain, the loneliness. My unicorn with no time left to him. Ending. All was now a final ending; he had stayed with me, walked with me, and had grown to care for me, until that time when he would be released from his duty by that special God; but now freedom was to be denied him; an ending.

The great transparent claimers all touched him, their ice fingers caressing his warm hide as we watched, helpless, Lizette's face buried in Paul's chest. Colors surged across my unicorn's body, as if by becoming more intense the chill touch of the claimers could be beaten off. Pulsing waves of rainbow color that lived in his hide for moments, then dimmed, brightened again and were bled off. Then the colors leaked away one by one, chroma weakening: purple-blue, manganese violet, discord, cobalt blue, doubt, affection, chrome green, chrome yellow, raw sienna, contemplation, alizarin crimson, irony, silver, severity, compassion, cadmium red, white.

They emptied him . . . he did not fight them . . . going colder and colder . . . flickers of yellow, a whisper of blue, pale as white . . . the tremors blending into one constant shudder . . . the wonderful golden eyes rolled in torment, went flat, brightness dulled, flat metal . . . the platinum hoofs caked with rust . . . and he stood, did not try to escape, gave himself for us . . . and he was emptied. Of everything. Then, like the claimers, we could see through him. Vapors swirled within the transparent husk, a fogged glass, shimmering . . . then nothing. And then they absorbed even the husk.

The chill blue light faded, and the claimers grew indistinct in our sight. The smoke within them seemed thicker, moved more slowly, horribly, as though they had fed and were sluggish and would go away, back across the line to that dark place where they waited, always waited, till their hunger was aroused again. And my unicorn was gone. I was alone with Lizette. I was alone with Paul. The mist died away, and the claimers were gone, and once more it was merely a cemetery as the first rays of the morning sun came easing through the tumble and disarray of headstones.

We stood together as one, her naked body white and virginal in my weary arms; and as the light of the sun struck us *we* began to fade, to merge, to mingle our bodies and our wandering spirits one into the other, forming one spirit that would neither love too much, nor too little, having taken our chance on the downhill side.

We faded and were lifted invisibly on the scented breath of that good god who had owned us, and were taken away from there. To be born again as one spirit, in some other human form, man or woman we did not know which. Nor would we remember. Nor did it matter.

This time, love would not destroy us. This time out, we would have luck.

The luck of silken mane and rainbow colors, platinum hoofs and spiral horn.

A LOT OF SAUCERS

I don't know about you, but I hate it when the coming attractions trailers at the Cineplex give away the whole plot of the flick they want me to pay megabucks to see next week. Same for when they do it on television, or in a review of some book, and they print one of those idiot "spoiler warning" lines—as if we had the self-control to stop reading, or watching. So I don't want to give away the punchline of this next story, but I need to put in right here what the troublemaker "lesson" is. So let me be even more obscure than usual. Pay attention: not everything in life is what it seems to be. On the other hand, this psychologist named Sigmund Freud once said, "Sometimes a cigar is just a cigar," meaning not everything is necessarily a symbol for something else, in this case a phallic symbol (you could look it up). We are usually afraid of, or suspicious of, that which we don't understand; that which is unfamiliar. So before you start seeing enemies under the bed, and thinking somebody who dresses or looks or sounds different from you is a threat, remember the old story about the mouse (or squirrel, or frog, whichever version you heard) who is out on this road at midnight in the wintertime, and he's freezing his mouse, squirrel or frog butt off, and along comes this big horse, and he sees the creature is turning blue and about to die (or in the case of the frog, to croak), and he drops a big, fat, steaming, smelly road muffin on him. It may be foul in there, but at least he's warm, and his life is saved. Until a fox comes along, sees him all nice and toasty, his head sticking out, and fox takes a bite and yanks out the itty-bitty critter, and eats him. The moral being: not everybody who dumps you *in* the sh-t is an enemy; not everybody who pulls you *out* of the sh-t is a friend. Sometimes things are simpler than they seem. Sometimes all you're afraid of is your own ignorance.

It wasn't just one sighting, or a covey, or a hundred. It was five thousand. Exactly five thousand of them, and all at the same time. They appeared in the skies over Earth instantaneously.

One instant the sky was empty and grey and flecked with cloud formations... the next they blotted out the clouds, and cast huge, elliptical shadows along the ground.

They were miles in diameter, and perfectly round, and there was no questioning—even for an incredulous second—that they were from outer space somewhere. They hung a mile above the Earth, over the 30th parallel. Over Los Angeles and the Sahara Desert and Baghdad and the Canary Islands and over Shanghai. There was no great empty space left between them, for they girdled the Earth with a band of discs. Where everyone could see them, so no one could doubt their power or their menace.

Yet they hung silently. As though waiting.

Waiting.

* * *

"The perplexing thing about it, General, is that every once in a while, one of them just goes *flick!* and disappears. In a little while another one *flicks!* and takes its place. Not the same one, either. We can tell. There are different markings on them. Nobody can figure it out."

Alberts was a Captain, properly deferential to the Commanding General. He was short, but dapper; clothes hung well on him; hair thinning across his skull; eyes alert, and a weariness in the softness and line of his body: a man who had been too long in grade, too long as Captain, with Colonel's rank out of reach. He folded his hands across his paunch, finished his speech, and settled back in the chair.

He stared across the desk at the General. The General steepled his blocky fingers, rocked back and forth in the big leather chair. He stared at his Adjutant with a veiled expression. Adjutant: the politically correct word for assistant, second-in-charge, gopher, the guy who actually got the job done. The General had found Alberts when he was a Second Looey, and knew he had a treasure when Alberts solved ten thorny problems in two days. He wasn't about to upgrade this Captain . . . he needed him right there, serving the General's needs. Adjutant: it sounded better than slave.

"How long—to the hour—have they been here now, Captain?" His tone was almost chiding, definitely aggressive.

He waited silently for an answer as the Adjutant leafed through a folder, consulted his watch, and closed his eyes in figuring. Finally the Adjutant leaned forward and said, "Three days, eight and one-half hours, General."

"And nothing has been done about them yet," the heavy-faced Air Force man replied. It was not a question; it was a statement, and one that demanded either an explanation or an alibi.

The Adjutant knew he had no explanation, so he offered the alibi. "But, General, what *can* we do? We don't dare scramble a flight of interceptors. Those things are almost four miles around, and there's no telling what they'd do if we made a hostile move . . . or even a move that *looked* hostile.

"We don't know where they come from or what they want. Or what's inside them. But if they were smart enough to *get* here, they're surely smart enough to stop any offensive action we might take. We're stuck, General. Our hands are tied."

The General leaned forward, and his sharp blue eyes caught the Adjutant's face in a vise-lock stare. "Captain, don't you *ever* use that word around me. The first thing I learned, when I was a plebe at West Point, was that the hands of the United States Air Force are *never* tied. You understand that?"

The Captain shifted uneasily, made an accepting motion with his hand. "Yes, but, General . . . what . . ."

"I said *never*, Captain Alberts! And by that I mean you'd better get out there and do something, right now."

The Adjutant rose hastily to his feet, slid the chair back an inch, and saluted briskly. Turning on his heel, he left the office, a frozen frown on his face. For the first time since he'd gotten this cushy job with the General, it looked as though there was going to be work involved. Worse, it might be dangerous.

Captain Harold Alberts, Adjutant, was terribly frightened, for the first time since he'd been appointed to the General's staff.

The saucers seemed to be holding a tight formation. They hovered, and lowered not an inch. They were separated by a half mile of empty space on either side, but were easily close enough to pick off anyone flying between them . . . should that be their intent.

They were huge things, without conning bubbles or landing gear, without any visible projections of any sort. Their skins were of some non-reflective metal, for it could be seen that the sun was glinting on them, yet was casting no burst of radiance. It made the possibility that this was some super-strong metal seem even more possible. They were silent behemoths, around which the air lanes of the world had had to be shifted. They did not move, nor did they show evidence of life. They were two cymbals, laid dead face-on-face.

They were simply *there*, and what sort of contesting could there be to that?

Every few hours, at irregular intervals (with no pattern that could be clocked or computed) one of the ships would disappear. Over the wasted sands of the Sahara, or above the crowded streets of Shanghai, or high over the neon of Las Vegas, one of the ships would waver for an instant, as though being washed by some invisible wave, then *flick!* and it would be gone. And in that moment the sun would stream through, covering the area that had been shadowed by the elliptical darkness. Shortly thereafter—but only sometimes shortly; occasionally a full hour or two would elapse—another ship would appear in the vanished one's spot. It would not be the same ship, because the one that had disappeared might have been ringed with blue lines, while this new one had a large green dot at its top-center.

But there it was, right in place, a half mile away from each neighbor on either side, and casting that fearful shadow along the ground.

Storm clouds formed above them, and spilled their contents down. The rain washed across their smooth, metallic tops, and ran off, to soak the ground a mile beneath.

They made no move, and they offered no hostility, but—as the hardware dealer in San Francisco said—"My God, the things could *blast* us at any second!" And—as the Berber tribesman, talking to his dromedary-mounted fellows said— "Even if they hang silent, they come from *somewhere,* and I'm frightened, terribly frightened."

So it went, for a week, with the terror clogging the throats of Earthmen around the world. This was not some disaster that happened in Mississippi, so the people of Connecticut could read about it and shake their heads, then worry no more. This was something that affected everyone, and a great segment of the Earth's population *lived* under those sleek metal vehicles from some far star.

This was terror incarnate.

Getting worse with each passing day.

The Adjutant felt his career frustration, his deep anger, his distaste for this pompous piss-ant of a General growing rapidly. He had worked as the General's aide for three years now, and been quite happy with the assignment. The General was an important man, and it was therefore surprising how few actual top-rung decisions had to be made by him, without first being checked and double-checked by underlings.

The Captain knew his General thought of him as his pride-and-joy. Certainly he did; the Adjutant made most of the decisions, and all the General had to do was hand out the orders. Without ever letting the General know his work was being done for him by an aide, the Adjutant had become indispensable. "A good man, that Alberts," the General said, at the Officers' Club.

But this crisis with the saucers was something else. It had been dumped in the General's lap, both from above, and from below, and he was sweating. He had to solve this problem, and for the first time in his life his rough-hewn good looks and military bearing and good name could not bluff him through.

He actually had to make a meaningful decision, and he was almost incapable of doing it. That made him edgy, and snappish, and dissatisfied, and it made the Adjutant's job not quite so cushy.

"Confound it, Alberts! This isn't some base maneuver you can stammer through! This is a nationwide emergency, and everyone is on my neck! God knows I'm doing all I can, but I need a little help! I've tried to impress upon you the—the—*seriousness* of the matter; this thing has got to be ended. It's got the world in an uproar. You're getting up my nose with this attitude, boy! It's starting to stink like subordination, Alberts . . ."

The Adjutant watched, his mouth a fine line. This was the first time the General had spoken to him in such demeaning manner. He didn't like it; a lot. But it was just another sign of the cracking facade of the old man.

The General had come from wealthy Army parents, been sent through West Point and graduated with top honors. He had joined the Air Force when the Army and Air Corps were one and the same, and stayed on after the separation. He had served in the air, and risen in the ranks almost faster than the eye could see. Mostly through his father's connections. The honors, the service duty, the medals . . . all through pull.

The man was a wealthy, sheltered, and vacillating individual, and the Adjutant had been making his decisions for three years. Alberts wondered what would happen when the rotation plan moved him to another job, next year. Would the new Adjutant catch on as fast as he had from the last one? Or would the General pull strings so he could stay on?

But that was all in the future, and this saucer decision

was one the General had to make for himself. It wasn't minor.

And the General was cracking. Badly.

"Now get up there and *do* something!" the General cried, slamming the empty desktop with a flattened hand.

His face was blotched with frustration and annoyance, and—naturally—Alberts saluted, swiveled, and left.

Thinking, *I hope the Pentagon lowers the boom right down his wattled throat, right down his gullet to his large colon!*

One saucer was a dirty affair. Not with the dust and filth of an atmosphere, for the saucer had obviously not been very long in air, but with the pocks and blazes of space. Here a small cluster of pits, where the saucer had encountered a meteor swarm; there a bright smear of oxidized metal. Its markings were slovenly, and there were obvious patchings on its metal hull.

Somehow, it seemed out of place among all the bright, shining, marvelously-intricate, painted saucers. It seemed to be a rather poor relation, and never, *never* flickered out of existence. All the others might be subject to that strange disappearing act, but not the poor relation. It stayed where it was, somewhere above the Fairchild Desert of Nevada.

Once a civilian pilot from Las Vegas, disregarding the orders of the C.A.P., flew very close to the dirty saucer. The pilot buzzed the ship several times, swooping in and over and back around in huge, swinging arcs. By the time he had made his fourteenth Immelmann and decided to land atop the saucer, just for yuks, the hurry-up bleep was out to interceptors based near Reno and Winnemucca, and they caught him high, blasting him from the sky in a matter of minutes.

With the fate of a world hanging in the balance, there could be no time for subtlety or reasoning with crackpots. He had been irrational, had defied the stay-grounded, keep-back orders, and so had fallen under the martial law which had ruled the country since the day after the five thousand had appeared.

Radio communication with the ships was impossibly fruitless.

Television transmission was equally worthless.

Bounced signals failed to come back; the metal of the ships sopped them up.

Telemetering devices brought back readings of the density—or *seeming* density—of the ships, and when they were reported, the situation looked bleaker than before.

The metal was, indeed, super-strong.

The only time things looked promising was when a philologist and a linguist were recruited to broadcast a complete course in English for thirty-six hours straight. The beam was directed at first one ship, then another, and finally when it was directed at the dirty saucer, was gulped in.

They continued broadcasting, till at the end of thirty-six hours, the dumpy, red-faced, runny-nosed, and sniffling Linguist, who had picked up his cold in the broadcasting shack, pushed back his chair, gathered his cashmere sweater from where it had fallen in the corner, and said there was no use.

No reply had come in. If the beings who had flown these saucers were intelligent enough to have gotten here, they would surely have been intelligent enough to have learned English by then. But there had been no reply, and spirits sank again.

Inter-channel memos slipped frantically down from President to Aide, to Secretary of Defense, to Undersecretary, to Chief of Staff, to the General, who passed the memos—bundled—to his Adjutant. Who worried.

It had been the only one where there was any slightest sign of contact. "Look, pilot, I want you to fly across that dirty one," the Adjutant said.

"Begging the Captain's permission . . ." the wide-eyed young pilot demanded, over his shoulder; he continued at the nod from Alberts ". . . but the last man who buzzed that big-O, sir, got himself scissored good and proper. What I mean, sir, is that we're way off bounds, and if our clearances didn't, uh, clear, we might have a flock of my buddies down our necks." He spoke in a faint Texas drawl that seemed to ease from between his thin lips.

The Adjutant felt the adrenaline flowing erratically. He had been taking slop from the General for three weeks, and now to be forced into flying up himself, into the very jaws of death (as he phrased it to himself), to look over the situation . . . he would brook no backtalk from a whey-faced flight boy fresh out of Floyd Bennett.

Alberts shooed him off, directed him back to the stick. "Don't worry yourself, pilot." He licked his lips, added, "They cleared, and all we have to worry about is that saucer line up ahead."

The discs were rising out of the late evening Nevada haze. The clouds seemed to have lowered, and the fog seemed to have risen, and the two intermingled, giving a wavering, indistinct appearance to the metallic line of saucers, stretching off beyond the horizon.

The Adjutant looked out through the curving bubble of the helicopter's control country, and felt the same twinges of fear rippling the hair along his neck that he had felt when the General had started putting the screws to him.

The Sikorsky rescue copter windmilled in toward the saucer, its rotors *flap-flap-flap-flapping* overhead.

The pilot sticked-in on the dirty saucer. It rose out of the mist abruptly, and they were close enough to see that there really *was* dust streaked with dirt along the dull metal surface of the ship. *Probably from one of these Nevada windstorms*, the Adjutant thought.

They scaled down, and came to a hovering stop two feet above the empty metal face of the disc.

"See anything?" the Adjutant asked.

The pilot craned off to one side, swept his gaze around, then turned on the searchbeam. The pole of light watered across the sleek saucer bulk, and picked up nothing. Not even a line of rivets, not even a break in the construction. Nothing but dirt and pockmarks, and what might be considered patches, were this a tire or an ordinary ship.

"Nothing, sir."

"Take us over there, right there, will you, pilot?"

The Adjutant indicated a lighter place on the metal of the ship. It seemed to be a different shade of chrome-color. The Sikorsky jerked, lifted a few inches, and slid over. The pilot brought it back down, and they looked over the hull of the saucer at that point.

It was, indeed, lighter in shade.

"This *could* be something, pi—"

The shaft rose up directly in front of the Sikorsky before he could finish the word.

It was a column of transparent, almost glass-like material, with a metal disc sealing off the top. It was rising out of the metal where there had been no break in the skin, and it kept rising till it towered over them.

"M-m-m—" the Adjutant struggled to get the word loose.

"*Move!*" More a snarl than a command. But before they could whip away, the *person* stepped up inside the column, stared straight out, his gigantic face on a line with their cab.

He must have been thirty feet tall, and completely covered with reddish-brown hair. His ears were pointed, and set almost atop his head. The eyes were pocketed by deep ridges of matted hair, and his nose was a pair of breather-slits. His hands hung far below his indrawn waist, and they were eight-fingered. Each finger was a tentacle that writhed with a separate life of its own. He wore a loose-fitting and wrinkled, dirty sort of toga affair, patched and covered with stains.

He stared at them unblinking. For he had no eyelids.

"*Gawd Almighty!*" the pilot squawked, and fumbled blindly at his controls for an instant, unable to tear his eyes away from the being before them. Finally his hand met the controls, and the Sikorsky bucked backward, tipped, and rose rapidly above the saucer, spiraling away into the night as fast as the rotors would windmill. In a minute the copter was gone.

The glassite pillar atop the dirty saucer remained raised for a few minutes, then slowly sank back into the ship.

No mark was left where it had risen.

Somehow, news of the *person* leaked out. And from then on, telescopes across the world were trained on the unbroken band of discs circling the Earth. They watched in shifts, not wanting to miss a thing, but there was nothing more to see. No further contact was made, in person or by radio.

There was no sign of life anywhere along the chain of discs. They could have been empty for all anyone knew. Going into the eighth week, no one knew any more about them than on the day they had arrived.

No government would venture an exploratory party, for the slightest hint of a wrong move or word might turn the unleashed wrath of the saucers on the Earth.

Stocks fell quickly and crazily. Shipping was slowed to a standstill, and production fell off terrifically in factories. No one wanted to work when they might be blown up at any moment. People began a disorganized exodus to the hills and swamps and lost places of the planet. If the saucers were going to wash the cities with fire and death, no one wanted to be there when it happened.

They were not hostile, and that was what kept the world moving in its cultural tracks; but they were *alien*, they were from the *stars*! And that made them objects of terror.

Tempers were short; memos had long since been replaced by curses and demands. Allegations were thrown back and forth across the oceans. Dereliction of duty proceedings were begun on dozens of persons in high places.

The situation was worsening every moment. In the tenth week the nasty remarks ceased, and there were rumors of a court-martial. And a firing squad.

"Got to *do* something, Alberts. Got to do *some*thing!"

The Adjutant watched the spectacle of his superior shattering with something akin to sorrow. There went the cushy job.

"But what, General?" He kept his voice low and modulated. No sense sending the old boy into another tantrum.

"I—I want to go up there . . . see what he looks like . . . see what I can d-do . . ."

An hour later the Sikorsky carried the General to the Maginot Line of silent saucers.

Twenty minutes later he was back, bathed in sweat, and white as a fish-belly. "Horrible. All hair and eyes. Horrible. Horrible." He croaked a few more words, and sank into a chair.

"Call Ordnance," he breathed gaspingly. "Prepare a missile.

"With an atomic warhead.

"Now!"

They attached the parasite missile beneath a night-fighter, checking and double-checking the release mechanism.

Before they released the ship, they waited for the General's okay. This wasn't just a test flight, this was an atomic missile, and whatever the repercussions, they wanted them on the General's head, not their own.

In the base office, the Adjutant was replacing the phone in its cradle. "What did Washington say, General?" he asked the trembling officer.

"They said the situation was in my hands. I was free to do as I saw fit. The President can't be located. They think he and his cabinet have been smuggled out West somewhere, to the mountains."

The General did not look at his Adjutant as he spoke the words. He stared at his clasped and shaking hands.

"Tell them to release the missile. We'll watch it on TV."

The Adjutant lifted the phone, clicked the connection buttons twice, spoke quickly, softly, into the mouthpiece. "Let it go."

A minute and a half later, from half a mile away on the launching strip, they heard the jet rev-up and split the evening sky with its fire.

Then they went to the television room and watched the lines of screens.

In one they saw the silent girdle of saucers. In another they were focused on the dirty saucer, with a sign above the screen that said INITIAL TARGET. In a third they had a line-of-sight to the night-fighter's approach pattern.

"There it comes!" one of the technicians yelled, pointing at the lighter dark of the jet as it streaked toward the massed saucers, leaving a trail of fire behind it. They watched silently as the plane swooped in high, dove, and they saw the parasite leave its belly, streak on forward. The jet sliced upward, did a roll, and was a mile away as the parasite homed in exactly.

They watched with held breath as the small atomic missile deaded-in on the dirty saucer, and they flinched as it struck.

A blinding flash covered all the screens for a moment, and a few seconds later they heard the explosion. Shock waves ripped outward and the concussion was great enough to knock out eighteen of the thirty telemetering cameras.

But they could see the dirty saucer clearly on one. In that one the smoke and blast were clearing slowly. A mushroom-shaped cloud was rising, rising, rising from the sloping dish of the saucer's upper side. As it moved away they could see oxidized smears and blast pattern of white jagged sunbursts. It looked as harmless as a kid's experiment with a match, potassium nitrate, and powdered magnesium. It had not harmed the saucer in the least. But . . .

There was a crack along the top face of the saucer. And from that gash spilled a bubbling white substance. The stuff frothed out and ran across the top of the saucer. It pitted and tore at the metal of the ship wherever it touched. There was a weird sound of clacking and coughing from the ship, as though some intricate mechanism within were erupting.

Then, as they watched, the glassite pillar rose up out of the ship . . .

. . . and the *person* was within.

Unmistakably, his face was a violence of rage and hatred. His fists beat against the glassite, and he roared— silently, for no sound could be picked up by the audio ears— inside the pillar. He spat, and blood—red and thick—dotted the clear glassite. His mouth opened screaming wide and long, sharp teeth could be seen.

He shook a fist at the emptiness beyond the saucer, and the pillar lowered into the ship.

A minute later, for the first time since it had arrived, the dirty saucer *flicked!* out of existence and was gone.

"That was perhaps the wrong move, General . . ."

The General, who had been fastened to the TV screen by some invisible linkage, tore his eyes away from the set, and whirled, glowering, on his Adjutant.

"That's for *me* to worry about, Captain Alberts. I told you the military mind can solve problems by the direct method, the uncomplicated method, while these scientists dawdle and doodle helplessly." He was speaking loudly, almost hysterically, and the Adjutant recognized relief in the officer's tones.

"They're on the run!" the General shouted, grinning hugely. "On the run, by George! Now, come on, Alberts, let's get a few antiaircraft battalions out there on the desert and pick off the rest of them in this area. Wait till the President hears of *this*!"

They were out on the desert, the ack-ack guns sniffing at the sky, pelting the saucers from six separate batteries. They were intent on what they were doing, certain that anyone in those other ships

(and why did the Adjutant keep getting the feeling that those other ships were *empty?*)

would turn tail and disappear as quickly as the dirty saucer had done an hour and a quarter before.

They had just lobbed five fast shells at a snow-white saucer with purple markings, when the dirty saucer reappeared.

Flick!

He was back, that hairy alien in the dirty, stained toga.

He was back in the same spot he had vacated, almost directly above the General's batteries.

The pillar rose, and the General watched stunned as the metal top slid off the pillar, and the alien stepped out.

He stepped onto the top of his ship, and they saw the gash in the hull had been repaired. Caulked with some sort of black sticky stuff that stuck to the alien's clawed feet as he walked along the top of the saucer. He carried a thick, gun-like object in his hands, cradled against his massive chest.

Then he screamed something in a voice like thunder. They could hear it only roughly, for it was in a guttural tongue. Then he switched to English, and screamed again, in more detail.

The General strained his ears. His hearing had never been the best, but the Adjutant heard, it was clear to see, from the look of horror and failure and frustration on his face. Then the Adjutant dove away from the antiaircraft gun, rolled over several times, and sprinted out into the desert.

The General hesitated only a moment before following, but that was enough.

The alien turned the gun-like object on the batteries, and a roar and a flash sent the metal screaming skyward, ripping and shredding. Bodies were flung in every direction, and a blue pallor settled across the landscape as a thirty-foot crater opened where the battery had been.

The General felt himself lifted, buffeted, and thrown. He landed face forward in the ditch, and saw his arm land five feet away. He screamed; the pain in his left side was excruciating.

He screamed again, and in a moment Alberts was beside him, dragging him away from the area of destruction. The alien was standing spraddle-legged atop his machine, blasting, blasting, scouring the Earth with blue fire.

The alien screamed in English again, and then he stepped into the pillar, which lowered into the ship once more. A few seconds later the ship *flicked!* away, and materialized in the sky ten miles off, above the air base.

There was more blasting. Blue pallor lit the sky for a full half hour.

The saucer *flicked!* and was gone. A few moments later the blue pallor—fainter yet, but strengthening all the time—was seen twenty miles further on, washing Las Vegas.

Flick! Flick! Flick!

And a dozen more saucers, dirtier than the first, materialized, paused a moment as though getting their bearings, then *flicked!* away.

For the next hours the blue pallor filled the sky, and it was easy to see the scouring was moving across the planet systematically.

The General's head was cradled in his Adjutant's lap. He was sinking so rapidly there was no hope at all. His entire left side had been scorched and ripped open. He lay there, looking up at the face of the once-dapper Adjutant, his eyes barely focusing. His tongue bulged from his mouth, and then a few words.

Haltingly, "I . . . c-couldn't hear . . . what he s-said, Al-b-berts. W-what . . . did . . . he . . . say?"

The General's eyes closed, but his chest still moved. The Adjutant felt all the hatred he had built for this man vanish. Though the blustering fool had caused the death of a world, still he was dying, and there was no sense letting him carry that guilt with him.

"Nothing, General. Nothing at all. You did your very best, sir."

Then he realized the last "sir" had been spoken uselessly. The General was dead.

"You did your best, sir," the Adjutant spoke to the night. "It wasn't your fault the attendant picked us.

"All the alien said was that there were destructive pests in this *parking lot*, and he was one attendant who was going to clear them out even if he had to work overtime for a century."

The words faded in the night, and only the blue pallor remained. Growing, flashing, never waning. Never.

S O L D I E R

If this next story seems a bit familiar, it's only because an ego-drenched movie director ripped it off when I adapted it in 1965 for a segment of *The Outer Limits*. So I brought a lawsuit against the film company. If you perceive a striking similarity here to a movie called *The Terminator*, well, go rent a VHS or DVD and watch at the end, when they roll the credits, to see something interesting. So this story has *two* good troublemaker lessons to be learned. The first one is so obvious I'm embarrassed even to be laying it on you: violence becomes a way of life. If you think a punch in the mouth really solves any problems, pretty soon that's the *only* way you can handle a problem, big or small. And finally, one day, you take a swing and someone puts out your lights for keeps. Smart is better than strong. Clever is better than clocking someone. Outthink the problem, don't let it bench-press you into making it *your* problem. The *other* lesson is the one the Academy award-winning director should have learned (and maybe he hasn't even learned it yet): don't let your ego get so hungry that it leads you to act unethically because you think you're such Hot Stuff and nobody can touch you. Don't think the rest of the world is as stupid as you'd like it to be: somebody is *always* watching. Sunny Jim, know this: there is *always* a faster gun out there; and there are *some* people whom you just cannot scare, no matter how big and loud you come on.

Qarlo hunkered down farther into the firmhole, gathering his cloak about him. Even the triple-lining of the cape could not prevent the seeping cold of the battlefield from reaching him; and even through one of those linings—lead impregnated—he could feel the faint tickle of dropout, all about him, eating at his tissues. He began to shiver again. The Push was going on to the South, and he had to wait, had to listen for the telepathic command of his superior officer.

He fingered an edge of the firmhole, noting he had not steadied it up too well with the firmer. He drew the small molecule-hardening instrument from his pouch, and examined it. The calibrater had slipped a notch, which explained why the dirt of the firmhole had not become as hard as he had desired.

Off to the left the hiss of an eighty-thread beam split the night air, and he shoved the firmer back quickly. The spider-web tracery of the beam lanced across the sky, poked tentatively at an armor center, throwing blood-red shadows across Qarlo's crag-like features.

The armor center backtracked the thread beam, retaliated with a blinding flash of its own batteries. One burst. Two. Three. The eighty-thread reared once more, feebly, then subsided. A moment later the concussion of its power chambers exploding shook the Earth around Qarlo, causing bits of unfirmed dirt and small pebbles to tumble in on him. Another moment, and the shrapnel came through.

Qarlo lay flat to the ground, soundlessly hoping for a bit more life amidst all this death. He knew his chances of coming back were infinitesimal. What was it? Three out of every thousand came back? He had no illusions. He was a common footman, and he knew he would die out here, in the midst of the Great War VII.

As though the detonation of the eighty-thread had been a signal, the weapons of Qarlo's company opened up, full-on. The webbings crisscrossed the blackness overhead with delicate patterns—appearing, disappearing, changing with every second, ranging through the spectrum, washing the bands of colors outside the spectrum Qarlo could catalog. Qarlo slid into a tiny ball in the slush-filled bottom of the firmhole, waiting.

He was a good soldier. He knew his place. When those metal and energy beasts out there were snarling at each other, there was nothing a lone foot soldier could do—but die. He waited, knowing his time would come much too soon. No matter how violent, how involved, how pushbutton-ridden Wars became, it always simmered down to the man on foot. It had to, for men fought men still.

His mind dwelled limply in a state between reflection and alertness. A state all men of war came to know when there was nothing but the thunder of the big guns abroad in the night.

The stars had gone into hiding.

Abruptly, the thread beams cut out, the traceries winked

off, silence once again descended. Qarlo snapped to instant attentiveness. This was the moment. His mind was now keyed to one sound, one only. Inside his head the command would form, and he would act; not entirely of his own voli-tion. The strategists and psychmen had worked together on this thing: the tone of command was keyed into each sol-dier's brain. Printed in, probed in, sunken in. It was there, and when the Regimenter sent his telepathic orders, Qarlo would leap like a puppet, and advance on direction.

Thus, when it came, it was as though he had anticipated it; as though he knew a second before the mental rasping and the *Advance!* erupted within his skull, that the moment had arrived.

A second sooner than he should have been, he was up, out of the firmhole, hugging his Brandelmeier to his chest, the weight of the plastic bandoliers and his pouch reassur-ing across his stomach, back, and hips. Even before the mental word actually came.

Because of this extra moment's jump on the command, it happened, and it happened just that way. No other chance coincidences could have done it but those, just those, just that way, done *just that way.*

When the first blasts of the enemy's zeroed-in batteries met the combined rays of Qarlo's own guns, also pin-pointed, they met at a point that should by all rights have been empty. But Qarlo had jumped too soon, and when they met, the soldier was at the focal point.

Three hundred distinct beams latticed down, joined in a coruscating rainbow, threw negatively charged particles five hundred feet in the air, shorted out . . . and warped the sol-dier off the battlefield.

Nathan Schwachter had his heart attack right there on the subway platform.

The soldier materialized in front of him, from nowhere, filthy and ferocious-looking, a strange weapon cradled to his body . . . just as the old man was about to put a penny in the candy machine.

Qarlo's long cape was still, the dematerialization and subsequent reappearance having left him untouched. He stared in confusion at the sallow face before him, and started violently at the face's piercing shriek.

Qarlo watched with growing bewilderment and terror as the sallow face contorted and sank to the littered floor of the platform. The old man clutched his chest, twitched and gasped several times. His legs jerked spasmodically, and his mouth opened wildly again and again. He died with mouth open, eyes staring at the ceiling.

Qarlo looked at the body disinterestedly for a moment; death . . . what did one death matter . . . every day during the War, ten thousand died . . . more horribly than this . . . this was as nothing to him.

The sudden universe-filling scream of an incoming express train broke his attention. The black tunnel that his War-filled world had become, was filled with the rusty wail of an unseen monster, bearing down on him out of the darkness.

The fighting man in him made his body arch, sent it into a crouch. He poised on the balls of his feet, his rifle levering horizontal instantly, pointed at the sound.

From the crowds packed on the platform, a voice rose over the thunder of the incoming train:

"*Him!* It was *him!* He shot that old man . . . he's crazy!" Heads turned; eyes stared; a little man with a dirty vest, his bald head reflecting the glow of the overhead lights, was pointing a shaking finger at Qarlo.

It was as if two currents had been set up simultaneously. The crowd both drew away and advanced on him. Then the train barreled around the curve, drove past, blasting sound into the very fibers of the soldier's body. Qarlo's mouth opened wide in a soundless scream, and more from reflex than intent, the Brandelmeier erupted in his hands.

A triple-thread of cold blue beams sizzled from the small bell mouth of the weapon, streaked across the tunnel, and blasted full into the front of the train.

The front of the train melted down quickly, and the vehicle ground to a stop. The metal had been melted like a coarse grade of plastic on a burner. Where it had fused into a soggy lump, the metal was bright and smeary—more like the gleam of oxidized silver than anything else.

Qarlo regretted having fired the moment he felt the Brandelmeier buck. He was not where he should be—*where* he was, that was still another, more pressing problem—and he knew he was in danger. Every movement had to be watched as carefully as possible . . . and perhaps he had gotten off to a bad start already. But that noise . . .

He had suffered the screams of the battlefield, but the reverberations of the train, thundering back and forth in that enclosed space, were a nightmare of indescribable horror.

As he stared dumbly at his handiwork, from behind him, the crowd made a concerted rush.

Three burly, charcoal-suited executives—each carrying an attaché case which he dropped as he made the lunge, looking like unhealthy carbon-copies of each other—grabbed Qarlo above the elbows, around the waist, about the neck.

The soldier roared something unintelligible and flung them from him. One slid across the platform on the seat of his pants, bringing up short, his stomach and face smashing into a tiled wall. The second spun away, arms flailing, into the crowd. The third tried to hang onto Qarlo's neck. The soldier lifted him bodily, arched him over his head—breaking the man's insecure grip—and pitched him against a stanchion. The executive hit the girder, slid down, and lay quite still, his back oddly twisted.

The crowd emitted scream after scream, drew away once more. Terror rippled back through its ranks. Several women, near the front, suddenly became aware of the blood pouring from the face of one of the executives, and keeled onto the dirty platform unnoticed. The screams continued, seeming echoes of the now-dead express train's squealing.

But as an entity, the crowd backed the soldier down the platform. For a moment Qarlo forgot he still held the Brandelmeier. He lifted the gun to a threatening position, and the entity that was the crowd pulsed back.

Nightmare! It was all some sort of vague, formless nightmare to Qarlo. This was not the War, where anyone he saw, he blasted. This was something else, some other situation, in which he was lost, disoriented. What was happening?

Qarlo moved toward the wall, his back prickly with fear sweat. He had expected to die in the War, but something as simple and direct and expected as that had not happened. He was *here*, not *there*—wherever *here* was, and wherever *there* had gone—and these people were unarmed, obviously civilians. Which would not have kept him from murdering them . . . but what was happening? Where was the battlefield?

His progress toward the wall was halted momentarily as he backed cautiously around a stanchion. He knew there were people behind him, as well as the white-faced knots before him, and he was beginning to suspect there was no way out. Such confusion boiled up in his thoughts, so close to hysteria was he—plain soldier of the fields—that his mind forcibly rejected the impossibility of being somehow transported from the War into this new—and in many ways more terrifying—situation. He concentrated on one thing only, as a good soldier should: *Out!*

He slid along the wall, the crowd flowing before him, opening at his approach, closing in behind. He whirled once, driving them back farther with the black hole of the Brandelmeier's bell mouth. Again he hesitated (not knowing why) to fire upon them.

He sensed they were enemies. But still they were unarmed. And yet, that had never stopped him before. The village in TetraOmsk Territory, beyond the Volga somewhere. They had been unarmed there, too, but the square had been filled with civilians he had not hesitated to burn. Why was he hesitating now?

The Brandelmeier continued in its silence.

Qarlo detected a commotion behind the crowd, above the crowd's inherent commotion. And a movement. Something was happening there. He backed tightly against the wall as a blue-suited, brass-buttoned man broke through the crowd.

The man took one look, caught the unwinking black eye of the Brandelmeier, and threw his arms back, indicating to the crowd to clear away. He began screaming at the top of his lungs, veins standing out in his temples, "Geddoudahere! The guy's a cuckaboo! Somebody'll get kilt! Beat it, run!"

The crowd needed no further impetus. It broke in the center and streamed toward the stairs.

Qarlo swung around, looking for another way out, but both accessible stairways were clogged by fighting commuters, shoving each other mercilessly to get out. He was effectively trapped.

The cop fumbled at his holster. Qarlo caught a glimpse of the movement from the corner of his eye. Instinctively he knew the movement for what it was; a weapon was about to be brought into use. He swung about, leveling the Brandelmeier. The cop jumped behind a stanchion just as the soldier pressed the firing stud.

A triple-thread of bright blue energy leaped from the weapon's bell mouth. The beam went over the heads of the crowd, neatly melting away a five foot segment of wall supporting one of the stairways. The stairs creaked, and the sound of tortured metal adjusting to poor support and an overcrowding of people rang through the tunnel. The cop looked fearfully above himself, saw the beams curve, then settle under the weight, and turned a wide-eyed stare back at the soldier.

The cop fired twice, from behind the stanchion, the booming of the explosions catapulting back and forth in the enclosed space.

The second bullet took the soldier above the wrist in his left arm. The Brandelmeier slipped uselessly from his good hand, as blood stained the garment he wore. He stared at his shattered lower arm in amazement. Doubled amazement.

What manner of weapon was this the blue-coated man had used? No beam, that. Nothing like anything he had ever seen before. No beam to fry him in his tracks. It was some sort of power that hurled a projectile . . . that had ripped his body. He stared stupidly as blood continued to flow out of his arm.

The cop, less anxious now to attack this man with the weird costume and unbelievable rifle, edged cautiously from behind his cover, skirting the edge of the platform, trying to get near enough to Qarlo to put another bullet into him, should he offer further resistance. But the soldier continued to stand, spraddle-legged, staring at his wound, confused at where he was, what had happened to him, the screams of the trains as they bulleted past, and the barbarian tactics of his blue-coated adversary.

The cop moved slowly, steadily, expecting the soldier to break and run at any moment. The wounded man stood rooted, however. The cop bunched his muscles and leaped the few feet intervening.

Savagely, he brought the barrel of his pistol down on the side of Qarlo's neck, near the ear. The soldier turned slowly, anchored in his tracks, and stared unbelievingly at the policeman for an instant.

Then his eyes glazed, and he collapsed to the platform.

As a gray swelling mist bobbed up around his mind, one final thought impinged incongruously: *he struck me . . . physical contact? I don't believe it!*

What have I gotten into?

Light filtered through vaguely. Shadows slithered and wavered, sullenly formed into solids.

"Hey, Mac. Got a light?"

Shadows blocked Qarlo's vision, but he knew he was lying on his back, staring up. He turned his head, and a wall oozed into focus, almost at his nose tip. He turned his head the other way. Another wall, about three feet away, blending in his sight into a shapeless gray blotch. He abruptly realized the back of his head hurt. He moved slowly, swiveling his head, but the soreness remained. Then he realized he was lying on some hard metal surface, and he tried to sit up. The pains throbbed higher, making him feel nauseated, and for an instant his vision receded again.

Then it steadied, and he sat up slowly. He swung his legs over the sharp edge of what appeared to be a shallow, sloping metal trough. It was a mattressless bunk, curved in its bottom, from hundreds of men who had lain there before him.

He was in a cell.

"Hey! I said you got a match there?"

Qarlo turned from the empty rear wall of the cell and looked through the bars. A bulb-nosed face was thrust up close to the metal barrier. The man was short, in filthy rags whose odor reached Qarlo with tremendous offensiveness. The man's eyes were bloodshot, and his nose was criss-crossed with blue and red veins. Acute alcoholism, reeking from every pore; *acne rosacea* that had turned his nose into a hideous cracked and pocked blob.

Qarlo knew he was in detention, and from the very look, the very smell of this other, he knew he was not in a military prison. The man was staring in at him, oddly.

"Match, Charlie? You got a match?" He puffed his fat, wet lips at Qarlo, forcing the bit of cigarette stub forward with his mouth. Qarlo stared back; he could not understand the man's words. They were so slowly spoken, so sharp and yet unintelligible. But he knew what to answer.

"Marnames Qarlo Clobregnny, pryt, sizfifwun-ohtootoonyn," the soldier muttered by rote, surly tones running together.

"Whaddaya mad at *me* for, buddy? I didn't putcha in here," argued the match-seeker. "All I wanted was a light for this here butt." He held up two inches of smoked stub. "How come they gotcha inna cell, and not runnin' around loose inna bull pen like us?" He cocked a thumb over his shoulder, and for the first time Qarlo realized others were in this jail.

"Ah, to hell wit ya," the drunk muttered. He cursed again, softly under his breath, turning away. He walked across the bull pen and sat down with the four other men—all vaguely similar in facial content—who lounged around a rough-hewn table-bench combination. The table and benches, all one piece, like a picnic table, were bolted to the floor.

"A screwloose," the drunk said to the others, nodding his balding head at the soldier in his long cape and metallic skintight suit. He picked up the crumpled remnants of an ancient magazine and leafed through it as though he knew every line of type, every girlie illustration, by heart.

Qarlo looked over the cell. It was about ten feet high by eight across, a sink with one thumb-push spigot running cold water, a commode without seat or paper, and metal trough, roughly the dimensions of an average-sized man, fastened to one wall. One enclosed bulb burned feebly in the ceiling. Three walls of solid steel. Ceiling and floor of the same, riveted together at the seams. The fourth wall was the barred door.

The firmer might be able to wilt that steel, he realized, and instinctively reached for his pouch. It was the first moment he had had a chance to think of it, and even as he reached, knew the satisfying weight of it was gone. His bandoliers also. His Brandelmeier, of course. His boots, too, and there seemed to have been some attempt to get his cape off, but it was all part of the skintight suit of metallic-mesh cloth.

The loss of the pouch was too much. Everything that had happened, had happened so quickly, so blurry, meshed, and the soldier was abruptly overcome by confusion and a deep feeling of hopelessness. He sat down on the bunk, the ledge of metal biting into his thighs. His head still ached from a combination of the blow dealt him by the cop, and the metal bunk where he had lain. He ran a shaking hand over his head, feeling the fractional inch of his brown hair, cut battle-style. Then he noticed that his left hand had been bandaged quite expertly. There was hardly any throbbing from his wound.

That brought back to sharp awareness all that had transpired, and the War leaped into his thoughts. The telepathic command, the rising from the firmhole, the rifle at the ready . . .

. . . then a sizzling shussssss, and the universe had exploded around him in a billion tiny flickering novas of color and color and color. Then suddenly, just as suddenly as he had been standing on the battlefield of Great War VII, advancing on the enemy forces of Ruskie-Chink, he was *not* there.

He was here.

He was in some dark, hard tunnel, with a great beast roaring out of the blackness onto him, and a man in a blue coat had shot him, and clubbed him. Actually *touched* him! Without radiation gloves! How had the man known Qarlo was not booby-trapped with radiates? He could have died in an instant.

Where was he? What war was this he was engaged in? Were these Ruskie-Chink or his own Tri-Continenters? He did not know, and there was no sign of an explanation.

Then he thought of something more important. If he had been captured, then they must want to question him. There was a way to combat *that*, too. He felt around in the hollow tooth toward the back of his mouth. His tongue touched each tooth till it hit the right lower bicuspid. It was empty. The poison glob was gone, he realized in dismay. *It must have dropped out when the blue-coat clubbed me*, he thought.

He realized he was at *their* mercy; who *they* might be was another thing to worry about. And with the glob gone, he had no way to stop their extracting information. It was bad. Very bad, according to the warning conditioning he had received. They could use Probers, or dyoxl-scopalite, or hypno-scourge, or any one of a hundred different methods, any one of which would reveal to them the strength of numbers in his company, the battery placements, the gun ranges, the identity and thought wave band of every officer . . . in fact, a good deal. More than he had thought he knew.

He had become a very important prisoner of War. He *had* to hold out, he realized!

Why?

The thought popped up, and was gone. All it left in its wake was the intense feeling: I despise War, all war and *the* War! Then, even that was gone, and he was alone with the situation once more, to try and decide what had happened to him . . . what secret weapon had been used to capture him . . . and if these unintelligible barbarians with the projectile weapons *could*, indeed, extract his knowledge from him.

I swear they won't get anything out of me but my name, rank, and serial number, he thought desperately.

He mumbled those particulars aloud, as reassurance: "Marnames Qarlo Clobregnny, pryt, sizfifwunohtootoonyn."

The drunks looked up from their table and their shakes, at the sound of his voice. The man with the rosedrop nose rubbed a dirty hand across fleshy chin folds, repeated his philosophy of the strange man in the locked cell.

"Screwloose!"

He might have remained in jail indefinitely, considered a madman or a mad rifleman. But the desk sergeant who had booked him, after the soldier had received medical attention, grew curious about the strangely shaped weapon.

As he put the things into security, he tested the Brandelmeier—hardly realizing what knob or stud controlled its power, never realizing what it could do—and melted away one wall of the safe room. Three inch plate steel, and it melted bluely, fused solidly.

He called the Captain, and the Captain called the F.B.I., and the F.B.I. called Internal Security, and Internal Security said, "Preposterous!" and checked back. When the Brandelmeier had been thoroughly tested—as much as *could* be tested, since the rifle had no seams, no apparent power source, and fantastic range—they were willing to believe. They had the soldier removed from his cell, transported along with the pouch, and a philologist named Soames, to the I.S. general headquarters in Washington, D.C. The Brandelmeier came by jet courier, and the soldier was flown in by helicopter, under sedation. The philologist named Soames, whose hair was long and rusty, whose face was that of a starving artist, whose temperament was that of a saint, came in by specially chartered lane from Columbia University. The pouch was sent by sealed Brinks truck to the airport, where it was delivered under heaviest guard to a mail plane. They all arrived in Washington within ten minutes of one another and, without seeing anything of the surrounding countryside, were whisked away to the subsurface levels of the I.S. Buildings.

When Qarlo came back to consciousness, he found himself again in a cell, this time quite unlike the first. No bars, but just as solid to hold him in, with padded walls. Qarlo paced around the cell a few times, seeking breaks in the walls, and found what was obviously a door, in one corner. But he could not work his fingers between the pads, to try and open it.

He sat down on the padded floor, and rubbed the bristled top of his head in wonder. Was he *never* to find out what had happened to himself? And *when* was he going to shake this strange feeling that he was being watched?

Overhead, through a pane of one-way glass that looked like a ventilator grille, the soldier was being watched.

Lyle Sims and his secretary knelt before the window in the floor, along with the philologist named Soames. Where Soames was shaggy, ill-kept, hungry-looking and placid . . . Lyle Sims was lean, collegiate-seeming, brusque and brisk.

He had been special advisor to an unnamed branch office of Internal Security, for five years, dealing with every strange or offbeat problem too outré for regulation inquiry. Those years had hardened him in an odd way: he was quick to recognize authenticity, even quicker to recognize fakery.

As he watched, his trained instincts took over completely, and he knew in a moment of spying, that the man in the cell below was out of the ordinary. Not so in any fashion that could be labeled—"drunkard," "foreigner," "psychotic"—but so markedly different, so *other*, he was taken aback.

"Six feet three inches," he recited to the girl kneeling beside him. She made the notation on her pad, and he went on calling out characteristics of the soldier below. "Brown hair, clipped so short you can see the scalp. Brown ... no, black eyes. Scars. Above the left eye, running down to center of left cheek; bridge of nose; three parallel scars on the right side of chin; tiny one over right eyebrow; last one I can see, runs from back of left ear, into hairline.

"He seems to be wearing an all-over, skintight suit something like, oh, I suppose it's like a pair of what do you call those pajamas kids wear ... the kind with the back door, the kind that enclosed the feet?"

The girl inserted softly, "You mean snuggies?"

The man nodded, slightly embarrassed for no good reason, continued, "Mmm. Yes, that's right. Like those. The suit encloses his feet, seems to be joined to the cape, and comes up to his neck. Seems to be some sort of metallic cloth.

"Something else ... may mean nothing at all, or on the other hand ..." He pursed his lips for a moment, then described his observation carefully. "His head seems to be oddly shaped. The forehead is larger than most, seems to be pressing forward in front, as though he had been smacked hard and it was swelling. That seems to be everything."

Sims settled back on his haunches, fished in his side

pocket, and came up with a small pipe, which he cold-puffed in thought for a second. He rose slowly, still staring down through the floor window. He murmured something to himself, and when Soames asked what he had said, the special advisor repeated, "I think we've got something almost too hot to handle."

Soames clucked knowingly, and gestured toward the window. "Have you been able to make out anything he's said yet?"

Sims shook his head. "No. That's why you're here. It seems he's saying the same thing, over and over, but it's completely unintelligible. Doesn't seem to be any recognizable language, or any dialect we've been able to pin down."

"I'd like to take a try at him," Soames said, smiling gently. It was the man's nature that challenge brought satisfaction; solution brought unrest, eagerness for a new, more rugged problem.

Sims nodded agreement, but there was a tense, strained film over his eyes, in the set of his mouth. "Take it easy with him, Soames. I have a strong hunch this is something completely new, something we haven't even begun to understand."

Soames smiled again, this time indulgently. "Come, come, Mr. Sims. After all ... he *is* only an alien of some sort ... all we have to do is find out what country he's from."

"Have you heard him talk yet?"

Soames shook his head.

"Then don't be too quick to think he's just a foreigner. The word *alien* may be more correct than you think—only not in the *way* you think."

A confused look spread across Soames's face. He gave a slight shrug, as though he could not fathom what Lyle Sims meant ... and was not particularly interested. He patted

Sims reassuringly, which brought an expression of annoyance to the advisor's face, and he clamped down on the pipestem harder.

They walked downstairs together; the secretary left them, to type her notes, and Sims let the philologist into the padded room, cautioning him to deal gently with the man. "Don't forget," Sims warned, "we're not sure *where* he comes from, and sudden movements may make him jumpy. There's a guard overhead, and there'll be a man with me behind this door, but you never know."

Soames looked startled. "You sound as though he's an aborigine or something. With a suit like that, he *must* be very intelligent. You suspect something, don't you?"

Sims made a neutral motion with his hands. "What I suspect is too nebulous to worry about now. Just take it easy . . . and above all, figure out what he's saying, where he's from."

Sims had decided, long before, that it would be wisest to keep the power of the Brandelmeier to himself. But he was fairly certain it was not the work of a foreign power. The trial run on the test range had left him gasping, confused.

He opened the door, and Soames passed through, uneasily.

Sims caught a glimpse of the expression on the stranger's face as the philologist entered. It was even more uneasy than Soames's had been.

It looked to be a long wait.

Soames was white as paste. His face was drawn, and the complacent attitude he had shown since his arrival in Washington was shattered. He sat across from Sims, and asked him in a quavering voice for a cigarette. Sims fished around in his desk, came up with a crumpled pack and idly slid them across to Soames. The philologist took one, put it in his mouth, then, as though it had been totally forgotten in the space of a second, he removed it, held it while he spoke.

His tones were amazed. "Do you know what you've got up there in that cell?"

Sims said nothing, knowing what was to come would not startle him too much; he had expected something fantastic.

"That man . . . do you know where he . . . that soldier—and by God, Sims, that's what he *is*—comes from, from—now you're going to think I'm insane to believe it, but somehow I'm convinced—he comes from the future!"

Sims tightened his lips. Despite himself, he *was* shocked. He knew it was true. It *had* to be true, it was the only explanation that fit all the facts.

"What can you tell me?" he asked the philologist.

"Well, at first I tried solving the communications problem by asking him simple questions . . . pointing to myself and saying 'Soames,' pointing to him and looking quizzical, but all he'd keep saying was a string of gibberish. I tried for hours to equate his tones and phrases with all the dialects and subdialects of every language I'd ever known, but it was no use. He slurred too much. And then I finally figured it out. He had to write it out—which I couldn't understand, of course, but it gave me a clue—and then I kept having him repeat it. Do you know what he's speaking?"

Sims shook his head.

The linguist spoke softly. "He's speaking English. It's that simple. Just English.

"But an English that has been corrupted and run together, and so slurred, it's incomprehensible. It must be the future trend of the language. Sort of an extrapolation of gutter English, just contracted to a fantastic extreme. At any rate, I got it out of him."

Sims leaned forward, held his dead pipe tightly. "What?"

Soames read it off a sheet of paper:

"My name is Qarlo Clobregnny. Private. Six-five-one-oh-two-two-nine."

Sims murmured in astonishment. "My God . . . name, rank and—"

Soames finished for him, "—and serial number. Yes, that's all he'd give me for over three hours. Then I asked him a few innocuous questions, like where did he come from, and what was his impression of where he was now."

The philologist waved a hand vaguely. "By that time, I had an idea what I was dealing with, though not where he had come from. But when he began telling me about the War, the War he was fighting when he showed up here, I knew immediately he was either from some other world—which is fantastic—or, or . . . well, I just don't know!"

Sims nodded his head in understanding. "From *when* do you think he comes?"

Soames shrugged. "Can't tell. He says the year he is in—doesn't seem to realize he's in the past—is K79. He doesn't know when the other style of dating went out. As far as he knows, it's been 'K' for a long time, though he's heard stories about things that happened during a time they dated 'GV.' Meaningless, but I'd wager it's more thousands of years than we can imagine."

Sims ran a hand nervously through his hair. This problem was, indeed, larger than he'd thought.

"Look, Professor Soames, I want you to stay with him, and teach him current English. See if you can work some more information out of him, and let him know we mean him no hard times.

"Though Lord knows," the special advisor added with a tremor, "*he* can give us a harder time than we can give him. What knowledge he must have!"

Soames nodded in agreement. "Is it all right if I catch a

few hours' sleep? I was with him almost ten hours straight, and I'm sure *he* needs it as badly as I do."

Sims nodded also, in agreement, and the philologist went off to a sleeping room. But when Sims looked down through the window, twenty minutes later, the soldier was still awake, still looking about nervously. It seemed he did *not* need sleep.

Sims was terribly worried, and the coded telegram he had received from the President, in answer to his own, was not at all reassuring. The problem was in his hands, and it was an increasingly worrisome problem.

Perhaps a deadly problem.

He went to another sleeping room, to follow Soames's example. It looked like sleep was going to be scarce.

Problem:

A man from the future. An ordinary man, without any special talents, without any great store of intelligence. The equivalent of "the man in the street." A man who owns a fantastic little machine that turns sand into solid matter, harder than steel—but who hasn't the vaguest notion of how it works, or how to analyze it. A man whose knowledge of past history is as vague and formless as any modern man's. A soldier. With no other talent than fighting. What is to be done with such a man?

Solution:

Unknown.

Lyle Sims pushed the coffee cup away. If he ever had to look at another cup of the disgusting stuff, he was sure he would vomit. Three sleepless days and nights, running on nothing but dexedrine and hot black coffee, had put his nerves more on edge than usual. He snapped at the clerks and secretaries, he paced endlessly, and he had ruined the stems of five pipes. He felt muggy and his stomach was queasy. Yet there was no solution.

It was impossible to say, "All right, we've got a man from the future. So what? Turn him loose and let him make a life for himself in our time, since he can't return to his own."

It was impossible to do that for several reasons: (1) What if he *couldn't* adjust? He was then a potential menace, of *incalculable* potential. (2) What if an enemy power—and God knew there were enough powers around anxious to get a secret weapon as valuable as Qarlo—grabbed him, and *did* somehow manage to work out the concepts behind the rifle, the firmer, the mono-atomic anti-gravity device in the pouch? What then? (3) A man used to war, knowing only war, would eventually *seek* or foment war.

There were dozens of others, they were only beginning to realize. No, something had to be done with him.

Imprison him?

For what? The man had done no real harm. He had not intentionally caused the death of the man on the subway platform. He had been frightened by the train. He had been attacked by the executives—one of whom had a broken neck, but was alive. No, he was just "a stranger and afraid, in a world I never made," as Housman had put it so terrifyingly clearly.

Kill him?

For the same reasons, unjust and brutal . . . not to mention wasteful.

Find a place for him in society?

Doing what?

Sims raged in his mind, mulled it over and tried every angle. It was an insoluble problem. A simple dogface, with no other life than that of a professional soldier, what good was he?

All Qarlo knew was war.

The question abruptly answered itself: If he knows no other life than that of a soldier . . . why, make him a soldier. (But . . . who was to say that, with his knowledge of futuristic tactics and weapons, he might not turn into another Hitler, or Genghis Khan?) No, making him a soldier would only heighten the problem. There could be no peace of mind were he in a position where he might organize.

As a tactician then?

It might work at that.

Sims slumped behind his desk, pressed down the key of his intercom, spoke to the secretary, "Get me General Mainwaring, General Polk and the Secretary of Defense."

He clicked the key back. It just might work at that. If Qarlo could be persuaded to detail fighting plans, now that he realized where he was, and that the men who held him were not his enemies and allies of Ruskie-Chink (and what a field of speculation *that* pair of words opened!).

It just might work . . .

. . . but Sims doubted it.

Mainwaring stayed on to report when Polk and the Secretary of Defense went back to their regular duties. He was a big man, with softness written across his face and body, and a pompous white moustache. He shook his head sadly, as though the Rosetta Stone had been stolen from him just before an all-important experiment.

"Sorry, Sims, but the man is useless to us. Brilliant grasp of military tactics, so long as it involves what he calls 'eighty-thread beams' and telepathic contacts.

"Do you know those wars up there are fought as much mentally as they are physically? Never heard of a tank or a mortar, but the stories he tells of brain-burning and spore-death would make you sick. It isn't pretty, the way they fight.

"I thank God I'm not going to be around to see it; I thought *our* wars were filthy and unpleasant. They've got us licked all down the line for brutality and mass death. And the strange thing is, this Qarlo fellow *despises* it! For a while there—felt foolish as hell—but for a while there, when he was explaining it, I almost wanted to chuck my career, go out and start beating the drum for disarmament."

The General summed up, and it was apparent Qarlo was useless as a tactician. He had been brought up with one way of waging war, and it would take a lifetime for him to adjust enough to be of any tactical use.

But it didn't really matter, for Sims was certain the General had given him the answer to the problem, inadvertently.

He would have to clear it with Security, and the President, of course. And it would take a great deal of publicity to make the people realize this man actually *was* the real thing, an inhabitant of the future. But if it worked out, Qarlo Clobregnny, the soldier and nothing *but* the soldier, could be the most valuable man Time had ever spawned.

He set to work on it, wondering foolishly if he wasn't too much the idealist.

Ten soldiers crouched in the frozen mud. Their firmers had been jammed, had turned the sand and dirt of their holes only to icelike conditions. The cold was seeping up through their suits, and the jammed firmers were emitting hard radiation. One of the men screamed as the radiation took hold in his gut, and he felt the organs watering away. He leaped up, vomiting blood and phlegm—and was caught across the face by a robot-tracked triple beam. The front of his face disappeared, and the nearly decapitated corpse flopped back into the firmhole, atop a comrade.

That soldier shoved the body aside carelessly, thinking

of his four children, lost to him forever in a Ruskie-Chink raid on Garmatopolis, sent to the bogs to work. His mind conjured up the sight of the three girls and the little boy with such long, long eyelashes—each dragging through the stinking bog, a mineral bag tied to the neck, collecting fuel rocks for the enemy. He began to cry softly. The sound and mental image of crying was picked up by a Ruskie-Chink telepath somewhere across the lines, and even before the man could catch himself, blank his mind, the telepath was on him.

The soldier raised up from the firmhole bottom, clutching with crooked hands at his head. He began to tear at his features wildly, screaming high and piercing, as the enemy telepath burned away his brain. In a moment his eyes were empty, staring shells, and the man flopped down beside his comrade, who had begun to deteriorate.

A thirty-eight thread whined its beam overhead, and the eight remaining men saw a munitions wheel go up with a deafening roar. Hot shrapnel zoomed across the field, and a thin, brittle, knife-edged bit of plasteel arced over the edge of the firmhole, and buried itself in one soldier's head. The piece went in crookedly, through his left earlobe, and came out skewering his tongue, half-extended from his open mouth. From the side it looked as though he were wearing some sort of earring. He died in spasms, and it took an awfully long while. Finally, the twitching and gulping got so bad, one of his comrades used the butt of a Brandelmeier across the dying man's nose. It splintered the nose, sent bone chips into the brain, killing the man instantly.

Then the attack call came!

In each of their heads, the telepathic cry came to advance, and they were up out of the firmhole, all seven of them, reciting their daily prayer, and knowing it would do no good. They advanced across the slushy ground, and overhead they could hear the buzz of leech bombs, coming down on the enemy's thread emplacements.

All around them in the deep-set night, the varicolored explosions popped and sugged, expanding in all directions like fireworks, then dimming the scene, again the blackness.

One of the soldiers caught a beam across the belly, and he was thrown sidewise for ten feet, to land in a soggy heap, his stomach split open, the organs glowing and pulsing wetly from the charge of the threader. A head popped out of a firmhole before them, and three of the remaining six fired simultaneously. The enemy was a booby—rigged to back-track their kill urge, rigged to a telepathic hookup—and even as the body exploded under their combined firepower, each of the men caught fire. Flames leaped from their mouths, from their pores, from the instantly charred spaces where their eyes had been. A pyrotic-telepath had been at work.

The remaining three split and cut away, realizing they might be thinking, might be giving themselves away. That was the horror of being just a dog-soldier, not a special telepath behind the lines. Out here all the options totaled nothing but death.

A doggie-mine slithered across the ground, entwined itself in the legs of one soldier, and blew his legs out from under him. He lay there clutching the shredded stumps, feeling the blood soaking into the mud, and then unconsciousness seeped into his brain. He died shortly thereafter.

Of the two left, one leaped a barbwall and blasted out a thirty-eight thread emplacement of twelve men, at the cost of the top of his head. He was left alive, and curiously, as though the war had stopped, he felt the top of himself, and his fingers pressed lightly against convoluted, slick matter for a second before he dropped to the ground.

His braincase was open, glowed strangely in the night, but no one saw it.

The last soldier dove under a beam that zzzzzzzed through the night and landed on his elbows. He rolled with the tumble, felt the edge of a leech-bomb crater, and dove in headfirst. The beam split up his passage, and he escaped charring by an inch. He lay in the hole, feeling the cold of the battlefield seeping around him, and drew his cloak closer.

The soldier was Qarlo . . .

He finished talking, and sat down on the platform . . .

The audience was silent . . .

Sims shrugged into his coat, fished around in the pocket for the cold pipe. The dottle had fallen out of the bowl, and he felt the dark grains at the bottom of the pocket. The audience was filing out slowly, hardly anyone speaking, but each staring at others around him. As though they were suddenly realizing what had happened to them, as though they were looking for a solution.

Sims passed such a solution. The petitions were there, tacked up alongside the big sign—duplicate of the ones up all over the city. He caught the heavy black type on them as he passed through the auditorium's vestibule:

SIGN THIS PETITION!
PREVENT WHAT YOU HAVE HEARD TONIGHT!

People were flocking around the petitions, but Sims knew it was only a token gesture at this point: the legislation had gone through that morning. No more war . . . under any conditions. And intelligence reported the long playing records, the piped broadcasts, the p.a. trucks, had all done their jobs. Similar legislation was going through all over the world.

It looked as though Qarlo had done it, single-handed.

Sims stopped to refill his pipe, and stared up at the big black-lined poster near the door.

HEAR QARLO, THE SOLDIER FROM THE FUTURE!
SEE THE MAN FROM TOMORROW,
AND HEAR HIS STORIES
OF THE WONDERFUL WORLD OF THE FUTURE!
FREE! NO OBLIGATIONS! HURRY!

The advertising had been effective, and it was a fine campaign.

Qarlo had been more valuable just telling about his Wars, about how men died in that day in the future, than he could ever have been as a strategist.

It took a real soldier, who hated war, to talk of it, to show people that it was ugly, and unglamorous. And there was a certain sense of foul defeat, of hopelessness, in knowing the future was the way Qarlo described it. It made you want to stop the flow of Time, say, "No. The future will *not* be like this! We will abolish war!"

Certainly enough steps in the right direction had been taken. The legislation was there, and those who had held back, who had tried to keep animosity alive, were being disposed of every day.

Qarlo had done his work well.

There was just one thing bothering special advisor Lyle Sims. The soldier had come back in time, so he was here. That much they knew for certain.

But a nagging worry ate at Sims's mind, made him say prayers he had thought himself incapable of inventing. Made him fight to get Qarlo heard by everyone . . .

Could the future be changed?

Or was it inevitable?

Would the world Qarlo left inevitably appear?

Would all their work be for nothing?

It couldn't be! It dare not be!

He walked back inside, got in line to sign the petitions again, though it was his fiftieth time.

RAIN, RAIN, GO AWAY

I had this pal when I was about fifteen or so, I'll call him Dandy, even though that wasn't his name. He's still around, and I see no reason to disrespect him, but I want to use him as the example of the troublemaker lesson embodied in the story that follows . . .an admittedly silly little story I wrote early in my career. Dandy was talented. He was whip-smart, and goodlooking and could talk to girls and adults with ease. He was the front-man for our bunch of weird geekazoids, because he got along with the basketball team and the social slicks and the cops, even. But he was one of us, because he liked to read, and he had a talent for writing, and he understood science and math and all like that, sort of an all-around Renais-sance High School kid. So we all thought he was going to be the one who became famous and rich and had the best-looking girls. (Remember, I was the one who was gonna wind up in the gutter or jail.) And soon after we all graduated high school, Dandy wrote this story that got published in one of the most prestigious magazines of the time, he got a book contract, he got a full scholarship to an atomic energy university, and he was courted and inducted into a top-line fraternity. And the book never got published, he bombed out of school, he drank too much, and he wound up writing copy for some mail order cata-logue. Spent a decade or so wandering around, and last time I heard of him he'd managed to find a happy berth, and was enjoying life. But now he's approaching seventy, and there was a lot of potential and grandeur that never got to show itself. He procrastinated. He put off till a decade later, that which he should've done today. Rain, rain, go away, come again . . .

*S*ometimes *I wish I were a duck,* mused Hobert Krouse.

Standing in front of his desk, looking out the window at the amount of water the black sky had begun to let flow, his thoughts rolled in the same trough made for them years before.

"Rain, rain, go away, come again another . . ." he began, *sotto voce.*

"Krouse! Come away from that window and get back to those weather analyses, man, or you'll be out *walking* in that, instead of just looking at it!" The voice had a sandpaper edge, and it rasped across Hobert's senses in much the same way real sandpaper might. Hobert gasped involuntarily and turned. Mr. Beigen stood, florid and annoyed, framed in the big walnut timbers of the entrance to his office.

"I—I was just looking at the rain, sir. You see, my predictions *were* correct. It *is* going to be a prolonged wet spell . . ." Hobert began, obsequiously sliding back into his swivel chair.

"*Balderdash*, man," Mr. Beigen roared. "Nothing of the sort! I've told you time and again, Krouse, leave the predictions to the men who are paid for that sort of thing. You just tend to your checking, and leave the brainwork to men who have the equipment. Prolonged rain, indeed! All my reports say fair.

"And let's have that be the *last* time we see you at something other than your job during work hours, Krouse. Which are eight-thirty to five, six days a week," he added.

With a quick glance across the rest of the office, immobilizing every person there with its rockiness, Beigen went back into his office, the door slamming shut with finality.

Hobert thought he caught a fragment of a sentence, just as the door banged closed. It sounded like "Idiot," but he couldn't be sure.

Hobert did not like the tone Mr. Beigen had used in saying it was the *last time* he wanted to see him away from his desk. It sounded more like a promise than a demand.

The steady pound of the rain on the window behind him made him purse his lips in annoyance. Even though his job was only checking the weather predictions sent down from the offices upstairs against the messages sent out by the teletype girls, still he had been around the offices of Havelock, Beigen and Elsesser long enough to take a crack at predicting himself.

Even though Mr. Beigen was the biggest man in the wholesale farm supply business, and Hobert was one small link in a chain employing many hundreds of people, still he didn't have to scream that way, did he? Hobert worried for a full three minutes, until he realized that the stack of invoices had been augmented by yet another pile from the Gloversville, Los Angeles and Topeka teletypes. He began furiously trying to catch up. Something which he would never quite be able to do.

Walking home in the rain, his collar turned up, his bowler pulled down tight over his ears, the tips of his shoes beginning to lose their shine from the water, Hobert's thoughts began to take on a consistency much like the angry sky above him.

Eight years in the offices of Havelock, Beigen and Elsesser had done nothing for him but put sixty-eight dollars and fifty-five cents into his hand each week. The work was an idiot's chore, and though Hobert had never finished college, still it was a job far beneath his capabilities.

Hobert's section of the firm was one of those little services rendered to farmers within the reach of the company's services. A long-range weather forecast for all parts of the country, sent free each week to thousands of subscribers.

A crack of thunder split Hobert's musings, forcing him to a further awareness of the foul weather. Rain had soaked him from hat crown to shoe soles and even gotten in through his upturned collar, to run down his back in chilly threads. He began to wish there might be someone waiting at home for him with the newspaper (the one he had bought at the corner was now a sodden mass) and his slippers, but he knew there would not be.

Hobert had never married—he had just not found *the* girl he told himself must come to him. In fact, the last affair he could recall having had was five years before, when he had gone up to Bear Mountain for two weeks. She had been a Western Union telegraph operator named Alice, with very silky chestnut hair, and for a while Hobert had thought perhaps. But he had gone back to New York and she had gone back to Trenton, New Jersey, without even a formal good-bye, and Hobert despaired of ever finding The One.

He walked down West 52nd to Seventh Avenue, scuffing his feet in irritation at the puddles which placed themselves so he could not fail to walk through them, soaking his socks. At 50th he boarded the subway uptown and all the way sat brooding.

Who does Beigen think he is, Hobert seethed within himself. I've been in that office eight years, three months and . . . well, I've been there well over eight years, three months. Who does he think he's pushing around like that? I may be a little smaller, but I'll be (his mind fortified itself) *damned* (his mind looked around in embarrassment to see if anyone had noticed) if I'll take treatment like that. I'll—I'll *quit*, that's what I'll do. I'll quit. Then where will he be? Who'll he get to fill my job as capably as I can?

But even as he said it, he could see the ad in the *Herald-Tribune* the night he would resign:

OFFICE Boy-clk, 18–20 exc. future $40 no exp. nec. Havelock, Beigen & Elsesser 229 W 52.

He could see it so clearly in his mind because that had been the ad to which he had replied, eight years, three months and an undetermined number of weeks before. The horror of it all was compounded by the fact that he couldn't even *answer* the ad now. He was no longer 18–20. He was caroming toward 50.

The mindless roar of the train hurtling through the subway dimmed for Hobert and, as happens to everyone occasionally, everything summed up for him. The eight years summed up. His life summed up.

"I'm a failure." He said it aloud, and heads turned toward him, but he didn't notice. He said it again in his mind, clearer this time, for it was true and he knew it: *I'm a failure.*

I've never been to Puerto Rico or India or even to Trenton, New Jersey, he thought. The farthest away from this city I've been is Bear Mountain, and that was only for two weeks. I've never really loved anyone—except Mother, he hastened to add; and she's been gone thirteen years now—and no one has ever really loved me.

When the line of thoughts had run itself out, Hobert looked up, misty-eyed, and saw that he had gone past his station. He got off, walked over and took the downtown train back to West 110th.

In his room, cramped by books and periodicals so that free space was nearly non-existent, Hobert removed his wet hat and coat, hung them near the radiator, and sat down on the bed, which served as a couch. I wish something truly unusual would happen to me, thought Hobert. I wish something so spectacular would happen that everyone would turn as I went down the street, and say, "There goes Hobert Krouse; what a *man!*" And they would have awe and wonder in their eyes. I wish it would happen to me just once. "Every man is entitled to fame at least once in his lifetime!" He said it with force, for he believed it. But nothing happened, and Hobert went to bed that night with the wind howling through the space between the apartment buildings and with the rain beating against his window.

Perhaps it will wash some of that dirt off the outside, he mused, thinking of the window that had not been clean since he had moved in. But then, it was five floors up and the custodian wouldn't hire a window-washer and it was too dangerous out there for Hobert to do it. Sleep began to press down on him, the sure feel of it washing away his worries of the day. Almost as an incantation he repeated the phrase he had remembered from his childhood, the phrase he had murmured thousands of times since. "Rain, rain, go away, come again another day." He began the phrase again, but sleep cut it off in mid-thought.

It rained all that week, and by Sunday morning, when Hobert emerged from the brownstone face of his building, the ground around the one lone tree growing slantwise on the sloping sidewalk of W. 110th Street was mushy and runny. The gutters were swollen with flowing torrents. Hobert looked up at the darkened sky which was angry even at eleven in the morning, with no trace of sun.

In annoyance he ran through the "Rain, rain, go away," nonsense and trudged up the hill to the corner of Broadway for breakfast.

In the little restaurant, his spread-bottom drooping over a stool too small for his pear shape, Hobert gave huge traditional leers to Florence, the redhead behind the counter, and ordered the usual: "Two up, ham steak, coffee, cream, Florence."

As he ate his eggs, Hobert returned again to his wistful dreams of a few evenings previous.

"Florence," he said, "you ever wish something spectacular would happen to you?" He pushed a mouthful of toast and ham around his tongue to get the sentence out.

Florence looked up from her duty; putting rock-hard butter squares on paper pads. "Yeah, I useta wish somethin'd happen ta me." She pushed a string of red hair back into place. "But it never did." She shrugged.

"Like what did you wish?" inquired Hobert.

"Oh, *you* know. Silly stuff, like whyn't Mahlon Brando come in here an' grab me an' like that. Or whyn't I win a millyun bucks in the Irish Sweepstakes and come back here some aftuhnoon wearin' a mink stole and flip the end of it in that stinkin' Erma Geller's kisser. *You* know." She went back to the butter.

Hobert knew. He had made equivalent wishes himself, with particulars slightly changed. It had been Gina Lollobrigida and a $250 silk shantung suit like Mr. Beigen owned, when *he* had daydreams.

He finished the eggs and ham, wiped up the last little

drippings of egg yellow, bolted his coffee, and, wiping his mouth with his paper napkin, said, "Well, see you tomorrow, Florence."

She accepted the exact change he left for the bill, noted the usual fifteen cents under the plate and said, "Ain'tcha comin' in for dinner tanight?"

Hobert assumed an air of bored detachment. "No, no, I think I shall go downtown and take in a show tonight. Or perhaps I shall dine at The Latin Quarter or Lindy's. With pheasant under glass and caviar and some of that famous Lindy's cheesecake. I shall decide when I get down there." He began to walk out, joviality in his walk.

"Oh, ya *such* a character," laughed Florence, behind him.

But the rain continued, and Hobert only went a few streets down Broadway where the storm had driven everyone off the sidewalks, with the exception of those getting the Sunday editions. "Lousy day," he muttered under his breath. Been like this all week, he observed to himself. That ought to teach that bigmouth Beigen that maybe I can predict as well as his high-priced boys upstairs. Maybe *now* he'll listen to me!

Hobert could see Mr. Beigen coming over to his desk, stammering for a moment, then, putting his arm around Hobert's shoulders—which Hobert carefully ignored—telling Hobert he was terribly sorry and he would never scream again, and would Hobert forgive him for his rudeness and here was a fifteen dollar raise and a job upstairs in the analysis department.

Hobert could see it all. Then the wetness of his socks, clinging to his ankles, made the vision fade. Oh, rain, rain!

The movie was just opening, and though Hobert despised Barbara Stanwyck, he went in to kill the time. It was lonely for a pot-bellied man of forty-six in New York without any close friends and all the current books and magazines read.

Hobert tsk-tsked all the way through the picture, annoyed at the simpleton plot. He kept thinking to himself that if he had one wish he would wish she never made another picture.

When he emerged, three hours later, it was afternoon and the rain whipped into the alcove behind the ticket booth drenching him even before he could get onto the street. It was a cold rain, wetter than any Hobert could remember, and thick, with no space between drops, it seemed. As though God were tossing down all the rain in the heavens at once.

Hobert began walking, humming to himself the little rain, rain ditty. His mind began trying to remember how many times he had uttered that series of words. He failed, for it stretched back to his childhood. Every time he had seen a rainfall he had made the same appeal. And he was surprised to realize now that it had worked almost uncannily, many times.

He could recall one sunny day when he was twelve, that his family had set aside for a picnic. It had suddenly darkened and begun to come down scant minutes before they were to leave.

Hobert remembered having pressed himself up flat against the front room windows, one after another, wildly repeating the phrase over and over. The windows had been cold, and his nose had felt funny, all flattened up that way. But after a few minutes it had worked. The rain had stopped, the sky had miraculously cleared, and they went to Huntington Woods for the picnic. It hadn't been a really good picnic, but that wasn't important. What *was* important was that *he* had stopped the rain with his own voice.

For many years thereafter Hobert had believed that.

And he had applied the rain, rain ditty as often as he could, which was quite often. Sometimes it never seemed to work, and others it did. But whenever he got around to saying it, the rain never lasted too long afterward.

Wishes, wishes, wishes, ruminated Hobert. If I had one wish, what would I wish? Would the wish really come true?

Or do you have to keep repeating your wish? Is that the secret? Is that why some people get what they want eventually, because they make the same wish, over and over, the same way till it comes true? Perhaps we all have the ability to make our wishes come true, but we must persist in them, for belief and the strength of your convictions is a powerful thing. If I had one wish, what would I wish? I'd wish that . . .

It was then, just as Hobert saw the Hudson River beginning to overflow onto Riverside Drive, rising up and up over the little park along the road, that he realized.

"Oh my goodness!" cried Hobert, starting up the hill as fast as he could.

"Rain, rain, go away, come again another day."

Hobert said it, sprayed his throat, and made one more chalk mark on the big board full of marks. He said it again, and once more marked.

It was odd. All that rain *had* gone away, only to come another day. The unfortunate part was that it *all* came back the same day. Hobert was—literally speaking—up the creek. He had been saying it since he was a child, how many times he had no idea. The postponements had been piling up for almost forty-six years, which was quite a spell of postponements. The only way he could now stop the flood of rain was to keep saying it, and say it one more time than all the times he had said it during those forty-six years. And the next time all forty-six years plus the one before plus another. And so on. And so on.

The water was lapping up around the cornice of his building, and Hobert crouched farther into his rubber raft on its roof, pulling the big blackboard toward him, repeating the phrase, chalking, spraying occasionally.

It wasn't bad enough that he was forced to sit there repeating, repeating, repeating all day, just to stop the rain; there was another worry nagging Hobert's mind.

Though it had stopped raining now, for a while, and though he was fairly safe on the roof of his building, Hobert was worried. For when the weather became damp, he invariably caught laryngitis.

NIGHT VIGIL

The lesson in this "space opera" should be apparent. If you're hired to do a job, DO THE DAMNED JOB! There are always punk-out reasons you can dream up why: "I'm not being paid enough" or "They work me too hard" or "How come s/he over there is doing the same job as I am, but s/he's getting paid twice as much" or "They don't respect me." You're supposed to *enjoy* the work you do, but if circumstances put you in the grease at a Mickey D's, or under a leaking tranny on somebody's Yugo, or working the stockroom at a K-Mart or Target, and you have to do it for the dough, and you hate the job, and you hate the hours, and you hate the fact that you can't be out hanging with the posse, well tough sh-t, Joker; you signed on to do the job, and they pay you to do it, so DO THE DAMNED JOB! If you don't like the gig, quit. Give 'em notice promptly, don't leave 'em in the lurch suddenly, don't trash the area out of baby-spite, and don't start shoplifting. Just DO THE DAMN JOB! That's how somebody with strength does it. Don't whine, don't piss'n'moan, don't jerk 'em around, just hang in there as long as it's ethically necessary, and then get in the wind. But if you sign on to do the job, no matter how onerous the chore, DO THE DAMNED JOB, just *do* it.

D arkness seeped in around the little quonset. It oozed out of the deeps of space and swirled around Ferreno's home. The automatic scanners turned and turned, whispering quietly, their message of wariness unconsciously reassuring the old man.

He bent over and plucked momentarily at a bit of lint on the carpet. It was the only speck of foreign matter on the rug, reflecting the old man's perpetual cleanliness and almost fanatical neatness.

The racks of bookspools were all binding-to-binding, set flush with the lip of the shelves; the bed was made with a military tightness that allowed a coin to bounce high three times; the walls were free of fingerprints—dusted and wiped clean twice a day; there was no speck of lint or dust on anything in the one room quonset.

When Ferreno had flicked the single bit of matter from his fingers, into the incinerator, the place was immaculate.

It reflected twenty-four years of watching, waiting, and living alone. Living alone on the edge of Forever, waiting for something that might never come. Tending blind, dumb machines that could say *Something is out here*, but also said, *We don't know what it is.*

Ferreno returned to his pneumo-chair, sank heavily into it, and blinked, his deep-set grey eyes seeking into the furthest rounded corner of the quonset's ceiling. His eyes seemed to be looking for something. But there was nothing there he did not already know. Far too well.

He had been on this asteroid, this spot lost in the darkness, for twenty-four years. In that time, nothing had happened.

There had been no warmth, no women, no feeling, and only a brief flurry of emotion for almost twenty of those twenty-four years.

Ferreno had been a young man when they had set him down on The Stone. They had pointed out there and said to him:

"Beyond the farthest spot you can see, there's an island universe. In that island universe, there's an enemy, Ferreno. One day he'll become tired of his home and come after yours.

"You're here to watch for him."

And they had gone before he could ask them.

Ask them: who *were* the enemy? Where would they come from, and why was he here, alone, to stop them? What could he do if they came? What were the huge, silent machines that bulked monstrous behind the little quonset? Would he ever go home again?

All he had known was the intricate dialing process for the inverspace communicators. The tricky-fingered method of sending a coded response half across the galaxy to a waiting Mark LXXXII brain—waiting only for his frantic pulsations.

He had known only that. The dialing process and the fact that he was to watch. Watch for he-knew-not-what!

There at first he had thought he would go out of his mind. It had been the monotony. Monotony intensified to a frightening degree. The ordeal of watching, watching, watching. Sleeping, eating from the self-replenishing supply of protofoods in the greentank, reading, sleeping again, re-reading the bookspools till their casings crackled, snapped, and lost panes. The re-binding—and re-re-reading. The horror of knowing every passage of a book by heart.

He could recite from Stendhal's LE ROUGE ET LE NOIR and Hemingway's DEATH IN THE AFTERNOON and Melville's MOBY DICK, till the very words lost meaning, sounded strange and unbelievable to his ears.

First had come living in filth and throwing things against the curving walls and ceilings. Things designed to give, and bounce—but not to break. Walls designed to absorb the impact of a flung drink-ball or a smashed fist. Then had come the extreme neatness, then a moderation, and finally back to the neat, prissy fastidiousness of an old man who wants to know where everything is at any time.

No women. That had been a persistent horror for the longest time. A mounting pain in his groin and belly, that had wakened him during the arbitrary night, swimming in his own sweat, his mouth and body aching. He had gotten over it slowly. He had even attempted emasculation. None of it had worked, of course, and it had only passed away with his youth.

He had taken to talking to himself. And answering himself. Not madness, just the fear that the ability to speak might be lost.

Madness had descended many times during the early years. The blind, clawing urgency to get out! Get out into the airless vastness of The Stone. At least to die, to end this nowhere existence.

But they had constructed the quonset without a door.

The plasteel-sealed slit his deliverers had gone out had been closed irrevocably behind them, and there *was* no way out.

Madness had come often.

But they had selected him wisely. He clung to his sanity, for he knew it was his only escape. He knew it would be a far more horrible thing to end out his days in this quonset a helpless maniac, than to remain sane.

He swung back over the line and soon grew content with his world in a shell. He waited, for there was nothing else he could do; and in his waiting a contentment grew out of frantic restlessness. He began to think of it as a jail, then as a coffin, then as the ultimate black of the Final Hole. He would wake in the arbitrary night, choking, his throat constricted, his hands warped into claws that crooked themselves into the foam rubber of the sleeping couch with fierceness.

The time was spent. A moment after it had passed, he could not tell *how* it had been spent. His life became dust-dry and at times he could hardly tell he *was* living. Had it not been for the protected, automatic calendar, he would hardly have known the years were passing.

And ever, ever, ever—the huge, dull, sleeping eye of the warning buzzer. Staring back at him, veiled, from the ceiling.

It was hooked up with the scanners. The scanners that hulked behind the quonset. The scanners in turn were hooked up to the net of tight inverspace rays that interlocked each other out to the farthest horizon Ferreno might ever know.

And the net, in turn, joined at stop-gap functions with the doggie-guards, also waiting, watching with dumb metal and plastic minds for that implacable alien enemy that might some day come.

They had known the enemy would come, for they had

found the remnants of those the enemy had destroyed. Remnants of magnificent and powerful cultures, ground to microscopic dust by the heel of a terrifying invader.

They could not chance roaming the universe with those Others somewhere. Somewhere ... waiting. They had formed the inverspace net, joining it with the doggie-guards. And they had hooked the system in with the scanners; and they had wired the scanners to the big, dull eye in the ceiling of the quonset.

Then they had set Ferreno to watching it.

At first Ferreno had watched the thing constantly. Waiting for it to make the disruptive noise he was certain it would emit. Breaking the perpetual silence of his bubble. He waited for the bloodiness of its blink to warp fantastic shadows across the room and furniture. He even spent five months deciding what shape those shadows would take, when they came.

Then he entered the period of nervousness. Jumping for no reason at all, to stare at the eye. The hallucinations: it was blinking, it was ringing in his ears. The sleeplessness: it might go off and he would not hear it.

Then as time progressed, he grew unaware of it, forgot it existed for long periods. Till it had finally come to the knowledge that it was there; a dim thing, an unremembered thing, as much a part of him as his own ears, his own eyes. He had nudged it to the back of his mind—but it was always there.

Always there, always waiting, always on the verge of disruption.

Ferreno never forgot why he was there. He never forgot the reason they had come for him. *The day they had come for him.*

The evening had been pale and laden with sound. The

flits clacking through the air above the city, the crickets in the grass, the noise of holograph from the living room of the house.

He had been sitting on the front porch, arms tight about his girl, on a creaking porch glider that smacked the wall every time they rocked back too far. He remembered the taste of the sweet-acidy lemonade in his mouth as the three men resolved out of the gloom.

They had stepped onto the porch.

"Are you Charles Jackson Ferreno, age nineteen, brown hair, brown eyes, five feet ten, 158 pounds, scar on right inner wrist?"

"Y-yes . . . why?" he had stammered.

The intrusion of these strangers on a thing as private as his love-making had caused him to falter.

Then they had grabbed him.

"What are you doing? Get your hands off him!" Marie had screamed.

They had flashed an illuminated card at her, and she had subsided into terrified silence before their authority. Then they had taken him, howling, into a flit—black and silent—and whirled him off to the plasteel block in the Nevada desert that had been Central Space Headquarters.

They had hypno-conditioned him to operate the inver-space communicators. A task he could not have learned in two hundred years—involving the billion alternate dialing choices—had they not planted it mechanically.

Then they had prepared him for the ship.

"Why are you doing this to me? Why have you picked me!" he had screamed at them, fighting the lacing-up of the pressure suit.

They had told him. The Mark LXXXII. He had been chosen best out of forty-seven thousand punched cards whipped through its platinum vitals. Best by selection. An infallible machine had said he was the least susceptible to madness, inefficiency, failure. He was the best, and the Service needed him.

Then, the ship.

The nose of the beast pointed straight up into a cloudless sky, blue and unfilmed as the best he had ever known. Then a rumble, and a scream, and the pressure as the ship had raced into space. And the almost imperceptible wrenching as the ship slipped scud wise through inverspace. The travel through the milky pinkness of that not-space. Then the gut-pulling again, and *there!* off to the right through the port—that bleak little asteroid with its quonset blemish.

When they had set him down and told him about the enemy, he had screamed at them, but they had pushed him back into the bubble, had sealed the pressure-lock, and had gone back to the ship.

They had left The Stone, then. Rushing up till they had popped out of sight around a bend in space.

His hands had been bloodied, beating against the resilient plasteel of the pressure-lock and the vista windows.

He never forgot why he was there.

He tried to conjure up the enemy. Were they horrible slug-like creatures from some dark star, ready to spread a ring of viscous, poisonous fluid inside Earth's atmosphere; were they tentacled spider-men who drank blood; were they perhaps quiet, well-mannered beings who would sublimate all of man's drives and ambitions; were they . . .

He went on and on, till it did not matter in the slightest to him. Then he forgot time. But he remembered he was here to watch. To watch and wait. A sentinel at the gate of the Forever, waiting for an unknown enemy that might streak out of nowhere bound for Earth and destruction. Or that might have died out millenia before—leaving him here on a worthless assignment, doomed to an empty life.

He began to hate. The hate of the men who had consigned him to this living death. He hated the men who had brought him here in their ship. He hated the men who had conceived the idea of a sentinel. He hated the Mark computer that had said:

"Get Charles Jackson Ferreno *only!*"

He hated them all. But most of all he hated the alien enemy. The implacable enemy that had thrown fear into the hearts of the men.

Ferreno hated them all with a bitter obsession verging on madness itself. Then, the obsession passed. Even that passed.

Now he was an old man. His hands and face and neck wrinkled with the skin-folding of age. His eyes had sunk back under ridges of flesh, his eyebrows white as the stars. His hair loose and uncombed, trimmed raggedly by an ultra-safe shaving device he had not been able to adapt for suicide. A beard of unkempt and foul proportions. A body slumped into a position that fitted his pneumo-chair exactly.

Thoughts played leap-frog with themselves. Ferreno was thinking. For the first time in eight years—since the last hallucination had passed—actually thinking. He sat humped into the pneumo-chair that had long ago formed itself permanently to his posture. The muted strains of some long since over-familiarized piece of taped music humming above him. Was the horrible repetition Vivaldi's *Gloria Mass* or a snatch of Monteverdi? He fumbled in the back of his mind, in the recess this music had lived for so long—consigned there by horrible repetition.

His thoughts veered before he found the answer. It didn't matter. Nothing mattered but the watching.

Beads of perspiration sprang out, dotting his upper lip and the receding arcs of sparse hair at his temples.

What if they never came?

What if they had gone already and through some failure of the mechanisms he had missed them? Even the subliminal persistence of the revolving scanners' workings was not assurance enough. For the first time in many years he was hearing the scanners again, and did they sound right?

Didn't ... they ... sound ... a ... bit ... off?

They didn't sound right! My God, all these years and now they weren't working! He had no way of repairing them, no way of getting out of here, he was doomed to lie here till he died—his purpose gone! Oh My God! All these years here nowhere and my youth gone and they've stopped running and no-good damned things failing now and the aliens've slipped through and Earth's gone and I'm no good here and it's all for nothing and Marie and everything ...

Ferreno! Good God, man! Stop yourself!

He grabbed control of himself abruptly, lurchingly. The machines were perfect. They worked on the basic substance of inverspace. They *couldn't* go wrong, once set running on the pattern.

But the uselessness of it all remained.

His head fell into his shaking hands. He felt tears bubbling behind his eyes. What could one puny man do here, away from all and everyone? They had told him more than one man would be dangerous. They would kill each other out of sheer boredom. The same for a man and a woman. Only one man could remain in possession of his senses, to tickle out the intricate warning on the inverspace communicator.

He recalled again what they had said about relief.

There could be none. Once sealed in, a man had begun the fight with himself. If they took him out and put in another man, they were upping the chances of a miscalculation—and a failure. By picking the very best man by infallible computer, they were putting all their eggs in one basket—but they were cutting risk to the bone.

He recalled again what they had said about a machine in his place.

Impossible. A robot brain, equipped to perform that remarkable task of sorting the warning factors, and recording it on the inverspace communicators—including any possible ramifications that might crop up in fifty years—would have to be fantastically large.

It would have had to be five hundred miles long by three hundred wide. With tapes and back-up circuits and tranversistors and punch-checks that, if laid end to end, would have reached halfway from The Stone to Earth.

He knew he was necessary, which had been one of the things that had somehow stopped him from finding a way to wreck himself or the whole quonset during those twenty-four years.

Yet, it still seemed so worthless, so helpless, so unnecessary. He didn't know, but he was certain the quonset bubble would inform them if he died or was helpless. Then they would try again.

He was necessary, if . . .

If the enemy was coming. *If* the enemy hadn't already passed him by. *If* the enemy hadn't died long ago. *If, if, if!*

He felt the madness walking again, like some horrible monster of the mind.

He pressed it back with cool argument.

He knew, deep inside himself, that he was a symbol. A gesture of desperation. A gesture of survival to the peoples of Earth. They wanted to live. But did they have to sacrifice him for their survival?

He could not come to an answer within himself.

Perhaps it was inevitable. Perhaps not. Either way, it just happened he had been the man.

Here at this junction of the galaxies; in this spot of most importance; here he was the key to a battle that must some-day be fought.

But what if he was wasted? What if they never came? What if there was no enemy at all? Only supposition by the learned ones. Tampering with the soul and life of a human being!

God! The horror of the thought! What if . . .

A soft buzz accompanied the steady ruby glow from the eye in the ceiling. Ferreno stared, open-mouthed. He could not look up at the eye itself. He stared at the bloody film that covered the walls and floor of the quonset. This was the time he had waited twenty-four years to come!

Was this it? No strident noises, no flickering urgency of the red light. Only a steady glow and a soft buzz.

And at the same time he knew that this was far more effective. It had prevented his death from heart attack.

Then he tried to move. Tried to finger the forty-three keys of the inverspace communicator on the underarm of the pneumo-chair. Tried to translate the message the way it had been impressed sub-cortically in his mind, in a way he could never have done consciously.

He was frozen in his seat.

He couldn't move. His hands would not respond to the frantic orders of his brain. The keys lay silent under the chair arm, the warning unsent. He was totally incapacitated. What if this was a dud? What if the machines were breaking down from the constant twenty-four years of use? Twenty-four years—and how many men before him? What if this was merely another hallucination? What if he was going insane at last?

He couldn't take the chance. His mind blocked him off. The fear was there. He couldn't be wrong, and send the warning now, crying wolf!

Then he saw it, and he knew it was not a dud.

Far out in the ever-dark dark of the space beyond The Stone, he could see a spreading point of light piercing the ebony of the void. And he knew. A calmness covered him.

Now he knew it had not been waste. This was the culmination of all the years of waiting. The privation, the hunger of loneliness, the torture of boredom, all of it. It was worth suffering all that.

He reached under, and closed his eyes, letting his hypno-training take over. His fingers flickered momentarily over the forty-three keys.

That done, he settled back, letting his thoughts rest on the calmed surface of his mind. He watched the spreading points of light in the vista window, knowing it was an armada advancing without pause on Earth.

He was content. He would soon die, and his job would be finished. It was worth all the years without. Without anything good he would have known on Earth. But it was worth all of it. The struggle for life was coming to his people.

His night vigil was finally ended.

The enemy was coming at last.

THE VOICE IN THE GARDEN

Trying to inject a subtextual "moral" into a story as brief as this one puts me in mind of a great quotation by the author of *Moby Dick*, Mr. Herman Melville. He once said: "No great and enduring volume can ever be written on the flea, though many there be who have tried it." (And even though the wonderful Don Marquis did a whole book about a cockroach named archy, and his swinging friend, the slut cat Mehitabel, a cockroach is certainly higher on the evolutionary scale than a flea, so what that tells us, hey, I don't have *all* the answers.) But though I'm writing this "troublemaker lesson" where it ain't necessary, because this short-short story is essentially the product of a smartass who never grew up, it *does*, in fact, suggest a lesson you deadbeats ought to heed. Which is this: if all you've got to back up your wisecracks and stupid jokes—the kind you make in the movie audience that gets everyone cheesed-off at you—is more smartmouth, you are very quickly going to look to everyone around you, everyone you want to be impressed by you, as what you truly are: a horse's patoot.

After the bomb, the last man on Earth wandered through the rubble of Cleveland, Ohio. It had never been a particularly jaunty town, nor even remotely appealing to aesthetes. But now, like Detroit and Rangoon and Minsk and Yokohama, it had been reduced to a petulantly shattered Tinkertoy of lath and brickwork, twisted steel girders and melted glass.

As he picked his way around the dust heap that had been the Soldiers and Sailors Monument in what had been Public Square, his eyes red-rimmed from crying at the loss of humanity, he saw something he had not seen in Beirut or Venice or London. He saw the movement of another human being.

Celestial choruses sang in his head as he broke into a run across the pitted and blasted remains of Euclid Avenue. It was a woman!

She saw him, and in the very posture of her body, he knew she was filled with the same glory he felt. She knew! She began running toward him, her arms outstretched. They seemed to swim toward each other in a ballet of slow motion. He stumbled once, but got to his feet quickly and went on. They detoured around the crumpled tin of tortured metal that had once been automobiles, and met in front of the shattered carcass that was, in a time seemingly eons before, The May Co.

"I'm the last man!" he blurted. He could not keep the words inside, they fought to fill the air. "I'm the last, the very last. They're all dead, everyone but us. I'm the last man, and you're the last woman, and we'll have to mate and start the race again, and this time we'll do it right. No war, no hate, no bigotry, nothing but goodness . . . we'll do it, you'll see, it'll be fine, a bright new shining world from all this death and terror."

Her face was lit with an ethereal beauty, even beneath the soot and deprivation. "Yes, yes," she said. "It'll be just like that. I love you, because we're all there is left to love, each other."

He touched her hand. "I love you. What is your name?"

She flushed slightly. "Eve," she said. "What's yours?"

"Bernie," he said.

DEEPER THAN THE DARKNESS

Since I was in trouble from the git-go (hell, I was taken to the Principal's Office on my first day in kindergarten; not ten minutes after my mother let go of my hand and left me in that classroom full of babies and sandboxes) (I'll tell you *that* tale another time, but I suspect Miss Whatever Her Name Was, the kindergarten teacher at Lathrop Grade School in 1939 or '40, whatever it was, in Painesville, Ohio, I'll bet she still has the marks of my fangs in her right hand), I knew early on that I would have to pretend to be one of the crowd, as best I could fake it, or get the crap kicked out of me at recess and after-school every day. Well, like Alf Gunnderson in this next story, I managed to hide my true personality a little...but not very well, and not for very long times at a stretch. Folks, believe me on this one: if you are what we call a "green monkey," the other apes are going to rip you a new one every time they smell you. Hiding out is an art. But don't hide yourself so well that others like you can't find you. And don't follow the crowd so much that eventually you're not playing at it. Don't wind up doing it so well that the mask you've worn to perfection becomes your real face. Protect yourself, but don't get assimilated. And never wage a land war in Asia. I just thought I'd throw that in. You never know.

They came to Alf Gunnderson in the Pawnee County jail.

He was sitting, hugging his bony knees, against the plasteel wall of the cell. On the plasteel floor lay an ancient, three-string mandolin he had borrowed from the deputy. He had been plunking, with some talent, all that hot, summer day. Under his thin buttocks the empty trough of his mattressless bunk curved beneath his weight. He was an extremely tall man, even hunched up that way.

He was more than tired-looking, more than weary. His was an inside weariness . . . he was a gaunt, empty-looking man. His hair fell lanky and drab and gray-brown in shocks over a low forehead. His eyes seemed to be peas, withdrawn from their pods and placed in a starkly white face. It was difficult to tell whether he could see from them.

Their blankness only accented the total cipher he seemed. There was no inch of expression or recognition on his face, in the line of his body.

More, he was a thin man. He seemed to be a man who

had given up the Search long ago. His face did not change its hollow stare at the plasteel-barred door opposite, even as it swung back to admit the two nonentities.

The two men entered, their stride as alike as the unobtrusive gray mesh suits they wore; as alike as the faces that would fade from memory moments after they had turned. The turnkey—a grizzled country deputy with a minus 8 rating—stared after the men with open wonder on his bearded face.

One of the gray-suited men turned, pinning the wondering stare to the deputy's face. His voice was calm and unrippled. "Close the door and go back to your desk." The words were cold and paced. They brooked no opposition. It was obvious: they were Mindees.

The roar of a late afternoon inverspace ship split the waiting moment outside, then the turnkey slammed the door, palming it loktite. He walked back out of the cell block, hands deep in his coverall pockets. His head was lowered as though he were trying to solve a complex problem. It, too, was obvious: he was trying to block his thoughts off from those goddammed Mindees.

When he was gone, the telepaths circled Gunnderson slowly. Their faces softly altered, subtly, and personality flowed in with quickness. They shot each other confused glances.

Him? the first man thought, nodding slightly at the still, knee-hugging prisoner.

That's what the report said, Ralph. The other man removed his forehead-concealing snapbrim and sat down on the edge of the bunk-trough. He touched Gunnderson's leg with tentative fingers. *He's not thinking, for God's sake!* the thought flashed. *I can't get a thing.*

Incredulousness sparkled in the thought.

He must be blocked off by trauma-barrier, came the reply from the telepath named Ralph.

"Is your name Alf Gunnderson?" the first Mindee inquired softly, a hand on Gunnderson's shoulder.

The expression never changed. The head swiveled slowly and the dead eyes came to bear on the dark-suited telepath. "I'm Gunnderson," he replied briefly. His tones indicated no enthusiasm, no curiosity.

The first man looked up at his partner, doubt wrinkling his eyes, pursing his lips. He shrugged his shoulders, as if to say, *Who knows?*

He turned back to Gunnderson.

Immobile, as before. Hewn from rock, silent as the pit.

"What are you in here for, Gunnderson?" He spoke as though he were unused to words. The halting speech of the telepath.

The dead stare swung back to the plasteel bars. "I set the woods on fire," he said shortly.

The Mindee's face darkened at the prisoner's words. That was what the report had said. The report that had come in from one of the remote corners of the country.

The American Continent was a modern thing, all plasteel and printed circuits, all relays and fast movement, but there had been areas of backwoods country that had never taken to civilizing. They still maintained roads and jails, and fishing holes and forests. Out of one of these had come three reports, spaced an hour apart, with startling ramifications— if true. They had been snapped through the primary message banks in Capitol City in Buenos Aires, reeled through the computalyzers, and handed to the Bureau for check-in. While the inverspace ships plied between worlds, while Earth fought its transgalactic wars, in a rural section of the American Continent, a strange thing was happening.

A mile and a half of raging forest fire, and Alf Gunnderson the one responsible. So they had sent two Bureau Mindees.

"How did it start, Alf?"

The dead eyes closed momentarily, in pain, opened, and he answered, "I was trying to get the pot to heat up. Trying to set the kindling under it to burning. I fired myself too hard." A flash of self-pity and unbearable hurt came into his face, disappeared just as quickly. Empty once more, he added, "I always do."

The first man exhaled sharply, got up and put on his hat. The personality flowed out of his face. He was a carbon copy of the other telepath once more.

"This is the one," he said.

"Come on, Alf," the Mindee named Ralph said. "Let's go."

The authority of his voice no more served to move Gunnderson than their initial appearance had. He sat as he was. The two men looked at one another.

What's the matter with him? the second one flashed.

If you had what he's got—you'd be a bit buggy yourself, the first one replied. They were no longer individuals; they were Bureau men, studiedly, exactly, precisely alike in every detail.

They hoisted the prisoner under his arms, lifted him off the bunk, unresisting. The turnkey came at a call, and still marveling at these men who had come in—shown Bureau cards, sworn him to deadly silence, and were now taking the tramp firebug with them—opened the cell door.

As they passed before him, the telepath named Ralph turned suddenly sharp and piercing eyes on the old guard. "This is government business, mister," he warned. "One word of this, and you'll be a prisoner in your own jail. Clear?"

The turnkey bobbed his head quickly.

"And stop thinking, mister." The Mindee added nastily, "We don't like to be referred to as slimy peekers!" The turnkey turned a shade paler and watched silently as they disappeared down the hall, out of the Pawnee County jailhouse. He waited, blanking fiercely, till he heard the whine of the Bureau solocab rising into the afternoon sky.

Now what the devil did they want with a crazy firebug hobo like that? He thought viciously, *Goddam Mindees!*

After they had flown him cross-continent to Buenos Aires, deep in the heart of the blasted Argentine desert, they sent him in for testing.

The testing was exhaustive. Even though he did not really cooperate, there were things he could not keep them from learning; things that showed up because they were there:

Such as his ability to start fires with his mind.

Such as the fact that he could not control the blazes.

Such as the fact that he had been bumming for fifteen years in an effort to find seclusion.

Such as the fact that he had become a tortured and unhappy man because of his strange mind-power.

"Alf," said the bodiless voice from the rear of the darkened auditorium, "light that cigarette on the table. Put it in your mouth and make it light, Alf. Without a match."

Alf Gunnderson stood in the circle of light. He shifted from leg to leg on the blazing stage, and eyed the cylinder of white paper on the table.

It was starting again. The harrying, the testing, the staring with strangeness. He was different—even from the other accredited psioid types—and they would try to put him away. It had happened before, it was happening now. There was no real peace for him.

"I don't smoke," he said, which was not true. But this was brother kin to the uncountable police line-ups he had gone through, all the way across the American Continent, across Earth, and from A Centauri IX back here. It annoyed him, and it terrified him, for he knew he was trapped.

Except this time, there were no tough, rock-faced cops out there in the darkness beyond his sight. This time there were tough, rock-faced Bureau men, and SpaceCom officials.

Even Terrence, head of SpaceCom, was sitting in one of those pneumoseats, watching him steadily.

Daring him to be what he was!

He lifted the cylinder hesitantly, almost put it back.

"Smoke it, Alf!" snapped a different voice, deeper in tone, from the ebony before him.

He put the cigarette between his lips. They waited.

He seemed to want to say something, perhaps to object. Alf Gunnderson's heavy brows drew down. His blank eyes became—if it were possible—even blanker. A sharp, denting V appeared between the brows.

The cigarette flamed into life.

A tongue of fire leaped up from the tip. In an instant it had consumed tobacco, paper, filter and de-nicotizer in one roar. The fire slammed against Gunnderson's lips, searing them, lapping at his nose, his face.

He screamed, fell on his face and beat at the flames with his hands.

Suddenly the stage was clogged with running men in the blue and charcoal suits of the SpaceCom. Gunnderson lay writhing on the floor, a wisp of charry smoke rising from his face. One of the SpaceCom officials broke the cap on an extinguisher vial and the spray washed over the body of the fallen man.

"Get the Mallaport! Get the goddammed Mallaport, willya!" A young Ensign with brush-cut blond hair, first to reach the stage—as though he had been waiting crouched below—cradled Gunnderson's head in his muscular arms, brushing with horror at the flakes of charred skin. He had the watery blue eyes of the spacemen, those who had seen terrible things; yet his eyes were more frightened now than any man's eyes were meant to be.

In a few minutes the angular, spade-pawed Malleable-Transporter was smoothing the skin on Gunnderson's face, realigning the atoms—shearing away the burned flesh, coating it with vibrant, healthy pink skin.

Another few moments and the psioid was finished; the burns had been erased; Gunnderson was new and whole, save for the patches of healthier-seeming skin that dotted his face.

All through it he had been murmuring. As the Mallaport finished his mental work, stood up with a sigh, the words filtered through to the young SpaceCom Ensign. He stared at Gunnderson a moment, then raised his watery blue eyes to the other officials standing about.

He stared at them with a mixture of fear and bewilderment.

Gunnderson had been saying: "Let me die, please let me die, I want to die, won't you let me die, please!"

The ship was heading toward Omalo, sun of the Delgart system. It had been translated into inverspace by a Driver named Carina Correia. She had warped the ship through, and gone back to her deep-sleep, till she was needed at Omalo snap-out.

Now the ship whirled through the crazy quilt of inverspace, cutting through to the star-system of Earth's adversary.

Gunnderson sat in the cabin with the brush-cut blond Ensign. All through the trip, since blast-off and snap-out, the pyrotic had been kept in his stateroom. This was the newest of the Earth SpaceCom ships, yet he had seen none of it. Just this tiny stateroom, in the constant company of the usually stoical Ensign.

The SpaceCom man's watery blue eyes swept between the pallid man and the teleport-proof safe set in the cabin's bulkhead.

"Any idea why they're sending us so deep into Delgart territory?" the Ensign fished. "It's pretty tight lines up this far. Must be something big. Any idea?"

Gunnderson's eyes came up from their focus on his boot-tops, and stared at the spaceman. He idly flipped the harmonica he had requested before blast-off, which he had used to pass away the long hours inverspace. "No idea. How long have you been at war with the Delgarts?"

"Don't you even know who your planet's at war with?"

"I've been rural for many years. But aren't they *always* at war with someone?"

The Ensign looked startled. "Not unless it's to protect the peace of the galaxies. Earth is a *peace*-loving . . ."

Gunnderson cut him off. "Yes, I know. But how long have you been at war with the Delgarts? I thought they were our allies under some Treaty Pact or other?"

The spaceman's face contorted in a picture of conditioned hatred. "We've been after the bastards since they jumped one of our mining planets outside their cluster." He twisted his lips in open loathing. We'll clean the bastards out soon enough! Teach *them* to jump peaceful Earthmen."

Gunnderson wished he could shut out the words. He heard the same story all the way from A Centauri IX and back. Someone had always jumped someone else . . . someone was always at war with someone else . . . there were always bastards to be cleaned out . . . never any peace . . . never any peace . . .

The invership whipped past the myriad odd-colors of

inverspace, hurtling through that not-space toward the alien cluster. Gunnderson sat in the teleport-proof stateroom, triple-coded loktite, and waited. He had no idea what they wanted of him, why they had tested him, why they had sent him through the pre-flight checkups, why he was in not-space. But he knew one thing: whatever it was, there was to be no peace for *him* . . . ever.

He silently cursed the strange mental power he had. The power to make the molecules of *anything* speed up tremendously, making them grind against one another, causing combustion. A strange, channeled teleport faculty that was useless for anything but the creation of fire. He damned it soulfully, wishing he had been born deaf, mute, blind, incapable of having to ward off the world.

From the first moment of his life when he had realized his strange power, he had been haunted. No control, no identification, no communication. Cut off. Tagged as an oddie. Not even the pleasures of being an acknowledged psioid, like the Mindees, or the invaluable Drivers, or the Blasters, or the Mallaports who could move the atoms of flesh to their design. He was an oddie. A strange-breed, and worse: he was a non-directive psioid. Tagged deadly and uncontrollable. He could set the fires, but he could not control them. The molecules were too tiny, too quickly imitative for him to stop the activity once it was started. It had to stop of its own volition . . . and occasionally it was too long in stopping.

Once he had thought himself normal, once he had thought of leading an ordinary life—of perhaps becoming a musician. But that idea had died aflaming, as all other normal ideas that had followed it.

First the ostracism, then the hunting, then the arrests and the prison terms, one after another. Now something new—something he could not understand. What did they want with him? It was obviously in connection with the mighty battle being fought between Earth and the Delgarts, but of what use could his unreliable powers be?

Why was he in this most marvelous of the new Space-Com ships, heading toward the central sun of the enemy cluster? And why should he help Earth in any case?

At that moment the locks popped, the safe broke open, and the clanging of the alarms was heard to the bowels of the invership.

The Ensign stopped him as he started to rise, started toward the safe. The Ensign thumbed a button on his wrist-console.

"Hold it, Mr. Gunnderson. I wasn't told what was in there, but I was told to keep you away from it until the other two got here."

Gunnderson slumped back hopelessly on the acceleration-bunk. He dropped the harmonica to the metal floor and lowered his head into his hands. "What other two?"

"I don't know, sir. I wasn't told."

The other two were psioids, naturally.

When the Mindee and the Blaster arrived, they motioned the Ensign to remove the contents of the safe. He walked over nervously, took out the tiny recorder and the single speak-tip.

"Play it, Ensign," the Mindee directed.

The spaceman thumbed the speak-tip into the hole, and the grating of the blank space at the beginning of the tip filled the room.

"You can leave now, Ensign," the Mindee said.

After the SpaceCom officer had securely loktited the door, the voice began. Gunnderson recognized it immediately as that of Terrence, head of SpaceCom. The man who had questioned him tirelessly at the Bureau building in Buenos Aires. Terrence, hero of another war, the Earth-

Kyben war, now head of SpaceCom. The words were brittle, almost without inflection and to the point, yet they carried a sense of utmost importance:

"Gunnderson," it began, "we have, as you already know, a job for you. By this time the ship will have reached central-point of your trip through inverspace.

"You will arrive in two days Earthtime at a slip-out point approximately five hundred million miles from Omalo, the enemy sun. You will be far behind enemy lines, but we are certain you will be able to accomplish your mission safely, that is why you have been given this new ship. It can withstand anything the enemy can throw.

"But we want you to get back for other reasons. You are the most important man in our war effort, Gunnderson, and it's tied up with your mission.

"We want you to turn the sun Omalo into a supernova."

Gunnderson, for the first time in thirty-eight years of bleak, gray life, was staggered. The very concept made his stomach churn. Turn another people's sun into a flaming, gaseous bomb of incalculable power, spreading death into space, burning off the very layers of its being, charring into nothing the planets of the system? Annihilate in one move an entire culture?

Was it possible they thought him mad?

What did they think he was capable of?

Could he direct his mind to such a task?

Could he do it?

Should he do it?

His mind boggled at the possibility. He had never really considered himself as having many ideals. He had set fires in warehouses to get the owners their liability insurance; he had flamed other hobos who had tried to rob him; he had used the unpredictable power of his mind for many things, but this . . .

This was the murder of a solar system!

He wasn't in any way sure he *could* turn a sun supernova. What was there to lead them to think he might be able to do it? Burning a forest and burning a giant red sun were two things fantastically far apart. It was something out of a nightmare. But even if he *could* . . .

"In case you find the task unpleasant, Mr. Gunnderson," the ice-chip voice of the SpaceCom head continued, "we have included in this ship's complement, a Mindee and a Blaster.

"Their sole job is to watch and protect you, Mr. Gunnderson. To make certain you are kept in the proper, er, *patriotic* state of mind. They have been instructed to read you from this moment on, and should you not be willing to carry out your assignment . . . well, I'm certain you are familiar with a Blaster's capabilities."

Gunnderson stared at the blank-faced telepath sitting across from him on the other bunk. The man was obviously listening to every thought in Gunnderson's head. A strange, nervous expression was on the Mindee's face. His gaze turned to the Blaster who accompanied him, then back to Gunnderson.

The pyrotic swiveled a glance at the Blaster, then swiveled away as quickly.

Blasters were men meant to do one job, one job only, and a certain type of man he became, he *had* to be, to be successful doing that job. They all looked the same, and Gunnderson found the look almost terrifying. He had not thought he could *be* terrified, any more.

"That is your assignment, Gunnderson, and if you have any hesitance, remember they are *not* human. They are extraterrestrials as unlike you as you are unlike a slug. And remember there's a war on . . . you will be saving the lives of many Earthmen by performing this task.

"This is your chance to become respected, Gunnderson.

"A hero, respected, and for the first time," he paused, as though not wishing to say what was next, "for the first time—worthy of your world."

The rasp-rasp-rasp of the silent record filled the state-room. Gunnderson said nothing. He could hear the phrase whirling, whirling in his head: *There's a war on,* There's a war on, *There's a war on,* THERE'S A WAR ON! He stood up and slowly walked to the door.

"Sorry, Mr. Gunnderson," the Mindee said emphatically, "we can't allow you to leave this room."

He sat down and lifted the battered mouth organ from where it had fallen. He fingered it for a while, then put it to his lips. He blew, but made no sound.

And he didn't leave.

They thought he was asleep. The Mindee—a cadaverously thin man with hair grayed at the temples and slicked back in strips on top, with a gasping speech and a nervous move-ment of hand to ear—spoke to the Blaster.

"He doesn't seem to be thinking, John!"

The Blaster's smooth, hard features moved vaguely, in the nearest thing to an expression, and a quirking frown split his ink-line mouth. "Can he do it?"

The Mindee rose, ran a hand quickly through the straight, slicked hair.

"Can he do it? No, he shouldn't be *able* to do it, but he's doing it! I can't figure it out . . . it's eerie, uncanny. Either I've lost it, or he's got something new."

"Trauma-barrier?"

"That's what they told me before I left, that he seemed to be blocked off. But they thought it was only temporary, once he was away from the Bureau buildings he would clear up.

"But he *isn't* cleared up."

The Blaster looked concerned. "Maybe it's you."

"I didn't get a Master's rating for nothing, John, and I tell you there isn't a trauma-barrier I can't at least get *some-thing* through. If only a snatch of gabble. But there's nothing . . . nothing!"

"Maybe it's you," the Blaster repeated, still concerned.

"Damn it! It's *not* me! I can read you, can't I—your right foot hurts from new boots, you wish you could have the bunk to lie down on, you . . . oh hell, I can read *you*—and I can read the Captain up front, and I can read the pitmen in the hold, but I *can't* read *him*!

"It's like hitting a sheet of glass in his head. There should be a reflection or some penetration, but it seems to be opaqued. I didn't want to say anything when he was awake, of course."

"Do you think I should twit him a little—wake him up and warn him we're on to his game?"

The Mindee raised a hand to stop the very thought of the Blaster. "Great Gods, no!" He gestured wildly. "This Gunnderson's invaluable. If they found out we'd done anything unauthorized to him, we'd both be Tanked."

Gunnderson lay on his acceleration-bunk, feigning sleep, listening to them. It was a new discovery to him, what they were saying. He had always suspected the pyrotic faculty of his mind. It was just too unstable to be a true-bred trait. There had to be side-effects, other differences from the norm. He knew *he* could not read minds; was this now another factor? Impenetrability by Mindees? He wondered.

Perhaps the Blaster was powerless, too.

It would never clear away his problem—that was something he could do only in his own mind—but it might make his position and final decision safer.

There was only one way to find out. He knew the Blaster

could not actually harm him severely, by SpaceCom's orders, but he wouldn't hesitate blasting off one of the pyrotic's arms—cauterizing it as it disappeared—to warn him, if the situation seemed desperate enough.

The Blaster had seemed to Gunnderson a singularly overzealous man, in any case. It was a terrible risk, but he had to know.

There was only one way to find out, and he took it . . . finding a startling new vitality in himself . . . for the first time in over thirty years . . .

He snapped his legs off the bunk, and lunged across the stateroom, shouldering aside the Mindee, and straight-arming the Blaster in the mouth. The Blaster, surprised by the rapid and completely unexpected movement, had a reflex thought, and one entire bulkhead was washed by bolts of power. They crackled, and the plasteel buckled. His direction had been upset, had been poor, but Gunnderson knew the instant he regained his mental balance, the power would be directed at him.

The bulkhead oxidized, and popped as it was broken, revealing the outer insulating hull of the invership; rivets snapped out of their holes and clattered to the floor.

Gunnderson was at the stateroom door, palming the loktite open—having watched the manner used by the Blaster when he had left on several occasions—and putting one foot into the companionway.

Then the Blaster struck. His fury rose, and he lost his sense of duty. This man had struck him; he was a psioid . . . an accepted psioid, not an oddie! His eyes deepened their black immeasurably, and his face strained. His cheekbones rose in a stricture of a grin, and the *force* materialized.

All around Gunnderson.

He could feel the heat.

He could see his clothes sparking and disappearing.

He could feel his hair charring at the tips.

He could feel the strain of psi power in the air.

But there was no effect on him.

He was safe.

Safe from the power of the Blasters.

Then he knew he didn't have to run.

He turned back to the cabin.

The two psioids were staring at him in open terror.

It was always night in inverspace.

The ship constantly ploughed through a swamp of black, with metal inside, and metal outside, and the cold, unchanging devil-dark beyond the metal. Men hated inverspace—they sometimes *took* the years-long journey through normal space, to avoid the chilling life of inverspace. For one moment the total black would surround the ship, and the next they would be sifting through a field of changing, flickering crazy-quilt colors. Then ebony again, then light, then dots, then shafts, then the dark once more. It was everchanging, like a madman's dream. But not interestingly changing, so one would wish to watch, as one might watch a kaleidoscope. This was strange, and unnatural, something beyond the powers of the mind, or the abilities of the eye to comprehend. Ports were allowed only in the officer's country, and those had solid lead shields that would slam down and dog closed at the slap of a button. Nothing could be done—men were only men, and space was their eternal enemy. But no man willingly stared back at the deep of inverspace.

In the officer's country, Alf Gunnderson reached with his sight and his mind into the coal soot that now lay beyond the ship. Since he had proved his invulnerability over the Blaster, he had been given the run of the ship. Where could he go? Nowhere that he could not be found.

Guards watched the egress ports at all times, so he was still, in effect, a prisoner on the invership. He had managed to secure time alone, however, and so with the Captain and his officers locked out of country, he stood alone, watching.

He stared; the giant quartz window, all shields open, all the darkness flowing in. The cabin was dark, but not half so dark as that darkness that was everywhere.

That darkness deeper than the darkness.

What was he? Was he man or was he machine . . . to be told he must turn a sun nova? What of the people on that sun's planets? What of the women and the children . . . alien or not? What of the people who hated war, and the people who served because they had been told to serve, and the people who wanted to be left alone? What of the men who went into the fields, while their fellow troops dutifully sharpened their war knives, and cried? Cried because they were afraid, and they were tired, and they wanted home without death. What of those men?

Was this war one of salvation or liberation or duty as they parroted the phrases of patriotism? Or was this still another of the unending wars for domination, larger holdings, richer worlds? Was this another dupe of the Universe, where men were sent to their deaths so one type of government, no better than another, could rule? He didn't know. He wasn't sure. He was afraid. He had a power beyond all powers in his hands, and he suddenly found himself not a tramp and a waste, but a man who could demolish a solar system at his own will.

Not even sure he *could* do it, he considered the possibility, and it terrified him, making his legs turn to ice water, his blood to steam. He was suddenly quite lost, and immersed into a deeper darkness than he had ever known. With no way out.

He spoke to himself, letting his words sound foolish to

himself, but sounding them just the same, knowing he had avoided sounding them for much too long:

"Can I do it?

"Should I? I've waited so long, so long, to find a place, and now they tell me I've found a place. Is this my final place? Is this what I've lived and searched for? I can be a valuable war weapon. I can be the man the men turn to when they want a job done. But what sort of job?

"Can I do it? Is it more important to me to find peace—even a peace such as this—and to destroy, than to go on with the unrest?"

Alf Gunnderson stared at the night, at the faint tinges of color beginning to form at the edges of his vision, and his mind washed itself in the water of thought. He had discovered much about himself in the past few days. He had discovered many talents, many ideals he had never suspected in himself.

He had discovered he had character, and that he was not a hopeless, oddie hulk, doomed to die wasted. He found he had a future.

If he could make the proper decision.

But what *was* the proper decision?

"Omalo! Omalo snap-out!"

The cry roared through the companionways, bounced down the halls and against the metal hull of the invership, sprayed from the speakers, and deafened the men asleep beside their squawk-boxes.

The ship ploughed through a maze of colors whose hues were unknown, skiiiiittered scud-wise, and popped out, shuddering. There it was. The sun of Delgart. Omalo. Big. And golden. With planets set about like boulders on the edge of the sea. The sea that was space, and from which this ship had come. With death in its hold, and death in its tubes, and death, nothing but death.

The Blaster and the Mindee escorted Alf Gunnderson to the bridge. They stood back and let him walk to the huge quartz portal. The portal before which the pyrotic had stood so long, so many hours, gazing so deep into inverspace. They left him there, and stood back, because they knew he was safe from them. No matter how hard they held his arms, no matter how fiercely they shouted at him, he was safe. He was something new. Not just a pyrotic, not just a mind-blocked, not just a Blaster-safe, he was something totally new.

Not a composite, for there had been many of those, with imperfect powers of several psi types. But something new, and something incomprehensible. Psioid+ with a + that might mean anything.

Gunnderson moved forward slowly, his deep shadow squirming out before him, sliding up the console, across the portal shelf, and across the quartz itself. Himself superimposed across the immensity of space.

The man who was Gunnderson stared into the night that lay without, and at the sun that burned steadily and high in that night. A greater fire raged within him than on that molten surface.

His was a power he could not even begin to estimate, and if he let it be used in this way, this once, it could be turned to this purpose over and over and over again.

Was there any salvation for him?

"You're supposed to flame that sun, Gunnderson," the slick-haired Mindee said, trying to assume an authoritative tone, a tone of command, but failing miserably. He knew he was powerless before this man. They could shoot him, of course, but what would that accomplish?

"What are you going to do, Gunnderson? What do you

have in mind?" the Blaster chimed in. "SpaceCom wants Omalo fired . . . are you going to do it, or do we have to report you as a traitor?"

"You know what they'll do to you back on Earth, Gunnderson. You know, don't you?"

Alf Gunnderson let the light of Omalo wash his sunken face with red haze. His eyes seemed to deepen in intensity. His hands on the console ledge stiffened and the knuckles turned white. He had seen the possibilities, and he had decided. They would never understand that he had chosen the harder way. He turned slowly.

"Where is the lifescoot located?"

They stared at him, and he repeated his question. They refused to answer, and he shouldered past them, stepped into the droptube to take him below decks. The Mindee spun on him, his face raging.

"You're a coward and a traitor, fireboy! You're a lousy no-psi freak and we'll get you! You can take the lifeboat, but someday we'll find you! No matter where you go out there, we're going to find you!"

He spat then, and the Blaster strained and strained and strained, but the power of his mind had no effect on Gunnderson.

The pyrotic let the dropshaft lower him, and he found the lifescoot some time later. He took nothing with him but the battered harmonica, and the red flush of Omalo on his face.

When they felt the *pop!* of the lifescoot being snapped into space, and they saw the dark gray dot of it moving rapidly away, flicking quickly off into inverspace, the Blaster and the Mindee slumped into relaxers, stared at each other.

"We'll have to finish the war without him."

The Blaster nodded. "He could have won it for us in one minute. He's gone."

"Do you think he could have done it?"

The Blaster shrugged his heavy shoulders. "I just don't know. Perhaps."

"He's gone," the Mindee repeated bitterly. "*He's* gone? Coward! Traitor! Some day . . . some day . . ."

"Where can he go?"

"He's a wanderer at heart. Space is deep, he can go anywhere."

"Did you mean that, about finding him some day?"

The Mindee nodded rapidly. "When they find out, back on Earth, what he did today, they'll start hunting him through all of space. He'll never have another moment's peace. They *have* to find him . . . he's the perfect weapon. But he can't run forever. They'll find him."

"A strange man."

"A man with a power he can't hide, John. A man who will sooner or later give himself away. He *can't* hide himself cleverly enough to stay hidden forever."

"Odd that he would turn himself into a fugitive. He could have had peace of mind for the rest of his life. Instead, he's got this . . ."

The Mindee stared at the closed portal shields. His tones were bitter and frustrated. "We'll find him some day."

The ship shuddered, reversed drives, and slipped back into inverspace.

Much sky winked back at him.

He sat on the bluff, wind tousling his gray hair, flapping softly at the dirty shirt-tail hanging from his pants top.

The Minstrel sat on the bluff watching the land fall slopingly away under him, down to the shining hide of the sprawling dragon, lying in the cup of the hills. The dragon slept—awake—across once lush grass and productive ground.

City.

On this far world, far from a red sun that shone high and steady, the Minstrel sat and pondered the many kinds of peace. And the kind that is not peace, can *never* be peace.

His eyes turned once more to the sage and eternal advice of the blackness above. No one saw him wink back at the silent stars. Deeper than the darkness.

With a sigh he slung the battered theremin over his frayed shoulders. It was a portable machine, with both rods bent, and its power-pack patched and soldered. His body almost at once assumed the half-slouch, round-shouldered walk of the wanderer. He ambled down the hill toward the rocket field.

They called it the rocket field, out here on the Edge, but they didn't use rockets any longer. Now they rode to space on a whistling tube that glimmered and sparkled behind itself like a small animal chuckling over a private joke. The joke was that the little animal knew the riders were never coming back.

It whistled and sparkled till it flicked off into some crazy-quilt not-space, and was gone forever.

Tarmac clicked under the heels of his boots. Bright, shining boots, kept meticulously clean by polishing over polishing till they reflected back the corona of the field kliegs and, ever more faintly, the gleam of the night. The Minstrel kept them cleaned and polished, a clashing note matched against his generally unkempt appearance.

He was tall, towering over almost everyone he had ever met in his homeless wanderings. His body was a lean and supple thing, like a high-tension wire; the merest suggestion of contained power and quickness. The man moved with an easy gait, accentuating his long legs and gangling arms, making his well-proportioned head seem a bubble precariously balanced on a neck too long and thin to support it.

He kept time to the click of the polished boots with a soft half-hum, half-whistle. The song was a dead song, long forgotten.

He, too, was a half-dead, half-forgotten thing.

He came from beyond the mountains. No one knew where. No one cared where. *He* had almost forgotten.

But they listened when he came. They listened almost reverently, having heard the stories about him, with a desperation born of men who know they are severed from their home worlds, who know they will go out and out and seldom come back. He sang of space, and he sang of land, and he sang of the nothing that is left for Man—all Men, no matter how many arms they have, or what their skin is colored—when he has expended the last little bit of Eternity to which he is entitled.

His voice had the sadness of death in it. The sadness of death before life has finished its work. But it had the joy of metal under quick fingers, the strength of turned nickel-steel, and the whip of heart and soul working through loneliness. They listened when his song came with the night wind; probing, crying, lonely through the darkness of a thousand worlds and in a thousand winds.

The pitmen stopped their work as he came, silent but for the hum of his song and the beat of his boots on the black-top. They watched as he came across the field.

There was no doubt who it was. He had been wandering the star-paths for many years now. He had appeared, and that was all; he was. They knew him as certainly as they knew themselves. They turned and he was like a pillar, set dark against the light and shadow of the field. He paced slowly, and they stopped the hoses feeding the radioactive food to the little animals, and stopped the torches they boiled on the metal skins; and they listened.

The Minstrel knew they were listening, and he unslung

his instrument, settling the narrow box with its tone-rods around his neck by its thong. As his fingers cajoled and pleaded and extracted the song of a soul, cast into the pit of the void, left to die, crying in torment not so much at death, but at the terror of being alone when the last calling came.

And the workmen cried.

They felt no shame as the tears coursed through the dirt on their faces and over the sweat-shine left from toil. They stood, silent and all-feeling, as he came toward them.

Then with many small crescendos, and before they even knew it was ended, and for seconds after the wail had fled back across the field into the mountains, they listened to the last notes of his lament.

Hands wiped clumsily across faces, leaving more dirt than before, and backs turned slowly as men resumed work. It seemed they could not face him, the nearer he came; as though he was too deep-seeing, too perceptive for them to be at ease close by. It was a mixture of respect and awe.

The Minstrel stood, waiting.

"Hey! You!"

The Minstrel stood waiting. The pad of soft-soled feet behind him. A spaceman; tanned, supple, almost as tall as the ballad-singer—reminding the ballad-singer of another spaceman, a blond-haired boy he had known long ago— came up beside the silent figure. The Minstrel had not moved.

"Whut c'n ah do for ya, Minstrel?" asked the spaceman, tones of the South of a long faraway Continent rich in his voice.

"What do they call this world?" the Minstrel asked. The voice was quiet, like a needle being drawn through velvet. He spoke in a hushed monotone, yet his voice was clear and bore traces of an uncountable number of accents.

"The natives call it Audi, and the charts call it Rexa Majoris XXIX, Minstrel. Why?"

"It's time to move on."

The Southerner grinned hugely, lines of amusement crinkling out around his watery brown eyes. "Need a lift?"

The Minstrel nodded, smiling back enigmatically.

The spaceman's face softened, the lines of squinting into the reaches of an eternal night broke and he extended his hand: "Mah name's Quantry; top dog on the *Spirit of Lucy Marlowe*. If y'doan mind workin' yer keep owff bah singin' fer the payssengers, we'd be pleased to hayve ya awn boward."

The tall man smiled, a quick radiance across the darkness the shadows made of his face. "That isn't work."

"Then done!" exclaimed the spaceman. "C'mon, ah'll fix ya a bunk in steerage."

They walked between the wiper gangs and the pitmen. They threaded their way between the glare of fluorotorches and the sputtering blast of robot welding instruments. The man named Quantry indicated the opening in the smooth side of the ship and the Minstrel clambered inside.

Quantry fixed the berth just behind the reactor feeder-bins, sealing off the compartment with an electrical blanket draped over a loading track bar. The Minstrel lay on his bunk—a repair bench—with a pillow under his head. He lay thinking.

The moments fled silently and his mind, deep in thought, hardly realized the ports were being dogged home, the radioactive additives were being sluiced through their tubes to the reactors, the blast tubes were being extruded. His mind did not leave its thoughts as the atomic motors warmed, turning the pit to green glass beneath the ship's bulk. Motors that would carry the ship to a height where the Driver would be wakened from his sleep—or *her* sleep, as was more often the case with that particular breed of psioid—to snap the ship through into inverspace.

As the ship came unstuck from solid ground, hurled itself outward on an unquenchable tail of fire, the Minstrel lay back, letting the reassuring hand of acceleration press him into deeper reverie. Thoughts spun, of the past, of the further past, and of all the pasts he had known.

Then the reactors cut off, the ship shuddered, and he knew they were in inverspace. The Minstrel sat up, his eyes far away. His thoughts deep inside the cloud-cover of a world billions of light years away, hundreds of years lost to him. A world he would never see again.

There was a time for running, and a time for resting, and even in the running, there could be resting. He smiled to himself so faintly it was not a smile.

Down in the reactor rooms, they heard his song. They heard the build to it, matching, sustaining, whining in tune with the inverspace drive. They grinned at each other with a sweet sadness their faces were never expected to wear.

"It's gonna be a good trip," said one to another.

In the officer's country, Quantry looked up at the tight-slammed shields blocking off the patchwork insanity of not-space, and *he* smiled. It *was* going to be a good trip.

In the saloons, the passengers listened to the odd strains of lonely music coming up from below, and even *they* were forced to admit, though they had no way of explaining how they knew, that this was indeed going to be a good trip.

And in steerage, his fingers wandering across the key-board of the battered theremin, no one noticed that the man they called "The Minstrel" had lit his cigarette without a match.

NEVER SEND TO KNOW FOR WHOM THE LETTUCE WILTS

So I'm watching the report on CNN about how little kids who've become enamoured of smackdown wrestling (which is *so* fulla crap bogus I can never figure how *any-body* can be dumb enough even to *watch* it, much less think of it as anything but staged stupidity, Three Stooges in ugly tights . . . but then I can also never understand why people who watch those weepy televangelists don't spot them as the con men they truly are), and the kids are so impressionable . . . not to mention dumb as a paving stone . . . that they're setting up these makeshift WWF play areas in their backyards. And they're jumping on each other, and they're hitting each other with chairs, and they're throwing smaller kids against walls, and they're dropping both knees into some other urchin's solar plexus, and in general going way beyond the kind of silly horseplay you and I engaged in when we were their age. (And *here's* a question: isn't there an adult in that time zone who can *see* what's going down, and maybe suggest that poking a garden hoe into another kid's eye might impair his career as an air traffic controller in later life?) But the chilling capper to this report is the moment when one of these doofus children, who has been—are you ready for this—videotaping the massacre, isn't satisfied with the "reality" of the scenario, and he takes a flippin' *cheese grater* to the face of his "opponent," slicing and dicing the kid for life, and he looks into the camera and grins and says, "See, now ya kin *see* the blood! Ain't it kewl!" The troublemaker lesson to be learned from this story is: curiosity about things that you shouldn't be curi-ous about can get you scarred for life. Oh, and the other lesson: stay away from people dumber than you. If such creatures exist.

Tuesday.

    Henry Leclair did a double-take. His eyes racked and reracked between the Chinese fortune cookie in his right hand and the Chinese fortune cookie *fortune* in his left. He read it again: **Tuesday.**

    Then again, querulously, "Tuesday?"

    That was all. Nothing more; no aphorism about meeting one's true love on Tuesday; no saccharine cliché denoting Tuesday as the advent of good fortune; no Tuesday-themed accompanying notation warning of investing in hi-tech stocks on Tuesday. Nothing. Just the narrow, slightly-gray slip of rectangular paper with the printed word **Tuesday** and a period immediately after it.

    Henry muttered to himself. "Why Tuesday? What Tuesday?" He absently let the fortune cookie slip from his fingers.

    "Damn!" he murmured, watching the cookie sink quickly to the bottom of his water glass.

    He returned his attention to the fortune. *Tuesday.* That

was today. Biting his lower lip, Harry reached for the second of the three cookies. He pulled at the edge of the fortune paper protruding from the convoluted pastry. Placing the cookie back on its plate carefully, he turned the slip over and read it:

You're the one.

Henry Leclair had been a premature baby. His mother, Martha Annette Leclair, had not carried him full term. Seven months, two days. Boom. Enter baby Henry. There was no explanation save the vagaries of female physiology. However, there *was* another explanation: Henry—even prenatal—had been curious. Pathologically, even pre-natally, curious. He had wanted free from the womb, had wanted to discover *what was out there*.

When he was two years old, Henry had been discovered, in trapdoor-bottom pajamas, in mid-winter, crouching in the snow outside his home, waiting to see whether the white stuff fell from above or came up through the ground.

At the age of seven they had to cut Henry down. He had been swinging from a clothesline strung in the basement, drying the family wash. Henry had been curious: what does it feel like to strangle?

By the time he was thirteen, Henry had read every volume of the ENCYLOPAEDIA BRITTANICA, copious texts on every phase of the sciences, all matter disseminated by the government for the past twenty-eight years, and biographies by the score. Also, somewhere between seven thousand, eight hundred, and seven thousand, nine hundred books on history, religion, and sociology. He avoided books of cartoons—and novels.

By the time he was twenty, Henry wore noticeably thick-lensed glasses; and he had migraine headaches. But his all-consuming curiosity had not been satiated.

On his thirty-first birthday, Henry was unmarried and digging for bits of a stone tablet in the remains of a lost city somewhere near the Dead Sea. Curiosity.

Henry Leclair was curious about almost everything. He wondered why a woman wore egret feathers in her hat, rather than those of the peacock. He wondered why lobsters turned red when they were cooked. He wondered why office buildings did not have thirteenth floors. He wondered why men left home. He wondered what the soot-accumulation rate in his city was. He wondered why he had a strawberry mark on his right knee. He wondered all sorts of things.

Curiosity. He was helpless, driven, doomed in its itching, overwhelming, adhesive grip.

You're the one.

"I'm the one?" Henry blurted incredulously. "Me? I'm the *what? What* am I? What the blazes are you talking about?" He spoke to the insensate, unresponsive fortune paper.

This was, suddenly, overpoweringly, a conundrum for Henry. He knew, deep in his soul-matter, that curiosity demanded he must solve this intrusive enigma. Two such fortunes—two such incomprehensible mind-troublers—were more than mere coyness on someone's part. There was something not quite right here. *Something*, as Henry put it to himself, with stunning originality, *more than meets the eye!*

Henry called for the waiter. The short, almost bald, and overly-contemptuous Oriental passed twice more—once in either direction—finally coming to a halt beside Henry's booth. Henry extended the two fortunes and said, "Who writes these?"

"我不知你講甚乜," answered the waiter, with a touch of insouciant, yet distingué, impudence.

"I beg your pardon," Henry said, removing his noticeably thick-lensed glasses, dangling them in his other hand, "but would you mind speaking English?"

The waiter wrinkled his nose in distaste, stroked the cloth napkin draped over his forearm, and pointed to the manager, lounging half-asleep behind the cash register.

"Thanks," said Henry absently, his attention to the chase now directed elsewhere. He started to rise as the waiter turned. "Oh—check, please." The waiter stopped dead in his tracks, drew his shoulders up as though he had been struck an especially foul blow, and returned to the table. He hurriedly scribbled the check, all in Chinese glyphs except the total, and plunked it on the table. Muttering Eastern epithets, he stalked away.

Henry absently dropped the remaining fortune cookie in his jacket pocket as he picked up the check—so anxious was he now to speak to the manager. Quickly slapping his hat on his head, he gathered his topcoat off the chair, dropped a dollar and some change, and headed for the manager. The old man was slumped across the glass case, one arm securely pressed against the cash register's drawer. He awakened at almost the instant Henry stopped in front of him. His hand extended automatically for check and cash.

While the fellow was placing his check on a spindle, Henry leaned across and asked, quietly, "Can you tell me where you get these little fortunes?" He showed one. Henry expected more misdirection and confusion, as he had experienced with the waiter, but the Chinese manager did not take his eyes off the change he was delivering as he said, "We buy in lots. From trading company that sell us cookies. You want buy dozen, take home with you?"

Henry fended him off, and asked the name and address of the company. After a few seconds of deliberation, the manager reached out of sight under the counter, dragged forth a large notebook. He opened it, ran a finger down a column of addresses, said, "Saigon-San Francisco Trading Company, 431 Bessemer Street."

Henry thanked him and strode out onto the sidewalk. "Taxi!" he called into the river of passing cars, and a few minutes later was riding toward 431 Bessemer Street. *The crimson clutching claw of cold curiosity.* Oh, my.

The Saigon-San Francisco Trading Company was located in a condemned warehouse on the desolate lower end of Bessemer Street. In the manufacturing and warehouse section of the city, Bessemer Street was regarded as the drop-off dead end of the known universe. On Bessemer Street, the lower end was regarded much the same. Henry had an idea this building was the last rung on the ladder of aversion. Beyond lay the dark, restless river.

The windows of the pathetic warehouse were, for the most part, broken and sightless; many were boarded up. The building itself leaned far out of plumb, dolorous, as though seeking impecunious support from some destitute relative on its west side. Its west side faced an empty, rat-infested lot.

So, for that matter, did the east, north, and south sides. Dolorous, pathetic, rat-infested.

"A pretty sorry place for an active trading company," murmured Henry, pulling his coat collar up about his ears. The wind ricocheting through the darkened warehouse canyons was rock-chilling, this late at night. Henry glanced at his wristwatch. Nearly eleven o'clock. It was the hour when the terminally curious talked to themselves:

"Um. Probably no one working at this time, no late shift, but at least I can get an idea of what the place is like, as long as I'm here." He mentally kicked himself for taking off in such a flurry of desire to solve the riddle of the fortune papers. "I should have waited till reasonable working hours, tomorrow morning. Ah, well . . ."

He walked across the street, stepping quickly in and out of the smudge of light thrown by a lone, remarkably, unshattered street lamp. Henry glanced nervously behind him.

Far off, back the way they had come, he could see the rapidly disappearing taillights of the taxi.

"Why the devil didn't I ask him to wait?" Henry had no answer for himself, though one did, in fact, exist: the mind-clouding power of curiosity. Now he would have to walk far in the wind, the cold, the dark, to the nearest hack stand or at least an inhabited thoroughfare.

The building loomed over him. He went up to the front door. Locked solid; steel bolts welded to the frame.

"Hmm. Locked up for good." He glanced at the dirty CONDEMNED sign beside the door. Then he muttered, "Odd," with uncertainty, because there were fresh truck tire treadmarks in the mud of the street. The tracks led around to the rear of the warehouse. Henry found his interest in this problem mounting. Piqued, piqued, piqued. Deserted, condemned: but still getting deliveries, or pickups? Curiouser and Curiouser.

He walked around to the rear of the warehouse, following the truck tracks. They stopped beside a number of square indentations in the mud. "Somebody left a bunch of crates here."

He looked around. The rear of the building bulked uglier than the front—if that was possible. All but one of the windows was boarded, and *that* one . . .

Henry realized he was looking at light streaming through the window, there on the top floor. It was blanked out for a moment, then came back. As though someone had walked in front of it. *But that light's in the ceiling,* Henry thought wildly. *I can see the edge of the fixture from here. How can anyone walk in front of it?*

His wonderment was cut short by still further signs of activity in the building. A circular opening in the wall next to the window—quite dark and obviously a pipe-shaft of some sort—was emitting large puffs of faintly phosphorescent green fog.

"There's someone up there," Henry concluded, ever the rocket scientist.

The Urge rose in Henry Leclair once more. The problem thumped and bobbed in his mind. Curiosity, now a *tsunami,* had utterly overwhelmed even the tiniest atoll of caution and self-preservation. *You're the one,* you say? *You'd better believe it because here I come!*

He carefully examined the rear of the building. No doors. But a first floor window was broken, and the boards were loose. As quietly as possible, he disengaged the nails' grip on the sill, and prized the boards off. Dragging two old crates from the dumpster across the alley, Henry stacked them, and climbed into the building. Curious is, as curious does. (Did anyone hear a cat being killed?)

It was pitch, night, ebony, lusterless, without qualification *dark* inside. Henry held his pipe lighter aloft and rasped it, letting the flame illuminate the place for a few seconds.

Broken crates, old newspapers, cobwebs, dust. The place looked deserted. But there *had* been the light from above.

He sought out the elevator. Useless. He sought out the stairs. Bricked off. He sat down on a packing crate. Annoyed.

Then the sound of glugging came to him.

Glug. Glug. And again, glug. Then a sort of washed-out, whimpery glug that even Henry could tell was a defective: Gluuuuuug!

"Plummis!" swore a voice in shivering falsetto.

Henry listened for a minute more, but no other sound came to him. "Oh, that was cursing, all right," murmured Henry to himself. "I don't know who's doing it, or where it's coming from, but that's unquestionably someone's equivalent of a damn or hell!" He began searching for the source of the voice.

As he neared one wall, the voice came again. "Plummis, valts er webbel er webbel er webbel . . ." the voice trailed off into muttered webbels.

Henry looked up. There was light shining through a ragged hole in the ceiling, very faintly shining. He stepped directly under it to assay a clearer view . . .

. . . and was yanked bodily and immediately up through many such holes in many such ceilings, till his head came into violent contact with a burnished metal plate in the ceiling of the top floor.

"Aaargh!" moaned Henry, crashing to the floor, clutching his banged head, clutching his crushed hat.

"Serves you qquasper!" the shivering falsetto voice remonstrated. Henry looked around. The room was filled with strangely-shaped machines resting on metal workbenches. They were all humming, clicking, gasping, winking and glugging efficiently. All, that is, but one, that emitted a normal glug then collapsed into a fit of prolonged *gluuuuu-uging.*

"Plummis!" Falsetto cursing: vehemently.

Henry looked around once more. The room was empty. He glanced toward the ceiling. The unie was sitting cross-legged in the air, about six inches below the ceiling.

"You're . . ." The rest of it got caught somewhere in Henry's throat.

"I'm Eggzaborg. You'd call me a unie, if you had the intelligence to call me."

"You're . . ." Henry tried again.

"I'm invading the Earth," he said snappishly. The unie completed the thought for Henry, even though that was not even remotely what Henry had been thinking.

Henry took a closer look at the unie.

He was a little thing, no more than two feet tall, almost a gnome, with long, knobbly arms and legs, a pointed head and huge, blue, owl-like eyes with nictitating eyelids. He had a fragile antenna swaying gently from the center of his forehead. It ended in a feather. A light-blue feather. *Almost robin's egg blue,* Henry thought inanely.

The unie's nose was thin and straight, with tripartite nostrils, overhanging a tight line of mouth, and bracketed by cherubic, puffy cheeks. He had no eyebrows. His ears were pointed and set very high on his skull. He was hairless.

The unie wore a form-fitting suit of bright yellow, and pinned to the breast was a monstrous button, half the size of his chest, which quite plainly read:

CONQUEROR.

The unie caught Henry's gaze. "The button. Souvenir. Made it up for myself. Can't help being pompous, giving in to hubris once in a while." He said it somewhat sheepishly. "Attractive, though, don't you think?"

Henry closed his eyes very tightly, pressing with the heels of both hands. He wrinkled his forehead, letting his noticeably thick-lensed glasses slide down his nose just a bit, to unfocus the unie. "I am not *well,*" he said, matter-of-factly. "Not well at all."

The shivering falsetto broke into chirping laughter.

"Well enough *now!*" Eggzaborg chortled. "But just wait three thousand years—just wait!" Henry opened his left eye a slit. Eggzaborg was rolling helplessly around in the air, clutching a place on his body roughly where his abdomen should have been. The unie bumped lightly against the ceiling, besotted with his revelry.

A thin shower of plaster fell across Henry's face. He felt the cool tickle of it on his eyelids and nose. *That plaster*, thought Henry, *was real. Ergo, this unie must be real.*

This is a lot like being in trouble.

"You wrote those fortunes?" Henry inquired, holding them up for the unie to see.

"Fortunes?" The unie spoke to himself. "For . . . *ohhh!* You must mean the mentality-crushers I've been putting in the cookies!" He rubbed long, thin fingers together. "I *knew*, I say, I just *knew* they would produce results!" He looked pensive for a moment, then sighed. "Things have been so slow. I've actually wondered once or twice if I'm really succeeding. Well, more than once or twice, actually. *Actually,* about ten or twenty *million* times! *Plummis!*"

He let his shoulders slump, and folded his knobbly hands in his knobbly lap, looking wistfully at Henry Leclair. "Poor thing," he said. (Henry wasn't sure if the unie meant his visitor . . . or himself.)

Henry ignored him for a moment, deciding to unravel this as he had always unraveled every conundrum in his search for information: calmly, sequentially, first things first. Since the unie's comments were baffling in the light of any historical conquests Henry had ever read about, he decided to turn his immediate attention elsewhere before trying to make sense of the nonsensical. First things first.

He crawled to his feet and unsteadily walked over to the machines. All the while glancing up to keep an eye on Eggzaborg. The machines hurt his eyes.

A tube-like apparatus mounted on an octagonal casing was spitting—through an orifice—buttons. The shape of the machine hurt his eyes. The buttons were of varying sizes, colors, shapes. Shirt buttons, coat buttons, industrial sealing buttons, watch-cap buttons, canvas tent buttons, exotic-purpose buttons. Many buttons, all kinds of buttons. Many of them were cracked, or the sides of the thread holes were sharpened enough to split the thread. They all fell into a trough with holes, graded themselves, and plunged through attached tubes into cartons on the floor. Henry blinked once.

The shape of the second machine hurt Henry's eyes; the device seemed to be grinding a thin line between the head and shank of twopenny nails. The small buzz-wheel ground away while the nail spun, held between pincers. As soon as an almost invisible line had been worn on the metal, the nail dropped into a bucket. Henry blinked twice.

The other machines, whose shapes *really* hurt Henry's eyes, were performing equally petty, yet subversive, procedures. One was all angles and glass sheets, leading to the hole in the wall Henry had seen from below. It was glugging frantically. The puffs of glowing green fog were still erupting sporadically.

"That one wilts lettuce," Eggzaborg said, with pride.

"It *what*?"

The unie looked shocked. "You don't think lettuce wilts of its own accord, do you?"

"Well, I never thought about it—that is—food rots, it goes bad of its own . . . uh, nature . . . entropy . . . doesn't it? It *doesn't*? Sure it does, yeah?"

"Poor thing," the unie repeated, looking even more wistful than before. Pity shone in his eyes. "It's almost like taking advantage of a very slow pony."

Henry felt this was the moment; but since the unie was obviously not human, he would have to handle things carefully. He was dealing with an alien intellect. Oh, yes, that was the long and short of it. An alien from another place in the universe. An e.t. sort of creature. Yes, indeed. He must never forget that. Probably a highly dangerous alien intellect. He didn't *look* very dangerous. But then, one couldn't tell with these alien intellects. One always has to be on one's toes with these devious, cunning alien intellects, Orson Welles knew that.

"All right, then," said Henry, nay, challenged Henry, "so you wilt lettuce. So what? How does that aid you in conquering the Earth?"

"Disorganization," the unie answered in a deeply significant tone of voice, pointing one ominous stick finger at Henry. "Disorganization and demoralization! Undercuts you! Unsettles, and unhinges, you! Makes you teeter, throws you off balance, makes you uncertain about the basic structure of things: gravity, entropy, cooking times. Strikes at the very fibers of your security! Heh!" He chuckled several times more, and folded his hands. There was a lot of that: folding and unfolding.

Henry began to realize just how alien this alien's thought-processes *really* were. Though he didn't recognize the psychological significance of wilted lettuce, it obviously meant something big to the unie. Big. He marked it down in his mind.

Still, he didn't seem to be getting anywhere meaningful. He decided to try another method to get the unie to talk, to reveal all. "I don't get this," Henry said. "I just don't *believe* it. You're just a demented magician or—or something. You aren't what you say at all. By the way," he added snidely, "just what the hell *are* you?"

The unie leaped to his feet in the air, bumping his pointed head on the ceiling. More plaster sifted down. *"Plummis!"* cursed the little being, massaging his skull. Like the lettuce, his antenna had begun to wilt noticeably.

He was furious. "You *dare* question the motives, machi-nations, methodology and . . . and . . ." he groped for an alliterative word, "*power* of Eggzaborg?" His face, normally an off-blue, not unpleasant sky tone, had slowly turned a fierce aquamarine. "Fool, dolt, imbecile, gleckbund, clod, bumpkin, jerk!" The words rolled off his tongue, spattered in Henry's face. Henry cringed.

He was beginning to think this might not be the most salutary approach.

He became convinced of his miscalculation as his feet left the floor and he found himself hanging upside-down in the air, vibrating madly, all the pocket-change and keys and bismuth tablets cascading from his pockets, plonking him on the head as gravity had its way with them. His notice-ably thick-lensed eyeglasses finally fell off. Everything became a blur. "S-s-s-stop! P-p-please s-s-s-stop!" Henry begged, twisting about in the air like a defective mixmaster. "U-u-u-uggedy-ug-ug!" he ugged as the unie bounced him, then pile-drove Henry's head against the floor, numerous times, with numerous painful clunks. His pipe lighter fell out of his vest pocket and cracked him under the chin.

Suddenly, it stopped. Henry felt his legs unstiffen, and he somersaulted over onto the floor, lying face up, quite a bit the worse for having been uniehandled. He was puffing with agony when the unie's face floated into what little was left of his blurred range of vision.

"Terribly sorry," the unie said, looking down. He appeared to be sincerely concerned about his actions. He picked up Henry's glasses and smoothly hooked them back in place on Henry's head. "It's just a result of waiting all these years. Six hundred years waiting. That's a long time to anticipate, to yearn for relief on a conquest-shift that, at best, would make anyone edgy. This planet isn't all that entertaining, meaning no offense; but you do only have the one moon, the one sun, no flemnall, and a mere four seasons. I'm three hundred and fifty years past due for the usual, standard rotation relief, and I really need some. I'm six hundred years total time on this unimportant tour of duty and, well, I'm feelin' mighty low." He sighed, bit what little there was of his lips, and sank into silent glumness.

Henry felt a bit of his strength coming back. At least enough to ask a few more questions.

"T-tell me the story, E-Eggzaborg."

The unie came to a floating halt above the prostrate Henry Lecalir. "Well . . ." he began, with reluctance to talk to this cretinous human, "the story is simple. I graduated with honors from Dorvis Lepham. One of the top phages, of course. First in quatt wunkery, first in padgett, sixteenth in crumbpf, but the professor had it in for me . . . well, anyway . . . I *am* a unie. I was thus assigned to—"

Henry cut him off, "What is a unie?"

"Shut up, stop interrupting!"

"But where did you come from?"

The unie purpled again, and Henry felt (with growing terror) his body twitch, as though it were about to ascend yet again. But it didn't, and he knew the unie had brought his temper under control. "*Plummis*, man! Let me finish! Stop your blasphemous interrupting!" Snappish. Very snappish. Probably not a congenial species, in the main. Likely did not play well with other species.

Henry quickly motioned him to continue, calming him with the same movement.

Eggzaborg huffed, then resumed. "Space, moron. Space. Out there." He pointed. Generally in the direction of some space. Not *all* space, but at least *some* space. "I came from space. Now don't interrupt—I come from out there where you have no idea a place exists. Both in space, and in *between* layers of space. Interstitial expanses. Voluminous voids. I am here because—I am here because—well, *plummis*, fellow, I'm here to *conquer!*" He vacillated his antenna helplessly, at a loss to embellish the explanation.

"But why?"

"Why? *Why?* How obstinately ignorant can you be? Haven't I told you: *I'm a unie!* What does that make you think of?"

"Fried shrimp," replied Henry.

"Oooooh!" The unie hurtled about the room, barely missing collisions with walls and machines. "The impertinence! *That's* one of the reasons I've stayed so well hidden! I can't stand the stupidity of you people! Rude! You're unconscionably rude! Probably the most insulting, rude, boorish species in this galaxy, possibly the entire expanding universe! When you think of *unie* you just naturally think of *conquest!*"

"I do?" asked Henry, still not quite convinced.

The unie subsided into muted sulfurous cursing.

Henry decided to try flattery. "You speak English very well."

"Why shouldn't I?" snapped the unie. "I *invented* it!"

That quieted Henry again. He wasn't quite sure for a moment whether he was lying on floor or ceiling. "And French? Did you invent French, too? What about Tagalog and Aramaic? Basque is nice. I've always wondered about Basque. So: Basque, too?"

The unie looked genuinely bewildered for a moment, then tried again, looking at Henry with piercing eyes, daring him to interrupt. "I was graduated in a large class. There was much talk that year (though we don't judge by your years, of course) (we don't even call them years) (in fact, 'years' is an ugly word, and sounds like pure gibberish if you say it over and over) (years years years years years years, years years years, see what I'm pointing out here) as I was saying, there was much talk of the coming Flib. Though I thought it was superfluous exhalations, I was worried by the rapidity with which my classmates were being sent out." He shivered fearfully, and mumbled, "The Flib . . . oh." He trembled again, then resumed. "When *my* placket was oiled, and I knew *I* was to go out, all other thoughts fled from my head.

"Now, I've been here three hundred and fifty years longer than my shift, six hundred years total, six *hundred* years, and I can't contact the Lephamaster. The Flib has likely already vastened longitudinally. It's not that I'm exactly frightened," he hastened to add, "it's just that I'm a little, well, *worried*, and I'd like a drink of yerbl. Oh yes," and he looked wistful, "just a melkh of pale, thick, moist yerbl."

"If you've been here six hundred years," asked Henry, beginning to rise to a sitting position, "why haven't you conquered us already?"

The unie looked at him strangely. "Who ever heard of conquering in less than four thousand years? It wouldn't be ethical. We're talking ethics here, you barbarian." He pouted and shined his button with a forearm.

Henry decided to risk another edgy question: "But how can writing cookie fortunes and wilting lettuce conquer us?"

"That isn't *all* I do," responded the unie. "Why, I make people smile (that's *very* important), and I rust water pipes, and I make pig's tails curl, and I cure colds, and I make shingles fall off roofs, and I stop wars, and I dirty white shoes, and I—" He seemed intending to continue for some time, but Henry, confused, stopped him.

"Excuse my interruption," he said, "but I don't understand. There's probably a point I've missed. What's the overall *plan*?"

The unie threw up his hands in exasperation, and Henry

noticed for the first time that the alien had only four fingers on each.

"That 'plan' as you so casually dismiss it, you meat-plug, has been deployed for millennia, by the unies," the little being said, "and no one has understood it but the top Lephamasters. How the blazes do you expect *me* to explain anything as complicated as that to a buffoon like *you*? That plan was formulated to handle four thousand years of exigencies, and you want a rundown in four *sentences*! Utter imbecile!"

"You've been here six hundred years," murmured Henry in awe.

"Yes. Rather clever the way I've kept out of sight, don't you think?"

"Oh, I don't know," Henry felt a spark of belligerence burning. All the slamming and jouncing and bouncing had finally overcome even his insatiable curiosity, and he was now more than slightly cheesed off. "I'll bet you're the basis for all those dumb legends about gnomes and gremlins and poltergeists; and flying saucers, too. Not such a terrific job if you ask me. Not to mention that your, what's his name, your Lephamaster seems to have forgotten you even exist!"

Eggzaborg spread his hands in unhappiness. "There are bound to be tiny slip-ups in six hundred years. Particularly with the defective screens on those," he cursed in an alien tongue, "raw-material trucks I use. They're very old now, pretty worn, and every once in a while some snoopy human will see one coming or going."

Henry realized he was, in fact, referring to UFOs, to flying saucers. Then, what the unie had said a minute before suddenly sank through to Henry's conscious: *"You say you stop wars?"* Amazement rang in his voice.

"Certainly. How else can I conquer you? If you keep killing each other off, what'll be left for me to conquer?" He looked at Henry appealingly. "I do wish you'd cease all that shooting and stabbing and blowing-up nonsense."

Any would-be tyrants Henry had ever read about had always *encouraged* inner strife. The unie seemed to have his wires crossed. "Are you sure you're supposed to *stop* wars?"

"Certainly!"

Henry finally decided it was the reverse-thinking of the strange alien intellect. He couldn't fathom the rationale, but it certainly seemed like a good deal for humanity.

"What are those button and nail machines over there doing?"

"Those are implement-cripplers," the unie said, with ill-concealed pride. "Have you ever stopped to wonder why you still use buttons, rather than—for instance—clasps, clamps, zippers, Velcro, seams and other much better contrivances? The button is easily lost, loses its center when sent through the laundry, breaks threads, isn't very attractive, and is difficult to open and close. Ever wonder why you still use them?" He didn't wait for Henry to answer. "Because I keep sifting supplies of them into stores, and they have to sell them, and that creates more of a demand.

"And there is, of course, the constant mindwashing of my 24-hour-a-day Coercive Brain Ray. That helps a lot."

Henry said, "Buttons. Insidious, no doubt about it. And the 'nail crippler' machine over there?

"The nails are treated so they go in at angles. You ever see anyone who could hit ten consecutive nails straight into a piece of wood? They slant, they bend, they break! That's what my sweet little machine over there does! Don't you just love it? The other machine, the trapezoidal one, helps keep the birthrate up, to offset the death-rate in your wars." He looked at Henry sternly. "It puts pin-sized holes in pro—"

Henry blanched, cut him off quickly. "Er—that's all

right; I understand. But what about those fortune cookies? Why the weird messages?"

"Demoralization. See how they bothered *you*? Just think of a million people opening fortune cookies and finding the message, *No way*, inside! They find a message, *Forget about it*, or *It's lost, you'll never find it*. What do you think happens to their frame of mind, their self-confidence, their *joie de vivre*? They don't know it, but it unnerves them for the rest of the week, throws them off-balance, to find a fortune cookie fortune, and all it says, enigmatically, maddeningly, is 'Tuesday!' "

"Do they all say 'Tuesday'?"

"The dated ones do. That's the only day I'm sure there will be no ominous omens of a Flib." He shuddered. Henry didn't know what Flib was, but the unie certainly seemed to be bothered, even terrified, of it. "Oh, I'm *so* pleased they're getting results! I think I'll step up production."

He walked down the air to a flat, multi-snake-armed machine, and punched a tip at one end. The machine began to *wonkle*.

Wonkle, wonkle, wonkle. *"Plummis!"* Eggzaborg swore, dealing the machine a vicious kick. The machine wonkled once more in agony, then began winkling. Winkle, winkle, winkle.

Eggzaborg looked relieved. "You'd think even this refurbished equipment would hold up better. It's only about a thousand years old. We don't judge in years, of course," he reminded Henry again. "No years. We're not *from* here, remember?"

"Why are you bothering to tell me all this?" asked Henry. "I should think you'd have to keep all this secret . . . or get rid of me." Suddenly Henry was very much more frightened. "Are you going to kill me . . . and . . . recycle my mortal flesh?"

The unie settled back in its cross-legged crouch. "Are you nuts? *Kill* you?!? I won't *be* here in another ten minutes, and you'll never find me again. Besides, who'd believe you if you told them what you'd seen? You people are such moles." He began to laugh. High, thin, squeaky. It rasped on Henry's nerves. "Kill you. Recycle you. Oh, that's rich! What ultra stupegoids you humans be!"

Henry lost his temper with flashing poor judgment. "You, sir," he began, from a lifetime of practicing the amenities, "are a charlatan and an egotistical . . ."

He never finished the epithet. Suddenly every coin in his pockets—every coin that was left from his previous jouncing—became screeching hot; every hair in every pore developed a life of its own, writhing and twisting, wrenching his skin over every inch of his agonized body; the soles of his shoes became peanut butter; his nose began to run; his pen leaked through his shirt. All at once.

Then he was turned upside-down, downside-up in the air yet again, and began to experience alternate hot and cold waves of stomach-convulsing nausea.

"You know something," the unie said, quietly, "if I didn't want to conquer you wretched gobbets so much, I'd—I'd *kill* the lot of you. You're an arrogant . . . *human being*!" He said the last, much as Henry would have said "leper," or "dog catcher," or "televangelist."

"Now scram, you nosey, rude simian! And just wait three thousand years! Just you wait—*you'll see*!"

An instant later, Henry found himself in an apartment at 6991 Perry Avenue, 5th Floor, sharing a bathtub with a very small naked child and her three plastic ducks. He sputtered several times, quacked once in hopes it might distract someone enough so they would not notice he wasn't a duck, clambered dripping from the tub, and was shortly thereafter taken into police custody, read his rights, casually but thoroughly bludgeoned, dragged down five flights of tenement stairs, and eventually transported to Incarceration Island. Not curiously, Henry was no longer curious.

The cell was drafty, and Henry was certain he was coming down with a beastly case of intestinal flu. His cellmate was ignoring him, while picking between his naked toes and eating what he discovered there. Henry was ill, he was nauseated, and he was still confused by the entire escapade. Nonetheless, he was desperately trying to cling to the impression that things were better than most people thought. (Some jobs are simply not worth the effort.)

Yet somehow, either because the unie had been sent out by the Lephamaster too quickly, or because there had been a glitch in the system and his people had forgotten he was here, or because this poor Earth had been an insignificant operation to begin with, or because he had gone mad having been left here too long, or perhaps, pathetically, the unie had been contaminated by human contact, or maybe, simply, just because of the normal alien viewpoint, humanity was getting Help From Outside. And Henry smiled.

Curiously, Henry was suddenly less troubled by his circumstance than common sense and pragmatism would have decreed. Yes, he had been through a physically unpleasant and unbelievable experience, one he could not convey to another human being lest he be put in a soft room dressed in clothing with sleeves too long for his arms. Yes, he was in jail waiting arraignment on a plethora of charges that only *began* with moral turpitude. And, yes, he was probably coming down with intestinal flu, not to mention that the goon across from him had started exploring elsewhere on his person for edibles. But . . .

His lifelong curiosity, which had gotten him into this wretched situation, had been well and truly cured; and it had been exchanged for something no one else on Earth possessed.

Something more valuable than freedom or sanity or the right to vote, which he would probably lose if convicted.

Every human being on the planet, whether a barrio child in La Paz or a multimillionaire in Lucerne, whether an igloo-dwelling Aleut or an iconoclastic Algerian, no matter old or young, male or female, rich or poor, *everyone* lived with some measure of terror about the future, some lesser or greater trepidation about war, the Bomb, global warming, meteors from space, crime in the streets, the pollution of the gene pool, the endless inhumanity of the human race toward itself.

Everyone harbored the fear of tomorrow.

But not Henry.

Henry was in on the secret.

Henry's curiosity had taken him to the source of the revelation that we were all going to do just fine, that there was a demented, all screwed-up, backward-thinking alien creature named Eggzaborg who, under the misconception that he was laying the groundwork for alien invasion, was actually looking out for the human race and this pitiful planet . . . at least for the next three thousand-plus years.

For the next three thousand-plus years nothing termi-nally awful could happen. The Flib, whatever horror *that* was, held fear for the unie, but probably was so alien it would have no effect on the human race.

Henry was in clover. One day he'd be out of jail. One day he'd be back in the world. And he'd be the happiest guy on the planet, because he was the only guy, the *only* guy . . . who *knew*!

His ruminations were cut short by the rumbling of his stomach. An hour earlier the inmates of cell block 4 had marched lockstep to lunch, and even though Henry had smiled at the scrap of wilted lettuce on his plate, he couldn't eat what had been doled out; he was still hungry.

Pretty miserable meal, he mused. Then the remembrance of the third fortune cookie in his pocket made him smile. Dessert! The guards had left it in his jacket pocket—clearly no "escape potential," any more than a stick of gum—when they had searched him and taken his belt and glasses and shoelaces and personal possessions.

He fished it out. It was still soggy from the bathwater in Apartment 5-C at 6991 Perry Avenue, but it *was* edible.

He pulled at the fortune. It came loose and he read it, choking on a slice of air. He remembered what the unie had said about the Flib. The fortune didn't say *Tuesday*. Horribly, ominously, it said:

Wednesday.

SENSIBLE CITY

The lesson here is pretty much like the lesson in the previous story, except it's stated differently. So don't give me a hard time; sometimes I have to write a piece of philosophy half a dozen different ways, just till my weary brain gets the message. Let us not forget that I was getting into trouble even worse than yours, years before you came out of yo momma, squealin' an' pukin', which makes me dumber than you, earlier than you. And it takes me a while to catch on. But one thing I know for certain: when I go to what my wife charmingly refers to as a "face-sucking alien" movie, and some actor we've come to like a lot ventures off by himself, or herself, into that dark room or down those basement stairs or, the way Harry Dean Stanton got offed in *Alien*, wandering into the storage bay with the water dripping down those clanking ceiling chains, and we just *know* the acid-drooling alien is out there somewhere, and he's just wandering around like a doofus in a Pauly Shore flick . . . well, I don't know about *you*, but I'm shouting at the top of my lungs in the theater, GET THE HELL OUTTA THERE!!! And even if he hadn't read the script, he should know from the creepy music and the *pro forma* pre–butchery scare of a cat jumping out of nowhere that within two beats there's going to be a blade at his throat, a fang at his ear, a power mower going for his wazoo. It's a convention of scarey movies. So I got this idea for a story, in which the protagonist (I won't call him a hero, because he's a creep) is aware of this time-weathered convention, and will not, absolutely *will not* go into the equivalent of "the dark room." Wherein lies the lesson to be learned here. Curiosity kills blah blah blah. More than that, though, the lesson is: what you do is gonna catch up with you, kid, no matter how far or fast your run, what you have done will always circle around behind you, get ahead of you, and power mow you in the wazoo.

During the third week of the trial, sworn under oath, one of the Internal Affairs guys the DA's office had planted undercover in Gropp's facility attempted to describe how terrifying Gropp's smile was. The IA guy stammered some; and there seemed to be a singular absence of color in his face; but he tried valiantly, not being a poet or one given to colorful speech. And after some prodding by the Prosecutor, he said:

"You ever, y'know, when you brush your teeth . . . how when you're done, and you've spit out the toothpaste and the water, and you pull back your lips to look at your teeth, to see if they're whiter, and like that . . . you know how you tighten up your jaws real good, and make that kind of death-grin smile that pulls your lips back, with your teeth lined up clenched in the front of your mouth . . . you know what I mean . . . well . . ."

Sequestered that night in a downtown hotel, each of the twelve jurors stared into a medicine cabinet mirror and skinned back a pair of lips, and tightened neck muscles till the cords stood out, and clenched teeth, and stared at a face grotesquely contorted. Twelve men and women then superimposed over the mirror reflection the face of the Defendant they'd been staring at for three weeks and approximated the smile they had *not* seen on Gropp's face all that time.

And in that moment of phantom face over reflection face, Gropp was convicted.

Police Lieutenant W. R. Gropp. Rhymed with *crop*. The meat-man who ruled a civic smudge called the Internment Facility when it was listed on the City Council's budget every year. Internment Facility: dripping wet, cold iron, urine smell mixed with sour liquor sweated through dirty skin, men and women crying in the night. A stockade, a prison camp, stalag, ghetto, torture chamber, charnel house, abattoir, duchy, fiefdom, Army co-op mess hall ruled by a neckless thug.

The last of the thirty-seven inmate alumni who had been supoenaed to testify recollected, "Gropp's favorite thing was to take some fool outta his cell, get him nekkid to the skin, then do this *rolling* thing t'him."

When pressed, the former tenant of Gropp's hostelry— not a felon, merely a steamfitter who had had a bit too much to drink and picked up for himself a ten-day Internment Facility residency for D&D—explained that this "rolling thing" entailed "Gropp wrappin' his big, hairy sausage arm aroun' the guy's neck, see, and then he'd *roll him* across the bars, real hard and fast. Bangin' the guy's head like a roulette ball around the wheel. Clank clank, like that. Usual, it'd knock the guy flat out cold, his head clankin' across the bars and spaces between, wham wham wham like that. See his eyes go up outta sight, all white; but

Gropp, he'd hang on with that sausage aroun' the guy's neck, whammin' and bangin' him and takin' some goddam kinda pleasure mentionin' how much bigger this criminal bastard was than *he* was. Yeah, fer sure. That was Gropp's fav'rite part, that he always pulled out some poor nekkid sonofabitch was twice his size.

"That's how four of these guys he's accused of doin', that's how they croaked. With Gropp's sausage 'round the neck. I kept my mouth shut; I'm lucky to get outta there in one piece."

Frightening testimony, last of thirty-seven. But as superfluous as feathers on an eggplant. From the moment of superimposition of phantom face over reflection face, Police Lieutenant W. R. Gropp was on greased rails to spend his declining years for Brutality While Under Color of Service— a *serious* offense—in a maxi-galleria stuffed chockablock with felons whose spiritual brethren he had maimed, crushed, debased, blinded, butchered, and killed.

Similarly destined was Gropp's gigantic Magog, Deputy Sergeant Michael "Mickey" Rizzo, all three hundred and forty pounds of him; brainless malevolence stacked six feet four inches high in his steel-toed, highly polished service boots. Mickey had only been indicted on seventy counts, as opposed to Gropp's eighty-four ironclad atrocities. But if he managed to avoid Sentence of Lethal Injection for having crushed men's heads underfoot, he would certainly go to the maxi-galleria mall of felonious behavior for the rest of his simian life.

Mickey had, after all, pulled a guy up against the inside of the bars and kept bouncing him till he ripped the left arm loose from its socket, ripped it off, and later dropped it on the mess hall steam table just before dinner assembly.

Squat, bullet-headed troll, Lieutenant W. R. Gropp, and

the mindless killing machine, Mickey Rizzo. On greased rails.

So they jumped bail together, during the second hour of jury deliberation.

Why wait? Gropp could see which way it was going, even counting on Blue Loyalty. The city was putting the abyss between the Dept., and him and Mickey. So, why wait? Gropp was a sensible guy, very pragmatic, no bullshit. So they jumped bail together, having made arrangements weeks before, as any sensible felon keen to flee would have done.

Gropp knew a chop shop that owed him a favor. There was a throaty and hemi-speedy, immaculately registered, four-year-old Firebird just sitting in a bay on the fifth floor of a seemingly abandoned garment factory, two blocks from the courthouse.

And just to lock the barn door after the horse, or in this case the Pontiac, had been stolen, Gropp had Mickey toss the chop shop guy down the elevator shaft of the factory. It was the sensible thing to do. After all, the guy's neck *was* broken.

By the time the jury came in, later that night, Lieut. W. R. Gropp was out of the state and somewhere near Boise. Two days later, having taken circuitous routes, the Firebird was on the other side of both the Snake River and the Rockies, between Rock Springs and Laramie. Three days after that, having driven in large circles, having laid over in Cheyenne for dinner and a movie, Gropp and Mickey were in Nebraska.

Wheat ran to the sun, blue storms bellowed up from horizons, and heat trembled on the edge of each leaf. Crows stirred inside fields, lifted above shattered surfaces of grain and flapped into sky. That's what it looked like: the words came from a poem.

They were smack in the middle of the Plains state, above Grand Island, below Norfolk, somewhere out in the middle of nowhere, just tooling along, leaving no trail, deciding to go that way to Canada, or the other way to Mexico. Gropp had heard there were business opportunities in Mazatlán.

It was a week after the jury had been denied the pleasure of seeing Gropp's face as they said, "Stick the needle in the brutal sonofabitch. Fill the barrel with a very good brand of weed-killer, stick the needle in the brutal sonofabitch's chest, and slam home the plunger. Guilty, your honor, guilty on charges one through eighty-four. Give 'im the weed-killer and let's watch the fat scum-bag do his dance!" A week of swift and leisurely driving here and there, doubling back and skimming along easily.

And somehow, earlier this evening, Mickey had missed a turnoff, and now they were on a stretch of superhighway that didn't seem to have any important exits. There were little towns now and then, the lights twinkling off in the mid-distance, but if they were within miles of a major metropolis, the map didn't give them clues as to where they might be.

"You took a wrong turn."

"Yeah, huh?"

"Yeah, *exactly* huh. Keep your eyes on the road."

"I'm sorry, Looten'nt."

"No. Not Lieutenant. I told you."

"Oh, yeah, right. Sorry, Mr. Gropp."

"Not Gropp. Jensen. Mister *Jensen*. You're *also* Jensen; my kid brother. Your name is Daniel."

"I got it, I remember: Harold and Daniel Jensen is us. You know what I'd like?"

"No, what would you like?"

"A box'a Grape-Nuts. I could have 'em here in the car, and when I got a mite peckish I could just dip my hand in an' have a mouthful. I'd like that."

"Keep your eyes on the road."

"So whaddya think?"

"About what?"

"About maybe I swing off next time and we go into one'a these little towns and maybe a 7-Eleven'll be open, and I can get a box'a Grape-Nuts? We'll need some gas after a while, too. See the little arrow there?"

"I see it. We've still got half a tank. Keep driving."

Mickey pouted. Gropp paid no attention. There were drawbacks to forced traveling companionship. But there were many culs-de-sac and landfills between this stretch of dark turnpike and New Brunswick, Canada, or Mazatlán, state of Sinaloa.

"What is this, the southwest?" Gropp asked, looking out the side window into utter darkness. "The Midwest? What?"

Mickey looked around, too. "I dunno. Pretty out here, though. Real quiet and pretty."

"It's pitch dark."

"Yeah, huh?"

"Just drive, for godsake. Pretty. Jeezus!"

They rode in silence for another twenty-seven miles, then Mickey said, "I gotta go take a piss."

Gropp exhaled mightily. Where were the culs-de-sac, where were the landfills? "Okay. Next town of any size, we can take the exit and see if there's decent accommodations. You can get a box of Grape-Nuts and use the toilet; I can have a cup of coffee and study the map in better light. Does that sound like a good idea, to you . . . Daniel?"

"Yes, Harold. See, I remembered!"

"The world is a fine place."

They drove for another sixteen miles and came nowhere in sight of a thruway exit sign. But the green glow had begun to creep up from the horizon.

"What the hell is that?" Gropp asked, running down his power window. "Is that some kind of a forest fire, or something? What's that look like to you?"

"Like green in the sky."

"Have you ever thought how lucky you are that your mother abandoned you, Mickey?" Gropp said wearily. "Because if she hadn't, and if they hadn't brought you to the county jail for temporary housing till they could put you in a foster home, and I hadn't taken an interest in you, and hadn't arranged for you to live with the Rizzos, and hadn't let you work around the lockup, and hadn't made you my deputy, do you have any idea where you'd be today?" He paused for a moment, waiting for an answer, realized the entire thing was rhetorical—not to mention pointless—and said, "Yes, it's green in the sky, pal, but it's also something odd. Have you ever seen 'green in the sky' before? Anywhere? Any time?"

"No, I guess I haven't."

Gropp sighed, and closed his eyes.

They drove in silence another nineteen miles, and the green miasma in the air had enveloped them. It hung above and around them like sea fog, chill and with tiny droplets of moisture that Mickey fanned away with the windshield wipers. It made the landscape on either side of the super-highway faintly visible, cutting the impenetrable darkness, but it also induced a wavering, ghostly quality to the terrain.

Gropp turned on the map light in the dome of the Firebird, and studied the map of Nebraska. He murmured, "I haven't got a rat's-fang of any idea where the hell we *are*!

There isn't even a freeway like this indicated here. You took some helluva wrong turn 'way back there, pal!" Dome light out.

"I'm sorry, Loo-Harold . . ."

A large reflective advisement marker, green and white, came up on their right. It said: **FOOD   GAS   LODGING 10 MILES.**

The next sign said: **EXIT   7 MILES.**

The next sign said: **OBEDIENCE   3 MILES.**

Gropp turned the map light on again. He studied the venue. "Obedience? What the hell kind of 'obedience'? There's nothing like that *anywhere*. What is this, an old map? Where did you get this map?"

"Gas station."

"Where?"

"I dunno. Back a long ways. That place we stopped with the root beer stand next to it."

Gropp shook his head, bit his lip, murmured nothing in particular. "Obedience," he said. "Yeah, huh?"

They began to see the town off to their right before they hit the exit turnoff. Gropp swallowed hard and made a sound that caused Mickey to look over at him. Gropp's eyes were large, and Mickey could see the whites.

"What'sa matter, Loo . . . Harold?"

"You see that town out there?" His voice was trembling.

Mickey looked to his right. Yeah, he saw it. Horrible.

Many years ago, when Gropp was briefly a college student, he had taken a warm-body course in Art Appreciation. One oh one, it was; something basic and easy to ace, a snap, all you had to do was show up. Everything you wanted to know about Art from aboriginal cave drawings to Diego Rivera. One of the paintings that had been flashed on the big screen for the class, a sleepy 8:00 A.M. class, had been

The Nymph Echo by Max Ernst. A green and smoldering painting of an ancient ruin overgrown with writhing plants that seemed to have eyes and purpose and a malevolently jolly life of their own, as they swarmed and slithered and overran the stone vaults and altars of the twisted, disturbingly resonant sepulcher. Like a sebaceous cyst, something corrupt lay beneath the emerald fronds and hungry black soil.

Mickey looked to his right at the town. Yeah, he saw it. Horrible.

"Keep driving!" Gropp yelled as his partner-in-flight started to slow for the exit ramp.

Mickey heard, but his reflexes were slow. They continued to drift to the right, toward the rising egress lane. Gropp reached across and jerked the wheel hard to the left. "I said: *keep driving!*"

The Firebird slewed, but Mickey got it back under control in a moment, and in another moment they were abaft the ramp, then past it, and speeding away from the nightmarish site beyond and slightly below the superhighway. Gropp stared mesmerized as they swept past. He could see buildings that leaned at obscene angles, the green fog that rolled through the haunted streets, the shadowy forms of misshapen things that skulked at every dark opening.

"That was a real scary-lookin' place, Looten . . . Harold. I don't think I'd of wanted to go down there even for the Grape-Nuts. But maybe if we'd've gone real fast . . ."

Gropp twisted in the seat toward Mickey as much as his muscle-fat body would permit. "Listen to me. There is this tradition, in horror movies, in mysteries, in tv shows, that people are always going into haunted houses, into graveyards, into battle zones, like assholes, like stone idiots! You know what I'm talking about here? Do you?"

Mickey said, "Uh . . ."

"All right, let me give you an example. Remember we went to see that movie *Alien*? Remember how scared you were?"

Mickey bobbled his head rapidly, his eyes widened in frightened memory.

"Okay. So now, you remember that part where the guy who was a mechanic, the guy with the baseball cap, he goes off looking for a cat or some damn thing? Remember? He left everyone else, and he wandered off by himself. And he went into that big cargo hold with the water dripping on him, and all those chains hanging down, and shadows everywhere . . . *do you recall that?*"

Mickey's eyes were chalky potholes. He remembered, oh yes; he remembered clutching Gropp's jacket sleeve till Gropp had been compelled to slap his hand away.

"And you remember what happened in the movie? In the theater? You remember everybody yelling, 'Don't go in there, you asshole! The thing's in there, you moron! Don't go in there!' But, remember, he *did*, and the thing came up behind him, all those teeth, and it bit his stupid head off! Remember that?"

Mickey hunched over the wheel, driving fast.

"Well, that's the way people are. They ain't sensible! They go into places like that, you can see are death places; and they get chewed up or the blood sucked outta their necks or used for kindling . . . but I'm no moron, I'm a sensible guy and I got the brains my mama gave me, and I don't go *near* places like that. So drive like a sonofabitch, and get us outta here, and we'll get your damned Grape-Nuts in Idaho or somewhere . . . if we ever get off this road . . ."

Mickey murmured, "I'm sorry, Lieuten'nt. I took a wrong turn or somethin'."

"Yeah, yeah. Just keep driv—" The car was slowing.

It was a frozen moment. Gropp exultant, no fool he, to

avoid the cliché, to stay out of that haunted house, that ominous dark closet, that damned place. Let idiot others venture off the freeway, into the town that contained the basement entrance to Hell, or whatever. Not he, not Gropp!

He'd outsmarted the obvious.

In that frozen moment.

As the car slowed. Slowed, in the poisonous green mist.

And on their right, the obscenely frightening town of Obedience, that they had left in their dust five minutes before, was coming up again on the superhighway.

"Did you take another turnoff?"

"Uh . . . no, I . . . uh, I been just driving fast . . ."

The sign read: **NEXT RIGHT   50 YDS   OBEDIENCE.**

The car was slowing. Gropp craned his neckless neck to get a proper perspective on the fuel gauge. He was a pragmatic kind of a guy, no nonsense, and very practical; but they were out of gas.

The Firebird slowed and slowed and finally rolled to a stop.

In the rearview mirror Gropp saw the green fog rolling up thicker onto the roadway; and emerging over the berm, in a jostling, slavering horde, clacking and drooling, dropping decayed body parts and leaving glistening trails of worm ooze as they dragged their deformed pulpy bodies across the blacktop, their snake-slit eyes gleaming green and yellow in the mist, the residents of Obedience clawed and slithered and crimped toward the car.

It was common sense any Better Business Bureau would have applauded: if the tourist trade won't come to your town, take your town to the tourists. Particularly if the freeway has forced commerce to pass you by. Particularly if your town needs fresh blood to prosper. Particularly if you have the civic need to share.

Green fog shrouded the Pontiac and the peculiar sounds that came from within. Don't go into that dark room is a sensible attitude. Particularly if one is a sensible guy, in a sensible city.

LIFE HUTCH

Okay. So not everyone who puts you *into* the sh-t is an enemy; and not everyone who pulls you *out* of the sh-t is a friend. So, okay; you got that. Now let me give you the troublemaker lesson that has made me the Golden Icon you see before you. The point of the story you're about to read is that even when they tell you "it can't be fixed, you got to buy a new one, a more expensive one, the latest model," they are jacking you around. Even when they tell you "it can't be done, it's never been done, nobody's ever done it that way," all they're revealing about themselves is that they are limited, minimally-talented, inept, lazy to the point where they'll let the job walk out the door then have to stretch their imagination to figure out a way the job *can* be done, and they are not people you should be dealing with, because they can't solve their *own* problems, much less yours. The world is full of dullards. Sad, sorry little ribbon clerks who fear taking responsibility for their *own* lives, so how the hell can you expect them to be brave or smart enough to take on a problem that emanates from *your* life? They cannot pull you out of the sh-t. They can only put you further into it. They just aren't very smart. The lesson here is the same lesson you find in *all* Art, whether book or story or movie or oil painting or classical symphony or great sculpture. (I cannot suggest that hip-hop or rap contain this message, because they're too illiterate or loud or just bad street doggerel, but that's *my* hang-up, so give it a pass, because I don't suggest you should agree with me, or even like me, because I'm too smart to give a damn if you think I'm kewl or not, 'cause we already got your money for this book.) What it is that *all* Art says is this: PAY ATTENTION. That's it. Nothing more profound or hard to understand. Pay attention. And if you do, just like the guy in this story, you will discover that there are many ways to solve a problem that most other, timid ribbon clerks will never pull down. The lesson of this story—and this book entire—is that you can never know enough, you can never be too smart, and you need to figure out the way the world works without believing that every rule you've been told is immutable—it can't be done, no one's ever done it, etcetera—just because some limited potatobrain believes it. The world is yours, go get it.

Terrence slid his right hand, the one out of sight of the robot, up his side. The razoring pain of the three broken ribs caused his eyes to widen momentarily in pain. Then he recovered himself and closed them till he was studying the machine through narrow slits.

If the eyeballs click, I'm dead, thought Terrence.

The intricate murmurings of the life hutch around him brought back the immediacy of his situation. His eyes again fastened on the medicine cabinet clamped to the wall next to the robot's duty-niche.

Cliché. So near yet so far. It could be all the way back on Antares-Base for all the good it's doing me, he thought, and a crazy laugh rang through his head. He caught himself just in time. *Easy! Three days is a nightmare, but cracking up will only make it end sooner.* That was the last thing he wanted. But it couldn't go on much longer.

He flexed the fingers of his right hand. It was all he *could* move. Silently he damned the technician who had passed the robot through. Or the politician who had let inferior robots get placed in the life hutches so he could get a rake-off from the government contract. Or the repairman who hadn't bothered checking closely his last time around. All of them; he damned them all.

They deserved it.

He was dying.

His death had started before he had reached the life hutch. Terrence had begun to die when he had gone into the battle.

He let his eyes close completely, let the sounds of the life hutch fade from around him. Slowly, the sound of the coolants hush-hushing through the wall-pipes, the relay machines feeding their messages without pause from all over the galaxy, the whirring of the antenna's standard, turning in its socket atop the bubble, slowly they melted into silence. He had resorted to blocking himself off from reality many times during the past three days. It was either that or existing with the robot watching, and eventually he would have had to move. To move was to die. It was that simple.

He closed his ears to the whisperings of the life hutch; he listened to the whisperings within himself.

"Good God! There must be a million of them!"

It was the voice of the squadron leader, Resnick, ringing in his suit intercom.

"What kind of battle formation is *that* supposed to be?" came another voice. Terrence looked at the radar screen, at the flickering dots signifying Kyben ships.

"Who can tell with those toadstool-shaped ships of theirs," Resnick answered. "But remember, the whole front umbrella-part is studded with cannon, and it has a helluva range of fire. Okay, watch yourselves, good luck—and give 'em Hell!"

The fleet dove straight for the Kyben armada.

To his mind came the sounds of war, across the gulf of space. It was all imagination; in that tomb there was no sound. Yet he could clearly detect the hiss of his scout's blaster as it poured beam after beam into the lead ship of the Kyben fleet.

His sniper-class scout had been near the point of that deadly Terran phalanx, driving like a wedge at the alien ships, converging on them in loose battle-formation. It was then it had happened.

One moment he had been heading into the middle of the battle, the left flank of the giant Kyben dreadnaught turning crimson under the impact of his firepower.

The next moment, he had skittered out of the formation which had slowed to let the Kyben craft overshoot, while the Earthmen decelerated to pick up maneuverability.

He had gone on at the old level and velocity, directly into the forward guns of a toadstool-shaped Kyben destroyer.

The first beam had burned the gun-mounts and directional equipment off the front of the ship, scorching down the aft side in a smear like oxidized chrome plate. He had managed to avoid the second beam.

His radio contact had been brief; he was going to make it back to Antares-Base if he could. If not, the formation would be listening for his homing-beam from a life hutch on whatever planetoid he might find for a crash-landing.

Which was what he had done. The charts had said the pebble spinning there was technically 1-333, 2-A, M & S, 3-804.39#, which would have meant nothing but three-dimensional coordinates had not the small # after the data indicated a life hutch somewhere on its surface.

His distaste for being knocked out of the fighting, being

forced onto one of the life hutch planetoids, had been offset only by his fear of running out of fuel before he could locate himself. Of eventually drifting off into space somewhere, to wind up, finally, as an artificial satellite around some minor sun.

The ship pancaked in under minimal reverse drive, bounced high twice and caromed ten times, tearing out chunks of the rear section, but had come to rest a scant two miles from the life hutch, jammed into the rocks.

Terrence had high-leaped the two miles across the empty, airless planetoid to the hermetically sealed bubble in the rocks. His primary wish was to set the hutch's beacon signal so his returning fleet could track him.

He had let himself into the decompression chamber, palmed the switch through his thick spacesuit glove, and finally removed his helmet as he heard the air whistle into the chamber.

He had pulled off his gloves, opened the inner door and entered the life hutch itself.

God bless you, little life hutch, Terrence had thought as he dropped the helmet and gloves. He had glanced around, noting the relay machines picking up messages from outside, sorting them, vectoring them off in other directions. He had seen the medicine chest clamped onto the wall; the refrigerator, he knew, would be well-stocked if a previous tenant hadn't been there before the stockman could refill it. He had seen the all-purpose robot, immobile in its duty-niche. And the wall-chronometer, its face smashed. All of it in a second's glance.

God bless, too, the gentlemen who thought up the idea of these little rescue stations, stuck all over the place for just such emergencies as this. He had started to walk across the room.

It was at this point that the service robot, that kept the

place in repair between tenants and unloaded supplies from the ships, had moved clankingly across the floor, and with one fearful smash of a steel arm thrown Terrence across the room.

The spaceman had been brought up short against the steel bulkhead, pain blossoming in his back, his side, his arms and legs. The machine's blow had instantly broken three of his ribs. He lay there for a moment, unable to move. For a few seconds he was too stunned to breathe, and it had been that, certainly, that had saved his life. His pain had immobilized him, and in that short space of time the robot had retreated with a muted internal clash of gears.

He had attempted to sit up straight, and the robot had hummed oddly and begun to move. He had stopped the movement. The robot had settled back.

Twice more had convinced him his position was as bad as he had thought.

The robot had worn down somewhere in its printed circuits. Its commands to lift had been erased or distorted so that now it was conditioned to smash, to hit, anything that moved.

He had seen the clock. He realized he should have suspected something was wrong when he saw its smashed face. Of course! The digital dials had moved, the robot had smashed the clock. Terrence had moved, the robot had smashed him.

And would again, if he moved again.

But for the unnoticeable movement of his eyelids, he had not moved in three days.

He had tried moving toward the decompression lock, stopping when the robot advanced and letting it settle back, then moving again, a little nearer. But the idea died with his first movement. His ribs were too painful. The pain was terrible. He was locked in one position, an uncomfortable, twisted position, and he would be there till the stalemate ended, one way or the other.

He was suddenly alert again. The reliving of his last three days brought back reality sharply.

He was twelve feet away from the communications panel, twelve feet away from the beacon that would guide his rescuers to him. Before he died of his wounds, before he starved to death, before the robot crushed him. It could have been twelve light-years, for all the nearer he could get to it.

What had gone wrong with the robot? Time to think was cheap. The robot could detect movement, but thinking was still possible. Not that it could help, but it was possible.

The companies that supplied the life hutch's needs were all government contracted. Somewhere along the line someone had thrown in impure steel or calibrated the circuit-cutting machines for a less expensive job. Somewhere along the line someone had not run the robot through its paces correctly. Somewhere along the line someone had committed murder.

He opened his eyes again. Only the barest fraction of opening. Any more and the robot would sense the movement of his eyelids. That would be fatal.

He looked at the machine.

It was not, strictly speaking, a robot. It was merely a remote-controlled hunk of jointed steel, invaluable for making beds, stacking steel plating, watching culture dishes, unloading spaceships and sucking dirt from rugs. The robot body, roughly humanoid, but without what would have been a head on a human, was merely an appendage.

The real brain, a complex maze of plastic screens and printed circuits, was behind the wall. It would have been too dangerous to install those delicate parts in a heavy-duty mechanism. It was all too easy for the robot to drop itself from a loading shaft, or be hit by a meteorite, or get caught under a wrecked spaceship. So there were sensitive units in the robot appendage that "saw" and "heard" what was going on, and relayed them to the brain—behind the wall.

And somewhere along the line that brain had worn grooves too deeply into its circuits. It was now mad. Not mad in any way a human being might go mad, for there were an infinite number of ways a machine could go insane. Just mad enough to kill Terrence.

Even if I could *hit the robot with something, it wouldn't stop the thing.* He could, perhaps, throw something at the machine before it could get to him, but it would do no good. The robot brain would still be intact, and the appendage would continue to function. It was hopeless.

He stared at the massive, blocky hands of the robot. It seemed he could see his own blood on the jointed work-tool fingers of one hand. He knew it must be his imagination, but the idea persisted. He flexed the fingers of his hidden hand.

Three days had left him weak and dizzy from hunger. His head was light and his eyes burned steadily. He had been lying in his own filth till he no longer noticed the discomfort. His side ached and throbbed, and the pain of a blast furnace roared through him every time he breathed.

He thanked God his spacesuit was still on, lest the movement of his breathing bring the robot down on him. There was only one solution, and that solution was his death. He was almost delirious.

Several times during the past day—as well as he could gauge night and day without a clock or a sunrise—he had heard the roar of the fleet landing outside. Then he had realized there was no sound in dead space. Then he had realized they were all inside the relay machines, coming through subspace right into the life hutch. Then he had realized that such a thing was not possible. Then he had come to his senses and realized all that had gone before was hallucination.

Then he had awakened and known it *was* real. He *was* trapped, and there was no way out. Death had come to live with him. He was going to die.

Terrence had never been a coward, nor had he been a hero. He was one of the men who fight wars because they are always fought by *some*one. He was the kind of man who would allow himself to be torn from wife and home and flung into an abyss they called Space to defend what he had been told needed defense. But it was in moments like this that a man like Terrence began to think.

Why here? Why like this? What have I done that I should finish in a filthy spacesuit on a lost rock—and not gloriously like they said in the papers back home, but starving or bleeding to death alone with a crazy robot? Why me? Why me? Why alone?

He knew there could be no answers. He expected no answers.

He was not disappointed.

When he awoke, he instinctively looked at the clock. Its shattered face looked back at him, jarring him, forcing his eyes open in after-sleep terror. The robot hummed and emitted a spark. He kept his eyes open. The humming ceased. His eyes began to burn. He knew he couldn't keep them open too long.

The burning worked its way to the front of his eyes, from the top and bottom, bringing with it tears. It felt as though someone was shoving needles into the corners. The tears ran down over his cheeks.

His eyes snapped shut. The roaring grew in his ears. The robot didn't make a sound.

Could it be inoperative? Could it have worn down to immobility? Could he take the chance of experimenting?

He slid down to a more comfortable position. The robot charged forward the instant he moved. He froze in mid-movement, his heart a chunk of ice. The robot stopped, confused, a scant ten inches from his outstretched foot. The machine hummed to itself, the noise of it coming both from the machine in front of him and from somewhere behind the wall.

He was suddenly alert.

If it had been working correctly, there would have been little or no sound from the appendage, and none whatsoever from the brain. But it was *not* working properly, and the sound of its thinking was distinct.

The robot rolled backward, its "eyes" still toward Terrence. The sense orbs of the machine were in the torso, giving the machine the look of a squat metal gargoyle, squared and deadly.

The humming was growing louder, every now and then a sharp *pfffft!* of sparks mixed with it. Terrence had a moment's horror at the thought of a short-circuit, a fire in the life hutch, and no service robot to put it out.

He listened carefully, trying to pinpoint the location of the robot's brain built into the wall.

Then he thought he had it. Or was it there? It was either in the wall behind a bulkhead next to the refrigerator, or behind a bulkhead near the relay machines. The two possible housings were within a few feet of each other, but they might make a great deal of difference.

The distortion created by the steel plate in front of the brain, and the distracting background noise of the robot broadcasting it made it difficult to tell exactly which was the correct location.

He drew a deep breath.

The ribs slid a fraction of an inch together, their broken ends grinding.

He moaned.

A high-pitched tortured moan that died quickly, but throbbed back and forth inside his head, echoing and building itself into a paean of sheer agony! It forced his tongue out of his mouth, limp in a corner of his lips, moving slightly. The robot rolled forward. He drew his tongue in, clamped his mouth shut, cut off the scream inside his head at its high point!

The robot stopped, rolled back to its duty-niche.

Oh, God! The pain! The God God where are you pain!

Beads of sweat broke out on his body. He could feel their tickle inside his spacesuit, inside his jumper, inside the bodyshirt, on his skin. The pain of the ribs was suddenly heightened by an irresistible itching of his skin.

He moved infinitesimally within the suit, his outer appearance giving no indication of the movement. The itching did not subside. The more he tried to make it stop, the more he thought about not thinking about it, the worse it became. His armpits, the crooks of his arms, his thighs where the tight service-pants clung—suddenly too tightly—were madness. He had to scratch!

He almost started to make the movement. He stopped before he started. He knew he would never live to enjoy any relief. A laugh bubbled into his head. *God Almighty, and I always laughed at the slobs who suffered with the seven-year itch, the ones who always did a little dance when they were at attention during inspection, the ones who could scratch and sigh contentedly. God, how I envy them.* His thoughts were taking on a wild sound, even to him.

The prickling did not stop. He twisted faintly. It got worse. He took another deep breath.

The ribs sandpapered again.

This time, blessedly, he fainted from the pain.

"Well, Terrence, how do you like your first look at a Kyban?"

Ernie Terrence wrinkled his forehead and ran a finger up the side of his face. He looked at his Commander and shrugged. "Fantastic things, aren't they?"

"Why fantastic?"

"Because they're just like us. Except, of course, the bright yellow pigmentation and the tentacle-fingers. Other than that they're identical. To a human being."

The Commander opaqued the examination-casket and drew a cigarette from a silver case, offering the Lieutenant one. He puffed it alight, staring with one eye closed against the smoke. "More than that, I'm afraid. Their insides look like someone had taken them out, liberally mixed them with spare parts from several other species, and jammed them back in any way that fitted conveniently. For the next twenty years we'll be knocking our heads together trying to figure out their metabolic *raison d'être*."

Terrence grunted, rolling his unlit cigarette absently between two fingers. "That's the least of it."

"You're right," agreed the Commander. "For the next *thousand* years we'll be trying to figure out how they think, why they fight, what it takes to get along with them, what motivates them."

If they let us live that long, thought Terrence.

"Why are we at war with the Kyben?" he asked the older man. "I mean *really*."

"Because the Kyben want to kill every human being they can recognize as a human being."

"What have they got against us?"

"Does it matter? Maybe it's because our skin isn't bright

179

yellow; maybe it's because our fingers aren't silken and flexible; maybe it's because our cities are too noisy for them. Maybe a lot of maybes. But it doesn't matter. Survival never matters until you have to survive.

Terrence nodded. He understood. So did the Kyben. It grinned at him and drew its blaster. It fired point-blank, crimsoning the hull of the Kyben ship.

He swerved to avoid running into his gun's own back-lash. The movement of the bucket seat sliding in its tracks, keeping his vision steady while maneuvering, made him dizzy. He closed his eyes for a moment.

When he opened them, the abyss was nearer, and he teetered, his lips whitening as they pressed together under his effort to steady himself. With a headlong gasp he fell sighing into the stomach. His long, silken fingers jointed steely humming clankingly toward the medicine chest over the plate behind the bulkhead.

The robot advanced on him grindingly. Small, fine bits of metal rubbed together, ashing away into a breeze that came from nowhere as the machine raised lead boots toward his face.

Onward and onward till he had no room to move

and

then

the light came on, bright, brighter than any star Terrence had ever seen, glowing, broiling, flickering, shining, bobbing a ball of light on the chest of the robot, who staggered,

stumbled,

stepped.

The robot hissed, hummed and exploded into a million flying, racing fragments, shooting beams of light all over the abyss over which Terrence again teetered, teetering. He flailed his arms wildly trying to escape but, at the last

moment, before
>the
>>fall
>he awoke with a start!

He saved himself only by his unconscious. Even in the hell of a nightmare he was aware of the situation. He had not moaned and writhed in his delirium. He had kept motionless and silent.

He knew it was true, because he was still alive.

Only his surprised jerking, as he came back to consciousness, started the monster rolling from its niche. He came fully awake and sat silent, slumped against the wall. The robot retreated.

Thin breath came through his nostrils. Another moment and he would have put an end to the past three days—three days or more now? how long had he been asleep?—days of torture.

He was hungry. Lord, how hungry he was. The pain in his side was worse now, a steady throbbing that made even shallow breathing torturous. He itched maddeningly. He was uncomfortably slouched against a cold steel bulkhead, every rivet having made a burrow for itself in his skin. He wished he was dead.

He didn't wish he was dead. It was all too easy to get his wish.

If he could only disable that robot brain. A total impossibility. If he could only wear Phobos and Deimos for watchfobs. If he could only shack-up with a silicon-deb from Penares. If he could only use his large colon for a lasso.

It would take a thorough destruction of the brain to do it enough damage to stop the appendage before it could roll over and smash Terrence again.

With a steel bulkhead between him and the brain, his chances of success totaled minus zero every time.

He considered which part of his body the robot would smash first. One blow of that tool-hand would kill him if it was used a second time. With the state of his present wounds, even a strong breath might finish him.

Perhaps he could make a break and get through the lock into the decompression chamber...

Worthless. (A) The robot would catch him before he had gotten to his feet, in his present condition. (B) Even allowing a miracle, even if he did get through the lock, the robot would smash the lock port, letting in air, ruining the mechanism. (C) Even allowing a double miracle and it didn't, what the hell good would it do him? His helmet and gloves were in the hutch itself, and there was no place to go on the planetoid. The ship was ruined, so no signal could be sent from there.

Doom suddenly compounded itself.

The more he thought about it, the more certain he was that soon the light would flicker out for him.

The light would flicker out.

The light would flicker...

The light...

...light...?

Oh God, is it possible? Can it be? Have I found an answer? He marveled at the simplicity of it. It had been there for more than three days waiting for him to use it. It was *so* simple it was magnificent. He could hardly restrain himself from moving, just out of sheer joy.

I'm not brilliant, I'm not a genius, why did this occur to me? For a few minutes the brilliance of the solution staggered him. Would a less intelligent man have solved the problem this easily? Would a *more* intelligent man have done it? Then he remembered the dream. The light in the dream. *He* hadn't solved the problem, his unconscious had. The answer had been there all the time, but he was too close to see it. His mind had been forced to devise a way to tell him. Luckily, it had.

And finally, he didn't care *how* he had uncovered it. His God, if he had had anything to do with it, had heard him. Terrence was by no means a religious man, but this was miracle enough to make him a believer. It wasn't over yet, but the answer was there—and it *was* an answer.

He began to save himself.

Slowly, achingly slowly, he moved his right hand, the hand away from the robot's sight, to his belt. On the belt hung the assorted implements a spaceman needs at any moment in his ship. A wrench. A packet of sleep-stavers. A compass. A geiger counter. A flashlight.

The last was the miracle. Miracle in a tube.

He fingered it almost reverently, then unclipped it in a moment's frenzy, still immobile to the robot's "eyes."

He held it at his side, away from his body by a fraction of an inch, pointing up over the bulge of his spacesuited leg.

If the robot looked at him, all it would see would be the motionless bulk of his leg, blocking off any movement on his part. To the machine, he was inert. Motionless.

Now, he thought wildly, *where is the brain?*

If it is behind the relay machines, I'm still dead. If it is near the refrigerator, I'm saved. He could afford to take no chances. He would have to move.

He lifted one leg.

The robot moved toward him. The humming and sparking were more distinct this time. He dropped the leg.

Behind the plates above the refrigerator!

The robot stopped, nearly at his side. Seconds had decided. The robot hummed, sparked, and returned to its niche.

Now he knew!

He pressed the button. The invisible beam of the flashlight leaped out, speared the bulkhead above the refrigerator. He pressed the button again and again, the flat circle of light appearing, disappearing, appearing, disappearing on the faceless metal of the life hutch's wall.

The robot sparked and rolled from its niche. It looked once at Terrence. Its rollers changed direction in an instant and the machine ground toward the refrigerator.

The steeled fist swung in a vicious arc, smashing with a deafening *clang!* at the spot where the light bubble flickered on and off.

It swung again and again. Again and again, till the bulkhead had been gouged and crushed and opened, and the delicate coils and plates and circuits and memorex modules behind it were refuse and rubble. Until the robot froze, with arm half-ready to strike again. Dead. Immobile. Brain and appendage.

Even then Terrence did not stop pressing the flashlight button. Wildly he thumbed it again and again and again.

Then he realized it was all over.

The robot was dead. He was alive. He would be saved. He had no doubts about that. *Now* he could cry.

The medicine chest grew large through the shimmering in his eyes. The relay machines smiled at him.

God bless you, little life hutch, he thought, before he fainted.

DJINN, NO CHASER

Wrote this one a couple of times, made it better each time I went after it. Then turned it into a TV segment on *Tales from the Darkside*. You may have seen it. Kareem Abdul-Jabbar played the Djinn. (Don't lose your day-job Kareem.) And the lesson passim this little tale is a good one for those of you who, like me, lead lives determinedly singular and oftimes cutting trail with trouble. The lesson is the same one Nelson Algren included in his famous three rules for living, as they were codified in a terrific novel called *The Man With the Golden Arm*. He said, "Never eat at a diner called "Mom's,' never play cards with a guy named 'Doc,' and never get involved with a woman who's got bigger troubles than you." (It was a "guy" novel, so if you're feeling foolishly Politically Correct, which is a pain in the patoot, you can substitute "never get involved with a *"guy"* for "woman.") If you learn nothing else from me in the course of reading this little tome, kiddies, let it be this: bad companions can drag your snout down into the mud faster than dope or drink or deep religious fervor. The world is full of leaners. People who are bone-stick-stone stupid, but they've got a low ratlike cunning. They know how to side you and smooth you and get into your pocket, and then give you 'tude about how you be hare-*assing* them when you call them and demand they repay you. They will involve you in idiot schemes, they will waste your time and your energy, they will mooch off you and eventually abandon you, step off when someone starts making static. They are the "bad companions" your momma and poppa warned you about. They are the yamps and shermheads, the biscuits and trife bums who will kill your waking hours and give you night fright when you lie down. The lesson is this: make your own way. Set your own pace. Do not get drawn into some non-productive lay-up that will sap your strength and let the air out of your dreams. In this story, a pretty nice guy and a pretty nice woman, who probably shouldn't have rolled on a duo, find themselves paying the price for each other's bad company. Yeah, sure, it's got a happy ending, but this is a *story*, gee, it's a piece of fiction! It ain't real.

W ho the hell ever heard of Turkish Period?" Danny Squires said. He said it at the top of his voice, on a city street.

"Danny! People are staring at us; lower your voice!" Connie Squires punched his bicep. They stood on the street, in front of the furniture store. Danny was determined not to enter.

"Come on, Connie," he said, "let's get away from these junk shops and go see some inexpensive modern stuff. You know perfectly well I don't make enough to start filling the apartment with expensive antiques."

Connie furtively looked up and down the street—she was more concerned with a "scene" than with the argument itself—and then moved in toward Danny with a determined air. "Now listen up, Squires. *Did* you or did you *not* marry me four days ago, and promise to love, honor and cherish and all that other good jive?"

Danny's blue eyes rolled toward Heaven; he knew he

was losing ground. Instinctively defensive, he answered, "Well, sure, Connie, but—"

"Well, then, I am your wife, and you have not taken me on a honeymoon—"

"I can't *afford* one!"

"—have not taken me on a honeymoon," Connie repeated with inflexibility. "Consequently, we will buy a little furniture for that rabbit warren you laughingly call our little love nest. And *little* is hardly the term: that vale of tears was criminally undersized when Barbara Fritchie hung out her flag.

"So to make my life *bearable*, for the next few weeks, till we can talk Mr. Upjohn into giving you a raise—"

"Upjohn!" Danny fairly screamed. "You've got to stay away from the boss, Connie. Don't screw around. He won't give me a raise, and I'd rather you stayed away from him—"

"Until then," she went on relentlessly, "we will decorate our apartment in the style I've wanted for years."

"Turkish Period?"

"Turkish Period."

Danny flipped his hands in the air. What was the use? He had known Connie was strong-willed when he'd married her.

It had seemed an attractive quality at the time; now he wasn't so sure. But he was strong-willed too: he was sure he could outlast her. Probably.

"Okay," he said finally, "I suppose Turkish Period it'll be. What the hell *is* Turkish Period?"

She took his arm lovingly, and turned him around to look in the store window. "Well, honey, it's not *actually* Turkish. It's more Mesopotamian. You know, teak and silk and . . ."

"Sounds hideous."

"So you're starting up again!" She dropped his arm, her eyes flashing, her mouth a tight little line. "I'm really ashamed of you, depriving me of the few little pleasures I need to make my life a blub, sniff, hoo-hoo . . ."

The edge was hers.

"Connie . . . Connie . . ." She knocked away his comforting hand, saying, "You beast." That was too much for him. The words were so obviously put-on, he was suddenly infuriated:

"Now, goddammit!"

Her tears came faster. Danny stood there, furious, helpless, outmaneuvered, hoping desperately that no cop would come along and say, "This guy botherin' ya, lady?"

"Connie, okay, okay, we'll *have* Turkish Period. Come on, come on. It doesn't matter what it costs, I can scrape up the money somehow."

It was not one of the glass-brick and onyx emporia where sensible furniture might be found (if one searched hard enough and paid high enough and retained one's senses long enough as they were trying to palm off modernistic nightmares in which no comfortable position might be found); no, it was not even one of those. This was an antique shop.

They looked at beds that had canopies and ornate metalwork on the bedposts. They looked at rugs that were littered with pillows, so visitors could sit on the floors. They looked at tables built six inches off the deck, for low banquets. They inspected incense burners and hookahs and coffers and giant vases until Danny's head swam with visions of the courts of long-dead caliphs.

Yet, despite her determination, Connie chose very few items; and those she did select were moderately-priced and quite handsome . . . for what they were. And as the hours passed, and as they moved around town from one dismal junk emporium to another, Danny's respect for his wife's taste grew. She was selecting an apartment full of furniture that wasn't bad at all.

They were finished by six o'clock, and had bills of sale that totaled just under two hundred dollars. Exactly thirty dollars less than Danny had decided could be spent to furnish the new household . . . and still survive on his salary. He had taken the money from his spavined savings account, and had known he must eventually start buying on credit, or they would not be able to get enough furniture to start living properly.

He was tired, but content. She'd shopped wisely. They were in a shabby section of town. How had they gotten here? They walked past an empty lot sandwiched in between two tenements—wet-wash slapping on lines between them. The lot was weed-overgrown and garbage-strewn.

"May I call your attention to the depressing surroundings and my exhaustion?" Danny said. "Let's get a cab and go back to the apartment. I want to collapse."

They turned around to look for a cab, and the empty lot was gone.

In its place, sandwiched between the two tenements, was a little shop. It was a one-storey affair, with a dingy facade, and its front window completely grayed-over with dust. A hand-painted line of elaborate script on the glass-panel of the door, also opaque with grime, proclaimed:

MOHANADUS MUKHAR, CURIOS.

A little man in a flowing robe, wearing a fez, plunged out the front door, skidded to a stop, whirled and slapped a huge sign on the window. He swiped at it four times with a big paste-brush, sticking it to the glass, and whirled back inside, slamming the door.

"No," Danny said.

Connie's mouth was making peculiar sounds.

"There's no insanity in my family," Danny said firmly. "We come from very good stock."

"We've made a visual error," Connie said.

"Simply didn't notice it," Danny said. His usually baritone voice was much nearer soprano.

"If there's crazy, we've both got it," Connie said.

"Must be, if you see the same thing I see."

Connie was silent a moment, then said, "Large seagoing vessel, three stacks, maybe the Titanic. Flamingo on the bridge, flying the flag of Lichtenstein?"

"Don't play with me, woman," Danny whimpered. "I think I'm losing it."

She nodded soberly. "Right. Empty lot?"

He nodded back, "Empty lot. Clothesline, weeds, garbage."

"Right."

He pointed at the little store. "Little store?"

"Right."

"Man in a fez, name of Mukhar?"

She rolled her eyes. "Right."

"So why are we walking toward it?"

"Isn't this what always happens in stories where weird shops suddenly appear out of nowhere? Something inexorable draws the innocent bystanders into its grip?"

They stood in front of the grungy little shop. They read the sign. It said:

BIG SALE! HURRY! NOW! QUICK!

"The word *unnatural* comes to mind," Danny said.

"Nervously," Connie said, "she turned the knob and opened the door."

A tiny bell went tinkle-tinkle, and they stepped across the threshold into the gloaming of Mohanadus Mukhar's shop.

"Probably not the smartest move we've ever made," Danny said softly. The door closed behind them without any assistance.

It was cool and musty in the shop, and strange fragrances chased one another past their noses.

They looked around carefully. The shop was loaded with junk. From floor to ceiling, wall to wall, on tables and in heaps, the place was filled with oddities and bric-a-brac. Piles of things tumbled over one another on the floor; heaps of things leaned against the walls. There was barely room to walk down the aisle between the stacks and mounds of things. Things in all shapes, things in all sizes and colors. Things. They tried to separate the individual items from the jumble of the place, but all they could perceive was stuff . . . things! Stuff and flotsam and bits and junk.

"Curios, effendi," a voice said, by way of explanation.

Connie leaped in the air, and came down on Danny's foot.

Mukhar was standing beside such a pile of tumbled miscellany that for a moment they could not separate him from the stuff, junk, things he sold.

"We saw your sign," Connie said.

But Danny was more blunt, more direct. "There was an empty lot here; then a minute later, this shop. How come?"

The little man stepped out from the mounds of dust-collectors and his little nut-brown, wrinkled face burst into a million-creased smile. "A fortuitous accident, my children. A slight worn spot in the fabric of the cosmos, and I have been set down here for . . . how long I do not know. But it never hurts to try and stimulate business while I'm here."

"Uh, yeah," Danny said. He looked at Connie. Her expression was as blank as his own.

"Oh!" Connie cried, and went dashing off into one of the side-corridors lined with curios. "This is perfect! Just what we need for the end table. Oh, Danny, it's a dream! It's absolutely the *ne plus ultra*!"

Danny walked over to her, but in the dimness of the aisle between the curios he could barely make out what it was she was holding. He drew her into the light near the door. It had to be:

Aladdin's lamp.

Well, perhaps not that *particular* person's lamp, but one of the ancient, vile-smelling oil burning jobs: long thin spout, round-bottom body, wide, flaring handle.

It was algae-green with tarnish, brown with rust, and completely covered by the soot and debris of centuries. There was no contesting its antiquity; nothing so time-corrupted could fail to be authentic. "What the hell do you want with that old thing, Connie?"

"But Danny, it's so *per*-fect. If we just shine it up a bit. As soon as we put a little work into this lamp, it'll be a beauty." Danny knew he was defeated . . . and she'd probably be right, too. It probably would be very handsome when shined and brassed-up.

"How much?" he asked Mukhar. He didn't want to seem anxious; old camel traders were merciless at bargaining when they knew the item in question was hotly desired.

"Fifty drachmae, eh?" the old man said. His tone was one of malicious humor. "At current exchange rates, taking into account the fall of the Ottoman Empire, thirty dollars."

Danny's lips thinned. "Put it down, Connie; let's get out of here."

He started toward the door, dragging his wife behind him. But she still clutched the lamp; and Mukhar's voice halted them. "All right, noble sir. You are a cunning shop-per, I can see that. You know a bargain when you spy it. But I am unfamiliar in this time-frame with your dollars and your strange fast-food native customs, having been set down here only once before; and since I am more at ease with the drachma than the dollar, with the shekel than the cent, I will cut my own throat, slash both my wrists, and offer you this magnificent antiquity for . . . uh . . . twenty dollars?" His voice was querulous, his tone one of wonder and hope.

"Jesse James at least had a horse!" Danny snarled, once again moving toward the door.

"Fifteen!" Mukhar yowled. "And may all your children need corrective lenses from too much tv-time!"

"Five; and may a hundred thousand syphilitic camels puke into your couscous," Danny screamed back over his shoulder.

"Not bad," said Mukhar.

"Thanks," said Danny, stifling a smile. Now he waited.

"Bloodsucker! Heartless trafficker in cheapness! Pimple on the fundament of decency! Graffito on the subway car of life! Thirteen; my last offer; and may the gods of ITT and the Bank of America turn a blind eye to your venality!" But *his* eyes held the golden gleam of the born haggler, at last, blessedly, in his element.

"Seven, not a penny more, you Arabic anathema! And may a weighty object drop from a great height, flattening you to the niggardly thickness of your soul." Connie stared at him with open awe and admiration.

"Eleven! Eleven dollars, a pittance, an outright theft we're talking about. Call the security guards, get a consumer advocate, gimme a break here!"

"My shadow will vanish from before the evil gleam of your rapacious gaze before I pay a penny more than six bucks, and let the word go out to every wadi and oasis across the limitless desert, that Mohanadus Mukhar steals maggots from diseased meat, flies from horse dung, and the hard-earned drachmae of honest laborers. Six, fuckface, and that's it!"

"My death is about to become a reality," the Arab bellowed, tearing at the strands of white hair showing under the fez. "Rob me, go ahead, rob me: drink my life's blood! Ten! A twenty dollar loss I'll take."

"Okay, okay." Danny turned around and produced his wallet. He pulled out one of the three ten dollar bills still inside and, turning to Connie, said, "You sure you want this ugly, dirty piece of crap?" She nodded, and he held the bill naked in the vicinity of the little merchant. For the first time Danny realized Mukhar was wearing pointed slippers that curled up; there was hair growing from his ears.

"Ten bucks."

The little man moved with the agility of a ferret, and whisked the tenner from Danny's outstretched hand before he could draw it back. "Sold!" Mukhar chuckled.

He spun around once, and when he faced them again, the ten dollars was out of sight. "And a steal, though Allah be the wiser; a hot deal, a veritable steal, blessed sir!"

Danny abruptly realized he had been taken. The lamp had probably been picked up in a junkyard and was worthless. He started to ask if it was a genuine antique, but the piles of junk had begun to waver and shimmer and coruscate with light. "Hey!" Danny said, alarmed, "What's this now?"

The little man's wrinkled face drew up in panic. "Out! Get out, quick! The time-frame is sucking back together! Out! Get out now if you don't want to roam the eternities with me and this shop ... and I can't afford any help! Out!"

He shoved them forward, and Connie slipped and fell,

flailing into a pile of glassware. None of it broke. Her hand went out to protect herself and went right through the glass. Danny dragged her to her feet, panic sweeping over him . . . as the shop continued to waver and grow more indistinct around them.

"Out! Out! Out!" Mukhar kept yelling.

Then they were at the door, and he was kicking them— literally planting his curl-slippered foot in Danny's backside and shoving—from the store. They landed in a heap on the sidewalk. The lamp bounced from Connie's hand and went into the gutter with a clang. The little man stood there grinning in the doorway, and as the shop faded and disappeared, they heard him mumble happily, "A clear nine-seventy-five profit. What a lemon! You got an Edsel, kid, a real lame piece of goods. But I gotta give it to you; the syphilitic camel bit was inspired."

Then the shop was gone, and they got to their feet in front of an empty, weed-overgrown lot.

A lame piece of goods?

"Are you asleep?"

"Yes."

"How come you're answering me?"

"I was raised polite."

"Danny, talk to me . . . come on!"

"The answer is no. I'm not going to talk about it."

"We have to!"

"Not only don't we *have* to, I don't *want* to, ain't *going* to, and shut up so I can go to sleep."

"We've been lying here almost an hour. Neither of us can sleep. We *have* to discuss it, Danny."

The light went on over his side of the bed. The single pool of illumination spread from the hand-me-down daybed they had gotten from Danny's brother in New Jersey, faintly limning the few packing crates full of dishes and linens, the three Cuisinarts they'd gotten as wedding gifts, the straight-back chairs from Connie's Aunt Medora, the entire bare and depressing reality of their first home together.

It would be better when the furniture they'd bought today was delivered. Later, it would be better. Now, it was the sort of urban landscape that drove divorcees and aging bachelors to jump down the airshaft at Christmastime.

"I'm going to talk about it, Squires."

"So talk. I have my thumbs in my ears."

"I think we should rub it."

"I can't hear you. It never happened. I deny the evidence of my senses. It never happened. I have these thumbs in my ears so I cannot hear a syllable of this craziness."

"For god's sake, Squires, I was *there* with you today. I saw it happen, the same as you. I saw that weird little old man and I saw his funky shop come and go like a big burp. Now, neither of us can deny it!"

"If I could hear you, I'd agree; and then I'd deny the evidence of my senses and tell you . . ." He took his thumbs from his ears, looking distressed. ". . . tell you with all my heart that I love you, that I have loved you since the moment I saw you in the typing pool at Upjohn, that if I live to be a hundred thousand years old I'll never love any one or any thing as much as I love you this very moment; and then I would tell you to fuck off and forget it, and let me go to sleep so that tomorrow I can con myself into believing it never happened the way I know it happened.

"Okay?"

She threw back the covers and got out of bed. She was naked. They had not been married that long.

"Where are you going?"

"You know where I'm going."

He sat up in the daybed. His voice had no lightness in it. "Connie!"

She stopped and stared at him, there in the light.

He spoke softly. "Don't. I'm scared. Please don't."

She said nothing. She looked at him for a time. Then, naked, she sat down cross-legged on the floor at the foot of the daybed. She looked around at what little they had, and she answered him gently. "I have to, Danny. I just have to . . . if there's a chance; I have to."

They sat that way, reaching across the abyss with silent imperatives, until—finally—Danny nodded, exhaled heavily, and got out of the daybed. He walked to one of the cartons, pulled out a dustrag, shook it clean over the box, and handed it to her. He walked over to the window ledge where the tarnished and rusted oil lamp sat, and he brought it to her.

"Shine the damned thing, Squires. Who knows, maybe we actually got ourselves a 24 carat genie. Shine on, oh mistress of my Mesopotamian mansion."

She held the lamp in one hand, the rag in the other. For a few minutes she did not bring them together. "I'm scared, too," she said, held her breath, and briskly rubbed the belly of the lamp.

Under her flying fingers the rust and tarnish began to come away in spots. "We'll need brass polish to do this right," she said; but suddenly the ruin covering the lamp melted away, and she was rubbing the bright skin of the lamp itself.

"Oh, Danny, look how nice it is, underneath all the crud!" And at that precise instant the lamp jumped from her hand, emitted a sharp, gray puff of smoke, and a monstrous voice bellowed in the apartment:

AH-HA! It screamed, louder than a subway train. AH-HA!

FREE AT LAST! FREE—AS FREE AS *I'LL* EVER BE—
AFTER TEN THOUSAND YEARS! FREE TO SPEAK AND
ACT, MY WILL TO BE KNOWN!

Danny went over backward. The sound was as mind-
throttling as being at ground zero. The window glass blew
out. Every light bulb in the apartment shattered. From the
carton containing their meager chinaware came the distinct
sound of hailstones as every plate and cup dissolved into
shards. Dogs and cats blocks away began to howl. Connie
screamed—though it could not be heard over the foghorn
thunder of the voice—and was knocked head over ankles
into a corner, still clutching the dustrag. Plaster showered in
the little apartment. The window shades rolled up.

Danny recovered first. He crawled over a chair and
stared at the lamp with horror. Connie sat up in the corner,
face white, eyes huge, hands over her ears. Danny stood and
looked down at the seemingly innocuous lamp.

"Knock off that noise! You want to lose us the lease?"

CERTAINLY, OFFSPRING OF A WORM!

"I said: stop that goddam bellowing!"

THIS WHISPER? THIS IS NAUGHT TO THE HURRICANE
I SHALL LOOSE, SPAWN OF PARAMECIUM!

"That's it," Danny yelled. "I'm not getting kicked out of
the only apartment in the city of New York I can afford just
because of some loudmouthed genie in a jug . . ."

He stopped. He looked at Connie. Connie looked back at
him.

"Oh, my god," she said.

"It's real," he said.

They got to their knees and crawled over. The lamp lay
on its side on the floor at the foot of the daybed.

"Are you really in there?" Connie asked.

WHERE ELSE WOULD I BE, SLUT!

"Hey, you can't talk to my wife that way—"

Connie shushed him. "If he's a genie, he can talk any way he likes. Sticks and stones; namecalling is better than poverty."

"Yeah? Well, *nobody* talks to my—"

"Put a lid on it, Squires. I can take care of myself. If what's in this lamp is even half the size of the genie in that movie you took me to the Thalia to see . . ."

"*The Thief of Bagdad* . . . 1939 version . . . but Rex Ingram was just an actor, they only made him *look* big."

"Even so. As big as he was, if this genie is only *half* that big, playing macho overprotective chauvinist hubby—"

SO HUMANS CONTINUE TO PRATTLE LIKE MONKEYS EVEN AFTER TEN THOUSAND YEARS! WILL NOTHING CLEANSE THE EARTH OF THIS RAUCOUS PLAGUE OF INSECTS?

"We're going to get thrown right out of here," Danny said. His face screwed up in a horrible expression of discomfort.

"If the cops don't beat the other tenants to it."

"Please, genie," Danny said, leaning down almost to the lamp. "Just tone it down a little, willya?"

OFFSPRING OF A MILLION STINKS! SUFFER!

"You're no genie," Connie said smugly. Danny looked at her with disbelief.

"He's no genie? Then what the hell do you *think* he is?"

She swatted him. Then put her finger to her lips.

THAT IS WHAT I AM, WHORE OF DEGENERACY!

"No you're not."

I AM.

"Am not."

AM.

"Am not."

AM SO, CHARNEL HOUSE HARLOT! WHY SAY YOU NAY?

"A genie has a lot of power; a genie doesn't need to shout like that to make himself heard. You're no genie, or you'd speak softly. You *can't* speak at a decent level, because you're a fraud."

CAUTION, TROLLOP!

"Foo, you don't scare me. If you were as powerful as you make out, you'd tone it way down."

is this better? are you convinced?

"Yes," Connie said, "I think that's more convincing. Can you keep it up, though? That's the question."

forever, if need be.

"And you can grant wishes?" Danny was back in the conversation.

naturally, but not to you, disgusting grub of humanity.

"Hey, listen," Danny replied angrily, "I don't give a damn what or *who* you are! You can't talk to me that way." Then a thought dawned on him. "After all, I'm your master!"

ah! correction, filth of primordial seas. there are some djinn who are mastered by their owners, but unfortunately for you i am not one of them, for i am not free to leave this metal prison. i was imprisoned in this accursed vessel many ages ago by a besotted sorcerer who knew nothing of molecular compression and even less of the binding forces of the universe. he put me into this thrice-cursed lamp, far too small for me, and i have been wedged within ever since. over the ages my good nature has rotted away. i am powerful, but trapped. those who own me cannot request anything and hope to realize their boon. i am unhappy, and an unhappy djinn is an evil djinn. were i free, i might be your slave; but as i am now, i will visit unhappiness on you in a thousand forms!

Danny chuckled. "The hell you will. I'll toss you in the incinerator."

ah! but you cannot. once you have bought the lamp, you cannot lose it, destroy it or give it away, only sell it. i am with you forever, for who would buy such a miserable lamp?

And thunder rolled in the sky.

"What are you going to do?" Connie asked.

do? just ask me for something, and you shall see!

"Not me," Danny said, "you're too cranky."

wouldn't you like a billfold full of money?

There was sincerity in the voice from the lamp.

"Well, sure, I want money, but—"

The djinn's laughter was gigantic, and suddenly cut off by the rain of frogs that fell from a point one inch below the ceiling, clobbering Danny and Connie with small, reeking, wriggling green bodies. Connie screamed and dove for the clothes closet. She came out a second later, her hair full of them; they were falling in the closet, as well. The rain of frogs continued and when Danny opened the front door to try and escape them, they fell in the hall. He slammed the door—he realized he was still naked—and covered his head with his hands. The frogs fell, writhing, stinking, and then they were knee-deep in them, with little filthy, warty bodies jumping up at their faces.

what a lousy disposition i've got! the djinn said, and then he laughed. And he laughed again, a clangorous peal that was silenced only when the frogs stopped, disappeared, and the flood of blood began.

It went on for a week.

They could not get away from him, no matter where they went. They were also slowly starving: they could not go out to buy groceries without the earth opening under their feet, or a herd of elephants chasing them down the street, or hundreds of people getting violently ill and vomiting on them. So they stayed in and ate what canned goods they had stored up in the first four days of their marriage. But who could eat with locusts filling the apartment from top to bottom, or snakes that were intent on gobbling them up like little white rats?

First came the frogs, then the flood of blood, then the whirling dust storm, then the spiders and gnats, then the snakes and then the locusts and then the tiger that had them backed against a wall and ate the chair they used to ward him off. Then came the bats and the leprosy and the hailstones and then the floor dissolved under them and they clung to the wall fixtures while their furniture—which had been quickly delivered (the moving men had brought it during the hailstones)—fell through, nearly killing the little old lady who lived beneath them.

Then the walls turned red hot and melted, and then the lightning burned everything black, and finally Danny had had enough. He cracked, and went gibbering around the room, tripping over the man-eating vines that were growing out of the light sockets and the floorboards. He finally sat down in a huge puddle of monkey urine and cried till his face grew puffy and his eyes flame-red and his nose swelled to three times normal size.

"I've got to get *away* from all this!" he screamed hysterically, drumming his heels, trying to eat his pants' cuffs.

you can divorce her, and that means you are voided out of the purchase contract: she wanted the lamp, not you, the djinn suggested.

Danny looked up (just in time to get a ripe Black Angus meadow muffin in his face) and yelled, "I won't! You can't make me. We've only been married a week and four days and I won't leave her!"

Connie, covered with running sores, stumbled to Danny and hugged him, though he had turned to tapioca pudding and was melting. But three days later, when ghost images of people he had feared all his life came to haunt him, he broke completely and allowed Connie to call the rest home on the boa constrictor that had once been the phone. "You can come and get me when this is over," he cried pitifully, kissing her poison ivy lips. "Maybe if we split up, he'll have some mercy." But they both doubted it.

When the downstairs buzzer rang, the men from the Home for the Mentally Absent came into the debacle that had been their apartment and saw Connie pulling her feet out of the swamp slime only with difficulty; she was crying in unison with Danny as they bundled him into the white ambulance. Unearthly laughter rolled around the sky like thunder as her husband was driven away.

Connie was left alone. She went back upstairs; she had nowhere else to go.

She slumped into the pool of molten slag, and tried to think while ants ate at her flesh and rabid rats gnawed off the wallpaper.

i'm just getting warmed up, the djinn said from the lamp.

Less than three days after he had been admitted to the Asylum for the Temporarily Twitchy, Connie came to get Danny. She came into his room; the shades were drawn, the sheets were very white; when he saw her his teeth began to chatter.

She smiled at him gently. "If I didn't know better, I'd swear you weren't simply overjoyed to see me, Squires."

He slid under the sheets till only his eyes were showing. His voice came through the covers. "If I break out in boils, it will definitely cause a relapse, and the day nurse hates mess."

"Where's my macho protective husband now?"

"I've been unwell."

"Yeah, well, that's all over. You're fit as a fiddle, so bestir your buns and let's get out of here."

Danny Squires' brow furrowed. This was not the tone of a woman with frogs in her hair. "I've been contemplating divorce or suicide."

She yanked the covers down, exposing his naked legs sticking out from the hem of the hospital gown. "Forget it, little chum. There are at least a hundred and ten positions we haven't tried yet before I consider dissolution. Now will you get out of that bed and *come on?*"

"But . . ."

". . . a thing I'll kick, if you don't move it."

Bewildered, he moved it.

Outside, the Rolls-Royce waited with its motor running. As they came through the front doors of the Institute for the Neurologically Flaccid, and Connie helped Danny from the discharge wheelchair, the liveried chauffeur leaped out and opened the door for them. They got in the back seat, and Connie said, "To the house, Mark." The chauffeur nodded, trotted briskly around and climbed behind the wheel. They took off to the muted roar of twin mufflers.

Danny's voice was a querulous squeak. "Can we afford a rented limo?"

Connie did not answer, merely smiled, and snuggled closer to him.

After a moment Danny asked, "What house?"

Connie pressed a button on the console in the armrest and the glass partition between front and back seats slid silently closed. "Do me a favor, will you," she said, "just hold the twenty questions till we get home? It's been a tough three days and all I ask is that you hold it together for another hour."

Danny nodded reluctantly. Then he noticed she was

dressed in extremely expensive clothes. "I'd better not ask about your mink-trimmed jacket, either, right?"

"It would help."

He settled into silence, uneasy and juggling more than just twenty unasked questions. And he remained silent until he realized they were not taking the expressway into New York. He sat up sharply, looked out the rear window, snapped his head right and left trying to ascertain their location, and Connie said, "We're not going to Manhattan. We're going to Darien, Connecticut."

"Darien? Who the hell do we know in Darien?"

"Well, Upjohn, for one, lives in Darien."

"Upjohn!?! Ohmigod, he's fired me and sent the car to bring me to him so he can have me executed! I *knew* it!"

"Squires," she said, "Daniel, my love, Danny heart of my heart, will you just kindly close the tap on it for a while! Upjohn has nothing to do with us any more. Nothing at all."

"But . . . but we live in New York!"

"Not no more we don't."

Twenty minutes later they turned into the most expensive section in Darien and sped down a private road.

They drove an eighth of a mile down the private road lined with Etruscan pines, beautifully maintained, and pulled into a winding driveway. Five hundred yards further, and the drive spiraled in to wind around the front of a huge, luxurious, completely tasteful Victorian mansion. "Go on," Connie said. "Look at your house."

"Who lives here?" Danny asked.

"I just told you: *we* do."

"I thought that's what you said. Let me out here, I'll walk back to the nuthouse."

The Rolls pulled up before the mansion, and a butler ran down to open the car door for them. They got out and the servant bowed low to Connie. Then he turned to Danny. "Good to have you home, Mr. Squires," he said. Danny was too unnerved to reply.

"Thank you, Penzler," Connie said. Then, to the chauffeur, "Take the car to the garage, Mark; we won't be needing it again this afternoon. But have the Porsche fueled and ready; we may drive out later to look at the grounds."

"Very good, Mrs. Squires," Mark said. Then he drove away.

Danny was somnambulistic. He allowed himself to be led into the house, where he was further stunned by the expensive fittings, the magnificent halls, the deep-pile rugs, the spectacular furniture, the communications complex set into an entire wall, the Art Deco bar that rose out of the floor at the touch of a button, the servants who bowed and smiled at him, as if he belonged there. He was boggled by the huge kitchen, fitted with every latest appliance; and the French chef who saluted with a huge ladle as Connie entered.

"Wh-where did all this *come* from?" He finally gasped out the question as Connie led him upstairs on the escalator.

"Come on, Danny; you know where it all came from."

"The limo, the house, the grounds, the mink-trimmed jacket, the servants, the Vermeer in the front hall, the cobalt-glass Art Deco bar, the entertainment center with the beam television set, the screening room, the bowling alley, the polo field, the Neptune swimming pool, the escalator and six-strand necklace of black pearls I now notice you are wearing around your throat . . . all of it came from the genie?"

"Sorta takes your breath away, don't it?" Connie said, ingenuously.

"I'm having a little trouble with this."

"What you're having trouble with, champ, is that

Mas'úd gave you a hard time, you couldn't handle it, you crapped out, and somehow I've managed to pull it all out of the swamp."

"I'm thinking of divorce again."

They were walking down a long hall lined with works of modern Japanese illustration by Yamazaki, Kobayashi, Takahiko Li, Kenzo Tanii and Orai. Connie stopped and put both her hands on Danny's trembling shoulders.

"What we've got here. Squires, is a bad case of identity reevaluation. Nobody gets through *all* the battles. We've been married less than two weeks, but we've known each other for three years. You don't know how many times I folded before that time, and I don't know how many times you triumphed before that time.

"What I've known of you for three years made it okay for me to marry you; to think 'This guy will be able to handle it the times I can't.' That's a lot of what marriage is, to my way of thinking. I don't have to score every time, and neither do you. As long as the unit maintains. This time it was my score. Next time it'll be yours. Maybe."

Danny smiled weakly. "I'm not thinking of divorce."

Movement out of the corner of his eye made him look over his shoulder.

An eleven foot tall black man, physically perfect in every way, with chiseled features like an obsidian Adonis, dressed in an impeccably-tailored three-piece Savile Row suit, silk tie knotted precisely, stood just in the hallway, having emerged from open fifteen-foot-high doors of a room at the juncture of corridors.

"Uh . . ." Danny said.

Connie looked over her shoulder. "Hi, Mas'úd. Squires, I would like you to meet Mas'úd Jan bin Jan, a Mazikeen djinn of the ifrit, by the grace of Sulaymin, master of *all* the jinni, though Allah be the wiser. Our benefactor. My friend."

"How *good* a friend?" Danny whispered, seeing the totem of sexual perfection looming eleven feet high before him.

"We haven't known each other carnally, if that's what I perceive your squalid little remark to mean," she replied. And a bit wistfully she added, "I'm not his type. I think he's got it for Lena Horne." At Danny's semi-annoyed look she added, "For god's sake, stop being so bloody suspicious!"

Mas'úd stepped forward, two steps bringing him the fifteen feet intervening, and proffered his greeting in the traditional Islamic head-and-heart salute, flowing outward, a smile on his matinee idol face. "Welcome home, Master. I await your smallest request."

Danny looked from the djinn to Connie, amazement and copelessness rendering him almost speechless. "But . . . you were stuck in the lamp . . . bad-tempered, oh boy were you bad-tempered . . . how did you . . . how did she . . ."

Connie laughed, and with great dignity the djinn joined in.

"You were in the lamp . . . you gave us all this . . . but you said you'd give us nothing but aggravation! Why?"

In deep, mellifluous tones Danny had come to associate with a voice that could knock high-flying fowl from the air, the djinn smiled warmly at them and replied, "Your good wife freed me. After ten thousand years cramped over in pain with an eternal bellyache, in that most miserable of dungeons, Mistress Connie set me loose. For the first time in a hundred times ten thousand years of cruel and venal master after master, I have been delivered into the hands of one who treats me with respect. We are friends. I look forward to extending that friendship to you, Master Squires." He seemed to be warming to his explanation, expansive and effusive. "Free now, permitted to exist among humans in a time where my kind are thought a legend, and thus able to live an interesting, new life, my gratitude knows no bounds, as my hatred and anger knew no bounds. Now I need no longer act as a Kako-daemon, now I can be the sort of ifrit Rabbi Jeremiah bin Eliazar spoke of in Psalm XLI.

"I have seen much of this world in the last three days as humans judge time. I find it most pleasing in my view. The speed, the shine, the light. The incomparable Lena Horne. Do you like basketball?"

"But how? How did you *do* it, Connie? How? No one could get him out . . ."

She took him by the hand, leading him toward the fifteen-foot-high doors. "May we come into your apartment, Mas'úd?"

The djinn made a sweeping gesture of invitation, bowing so low his head was at Danny's waist as he and Connie walked past.

They stepped inside the djinn's suite and it was as if they had stepped back in time to ancient Basra and the Thousand Nights and a Night. Or into a Cornel Wilde costume epic.

But amid all the silks and hangings and pillows and tapers and coffers and brassware, there in the center of the foyer, in a Lucite case atop an onyx pedestal, lit from an unknown source by a single glowing spot of light, was a single icon.

"Occasionally magic has to bow to technology," Connie said. Danny moved forward. He could not make out what the item lying on the black velvet pillow was. "And sometimes ancient anger has to bow to common sense."

Danny was close enough to see it now.

Simple. It had been so simple. But no one had thought of it before. Probably because the last time it had been needed, by the lamp's previous owner, it had not existed.

"A can opener," Danny said. "A can opener!?! A simple,

stupid, everyday can opener!?! That's all it took? I had a nervous breakdown, and you figured out a can opener?"

"Can do," Connie said, winking at Mas'úd.

"Not cute, Squires," Danny said. But he was thinking of the diamond as big as the Ritz.

"REPENT, HARLEQUIN!" SAID THE TICKTOCKMAN

Got to be careful about codifying the "lesson" in this one, because it is, in some ways, a statement about the way I live *my* life, and if you follow the trail too closely, you'll get into more trouble than you deserve, which is the opposite of what this book is supposed to do . . . according to my publisher, who says this book is intended to make you better citizens and happier individuals, with an understanding that if you litter your Taco Bell and Burger King garbage in the streets I will seek you out no matter where you live, and I will nail your head to a coffee table. At least that's what my publisher tells me this book is supposed to do. But I haven't lied to you yet, not as far as I can tell; and I'm not about to start now. As if I gave a— Well, the point of the lesson in this story—which I'm told, by academics who teach it in literally hundreds of college English and Modern American Writing classes, is one of the most reprinted stories in the English Language—have you noticed, it's only my charming humility that has held me back from true stardom— the lesson is that if they suck you into the System, extricating yourself may be damned near impossible. Letting your life be set to other people's schedules may satisfy *their* needs, but you'll be trading off bits and pieces of your own life to placate others who do not, in actuality, care much about you or your problems or desires or potentialities. They mumble "I know how tough it is for you" or "I understand" but when it comes right down to it, it is *their* production schedule or swing shift time or actuarial table that mesmerizes them. Their hearts bleed that you're lying on an operating table having your stomach replaced with a vacuum cleaner or a bidet or somedamnthing, but that pulmonary drip-drip-drip only masks their annoyance that, like the mule you are, you've fallen to your knees under the yoke of their schedule. Yes, as I told you before, DO THE DAMN JOB, just *do* it; nonetheless, Life keeps getting in the way of Being On Time, and once in a great while you just have to say *screwit*! And bear this in mind, folks: if you work at their pace for twenty-seven years, do 1,444 jobs well, and do them to the deadline, if you ain't got the juice and you mess up on the 1,445th gig, you will catch the same amount of flak and the same amount of guilt and the same amount of badmouth and opprobrium you would snag if you'd been late *every* time. The lesson here is one that will get you clobbered if you follow it. Run your life at your own pace, not that of the Man.

T here are always those who ask, what is it all about? For those who need to ask, for those who need points sharply made, who need to know "where it's at," this:

The mass of men serve the state thus, not as men mainly, but as machines, with their bodies. They are the standing army, and the militia, jailors, constables, posse comitatus, *etc. In most cases there is no free exercise whatever of the judgment or of the moral sense; but they put themselves on a level with wood and earth and stones; and wooden men can perhaps be manufactured that will serve the purpose as well. Such command no more respect than men of straw or a lump of dirt. They have the same sort of worth only as horses and dogs. Yet such as these even are commonly esteemed good citizens. Others— as most legislators, politicians, lawyers, ministers, and officeholders—serve the state chiefly with their heads; and, as they rarely make any moral distinc-*

tions, they are as likely to serve the Devil, without intending it, as God. A very few, as heroes, patriots, martyrs, reformers in the great sense, and men, serve the state with their consciences also, and so necessarily resist it for the most part; and they are commonly treated as enemies by it.

Henry David Thoreau
CIVIL DISOBEDIENCE

That is the heart of it. Now begin in the middle, and later learn the beginning; the end will take care of itself.

But because it was the very world it was, the very world they had allowed it to *become*, for months his activities did not come to the alarmed attention of The Ones Who Kept The Machine Functioning Smoothly, the ones who poured the very best butter over the cams and mainsprings of the culture. Not until it had become obvious that somehow, someway, he had become a notoriety, a celebrity, perhaps even a hero for (what officialdom inescapably tagged) "an emotionally disturbed segment of the populace," did they turn it over to the Ticktockman and his legal machinery. But by then, because it was the very world it was, and they had no way to predict he would happen—possibly a strain of disease long-defunct, now, suddenly, reborn in a system where immunity had been forgotten, had lapsed—he had been allowed to become too real. Now he had form and substance.

He had become a *personality*, something they had filtered out of the system many decades before. But there it was, and there *he* was, a very definitely imposing personality. In certain circles—middle-class circles—it was thought disgusting. Vulgar ostentation. Anarchistic. Shameful. In others, there was only sniggering: those strata where thought is subjugated to form and ritual, niceties, proprieties. But down below, ah, down below, where the people always needed their saints and sinners, their bread and circuses, their heroes and villains, he was considered a Bolivar; a Napoleon; a Robin Hood; a Dick Bong (Ace of Aces); a Jesus; a Jomo Kenyatta.

And at the top—where, like socially-attuned Shipwreck Kellys, every tremor and vibration threatening to dislodge the wealthy, powerful and titled from their flagpoles—he was considered a menace; a heretic; a rebel; a disgrace; a peril. He was known down the line, to the very heart-meat core, but the important reactions were high above and far below. At the very top, at the very bottom.

So his file was turned over, along with his time-card and his cardioplate, to the office of the Ticktockman.

The Ticktockman: very much over six feet tall, often silent, a soft purring man when things went timewise. The Ticktockman.

Even in the cubicles of the hierarchy, where fear was generated, seldom suffered, he was called the Ticktockman. But no one called him that to his mask.

You don't call a man a hated name, not when that man, behind his mask, is capable of revoking the minutes, the hours, the days and nights, the years of your life. He was called the Master Timekeeper to his mask. It was safer that way.

"This is *what* he is," said the Ticktockman with genuine softness, "but not *who* he is. This time-card I'm holding in my left hand has a name on it, but it is the name of *what* he is, not *who* he is. The cardioplate here in my right hand is also named, but not *whom* named, merely *what* named. Before I can exercise proper revocation, I have to know *who* this *what* is."

To his staff, all the ferrets, all the loggers, all the finks, all the commex, even the mineez, he said, "Who is this Harlequin?"

He was not purring smoothly. Timewise, it was jangle.

However, it *was* the longest speech they had ever heard him utter at one time, the staff, the ferrets, the loggers, the finks, the commex, but not the mineez, who usually weren't around to know, in any case. But even they scurried to find out.

Who is the Harlequin?

High above the third level of the city, he crouched on the humming aluminum-frame platform of the air-boat (foof! air-boat, indeed! swizzleskid is what it was, with a tow-rack jerry-rigged) and he stared down at the neat Mondrian arrangement of the buildings.

Somewhere nearby, he could hear the metronomic left-right-left of the 2:47 PM shift, entering the Timkin roller-bearing plant in their sneakers. A minute later, precisely, he heard the softer right-left-right of the 5:00 AM formation, going home.

An elfin grin spread across his tanned features, and his dimples appeared for a moment. Then, scratching at his thatch of auburn hair, he shrugged within his motley, as though girding himself for what came next, and threw the joystick forward, and bent into the wind as the air-boat dropped. He skimmed over a slidewalk, purposely dropping a few feet to crease the tassels of the ladies of fashion, and—inserting thumbs in large ears—he stuck out his tongue, rolled his eyes and went wugga-wugga-wugga. It was a minor diversion. One pedestrian skittered and tumbled, sending parcels every-whichway, another wet herself, a third keeled slantwise and the walk was stopped automatically by the servitors till she could be resuscitated. It was a minor diversion.

Then he swirled away on a vagrant breeze, and was gone. Hi-ho. As he rounded the cornice of the Time-Motion Study Building, he saw the shift, just boarding the slide-walk. With practiced motion and an absolute conservation of movement, they sidestepped up onto the slow-strip and (in a chorus line reminiscent of a Busby Berkeley film of the antediluvian 1930s) advanced across the strips ostrich-walking till they were lined up on the expresstrip.

Once more, in anticipation, the elfin grin spread, and there was a tooth missing back there on the left side. He dipped, skimmed, and swooped over them; and then, scrunching about on the air-boat, he released the holding pins that fastened shut the ends of the home-made pouring troughs that kept his cargo from dumping prematurely. And as he pulled the trough-pins, the air-boat slid over the factory workers and one hundred and fifty thousand dollars' worth of jelly beans cascaded down on the expresstrip.

Jelly beans! Millions and billions of purples and yellows and greens and licorice and grape and raspberry and mint and round and smooth and crunchy outside and soft-mealy inside and sugary and bouncing jouncing tumbling clittering clattering skittering fell on the heads and shoulders and hard-hats and carapaces of the Timkin workers, tinkling on the slidewalk and bouncing away and rolling about underfoot and filling the sky on their way down with all the colors of joy and childhood and holidays, coming down in a steady rain, a solid wash, a torrent of color and sweetness out of the sky from above, and entering a universe of sanity and metro-nomic order with quite-mad coocoo newness. Jelly beans!

The shift workers howled and laughed and were pelted, and broke ranks, and the jelly beans managed to work their way into the mechanism of the slidewalks after which there was a hideous scraping as the sound of a million fingernails rasped down a quarter of a million blackboards, followed by a coughing and a sputtering, and then the slidewalks all stopped and everyone was dumped thisawayandthataway in a jackstraw tumble, still laughing and popping little jelly bean eggs of childish color into their mouths. It was a holiday, and a jollity, an absolute insanity, a giggle. But . . .

The shift was delayed seven minutes.

They did not get home for seven minutes.

The master schedule was thrown off by seven minutes.

Quotas were delayed by inoperative slidewalks for seven minutes.

He had tapped the first domino in the line, and one after another, like chik chik chik, the others had fallen.

The System had been seven minutes' worth of disrupted. It was a tiny matter, one hardly worthy of note, but in a society where the single driving force was order and unity and equality and promptness and clocklike precision and attention to the clock, reverence of the gods of the passage of time, it was a disaster of major importance.

So he was ordered to appear before the Ticktockman. It was broadcast across every channel of the communications web. He was ordered to be *there* at 7:00 dammit on time. And they waited, and they waited, but he didn't show up till almost ten-thirty, at which time he merely sang a little song about moonlight in a place no one had ever heard of, called Vermont, and vanished again. But they had all been waiting since seven, and it wrecked *hell* with their schedules. So the question remained: Who is the Harlequin?

But the *unasked* question (more important of the two) was: how did we get *into* this position, where a laughing, irresponsible japer of jabberwocky and jive could disrupt our entire economic and cultural life with a hundred and fifty thousand dollars' worth of jelly beans . . .

Jelly for God's sake *beans!* This is madness! Where did he get the money to buy a hundred and fifty thousand dollars' worth of jelly beans? (They knew it would have cost that much, because they had a team of Situation Analysts pulled off another assignment, and rushed to the slidewalk scene to sweep up and count the candies, and produce findings, which disrupted *their* schedules and threw their entire branch at least a day behind.) Jelly beans! Jelly ... *beans?* Now wait a second—a second accounted for—no one has manufactured jelly beans for over a hundred years. Where did he get jelly beans?

That's another good question. More than likely it will never be answered to your complete satisfaction. But then, how many questions ever are?

The middle you know. Here is the beginning. How it starts:

A desk pad. Day for day, and turn each day. 9:00—open the mail. 9:45—appointment with planning commission board. 10:30—discuss installation progress charts with J. L. 11:45—pray for rain. 12:00—lunch. *And so it goes.*

"I'm sorry, Miss Grant, but the time for interviews was set at 2:30, and it's almost five now. I'm sorry you're late, but those are the rules. You'll have to wait till next year to submit application for this college again." *And so it goes.*

The 10:10 local stops at Cresthaven, Galesville, Tonawanda Junction, Selby and Farnhurst, but not at Indiana City, Lucasville and Colton, except on Sunday. The 10:35 express stops at Galesville, Selby and Indiana City, except on Sundays & Holidays, at which time it stops at... *and so it goes.*

"*I couldn't wait, Fred. I had to be at Pierre Cartain's by 3:00, and you said you'd meet me under the clock in the terminal at 2:45, and you weren't there, so I had to go on. You're always late, Fred. If you'd been there, we could have sewed it up together, but as it was, well, I took the order alone ... And so it goes.*"

Dear Mr. and Mrs. Atterley: In reference to your son Gerold's constant tardiness, I am afraid we will have to suspend him from school unless some more reliable method can be instituted guaranteeing he will arrive at his classes on time. Granted he is an exemplary student, and his marks are high, his constant flouting of the schedules of this school makes it impractical to maintain him in a system where the other children seem capable of getting where they are supposed to be on time *and so it goes.*

YOU CANNOT VOTE UNLESS YOU APPEAR AT 8:45 AM.

"I don't care if the script is good, I need it Thursday!"

CHECK-OUT TIME IS 2:00 PM.

"You got here late. The job's taken. Sorry."

YOUR SALARY HAS BEEN DOCKED FOR TWENTY MINUTES TIME LOST.

"God, what time is it, I've gotta run!"

And so it goes. And so it goes. And so it goes. And so it goes goes goes goes goes tick tock tick tock tick tock and one day we no longer let time serve us, we serve time and we are slaves of the schedule, worshipers of the sun's passing, bound into a life predicated on restrictions because the system will not function if we don't keep the schedule tight.

Until it becomes more than a minor inconvenience to be late. It becomes a sin. Then a crime. Then a crime punishable by this:

EFFECTIVE 15 JULY 2389 12:00:00 midnight, the office of the Master Timekeeper will require all citizens to submit their time-cards and cardioplates for processing. In accordance with Statute 555-7-SGH-999 governing the revocation of time per capita, all cardioplates will be keyed to the individual holder and—

What they had done was devise a method of curtailing the amount of life a person could have. If he was ten minutes late, he lost ten minutes of his life. An hour was proportionately worth more revocation. If someone was consistently tardy, he might find himself, on a Sunday receiving a communiqué from the Master Timekeeper that his time had run out, and he would be "turned off" at high noon on Monday, please straighten your affairs, sir, madame or bisex.

And so, by this simple scientific expedient (utilizing a scientific process held dearly secret by the Ticktockman's office) the System was maintained. It was the only expedient thing to do. It was, after all, patriotic. The schedules had to be met. After all, there *was* a war on!

But, wasn't there always?

"Now that is really disgusting," the Harlequin said, when Pretty Alice showed him the wanted poster. "Disgusting and *highly* improbable. After all, this isn't the Day of the Desperado. A *wanted* poster!"

"You know," Pretty Alice noted, "you speak with a great deal of inflection."

"I'm sorry," said the Harlequin, humbly.

"No need to be sorry. You're always saying 'I'm sorry.' You have such massive guilt, Everett, it's really very sad."

"I'm sorry," he said again, then pursed his lips so the dimples appeared momentarily. He hadn't wanted to say that at all. "I have to go out again. I have to *do* something."

Pretty Alice slammed her coffee-bulb down on the counter. "Oh for God's sake, Everett, can't you stay home just one night! Must you always be out in that ghastly clown suit, running around an*noy*ing people?"

"I'm—" He stopped, and clapped the jester's hat onto his auburn thatch with a tiny tinkling of bells. He rose, rinsed out his coffee-bulb at the spray, and put it into the dryer for a moment. "I have to go."

She didn't answer. The faxbox was purring, and she pulled a sheet out, read it, threw it toward him on the counter. "It's about you. Of course. You're ridiculous."

He read it quickly. It said the Ticktockman was trying to locate him. He didn't care, he was going out to be late again. At the door, dredging for an exit line, he hurled back petulantly, "Well, *you* speak with inflection, *too!*"

Pretty Alice rolled her pretty eyes heavenward. "You're ridiculous."

The Harlequin stalked out, slamming the door, which sighed shut softly, and locked itself.

There was a gentle knock, and Pretty Alice got up with an exhalation of exasperated breath, and opened the door. He stood there. "I'll be back about ten-thirty, okay?"

She pulled a rueful face. "Why do you tell me that? Why? You *know* you'll be late! You *know* it! You're *always* late, so why do you tell me these dumb things?" She closed the door.

On the other side, the Harlequin nodded to himself. *She's right. She's always right. I'll be late. I'm always late. Why* do *I tell her these dumb things?*

He shrugged again, and went off to be late once more.

He had fired off the firecracker rockets that said: I will attend the 115th annual International Medical Association Invocation at 8:00 PM precisely. I do hope you will all be able to join me.

The words had burned in the sky, and of course the authorities were there, lying in wait for him. They assumed, naturally, that he would be late. He arrived twenty minutes early, while they were setting up the spiderwebs to trap and hold him. Blowing a large bullhorn, he frightened and unnerved them so, their own moisturized encirclement webs sucked closed, and they were hauled up, kicking and shrieking, high above the amphitheater's floor. The Harlequin laughed and laughed, and apologized profusely. The physicians, gathered in solemn conclave, roared with laughter, and accepted the Harlequin's apologies with exaggerated bowing and posturing, and a merry time was had by all, who thought the Harlequin was a regular foofaraw in fancy pants; all, that is, but the authorities, who had been sent out by the office of the Ticktockman; they hung there like so much dockside cargo, hauled up above the floor of the amphitheater in a most unseemly fashion.

(In another part of the same city where the Harlequin carried on his "activities," totally unrelated in every way to what concerns us here, save that it illustrates the Ticktockman's power and import, a man named Marshall Delahanty received his turn-off notice from the Ticktockman's office. His wife received the notification from the gray-suited minee who delivered it, with the traditional "look of sorrow" plastered hideously across his face. She knew what it was, even without unsealing it. It was a billet-doux of immediate recognition to everyone these days. She gasped, and held it as though it were a glass slide tinged with botulism, and prayed it was not for her. Let it be for Marsh, she thought, brutally, realistically, or one of the kids, but not for me, please dear God, not for me. And then she opened it, and it *was* for Marsh, and she was at one and the same time horrified and relieved. The next trooper in the line had caught the bullet. "Marshall," she screamed, "Marshall! Termination, Marshall! OhmiGod, Marshall, whattl we do, whattl we do, Marshall omigodmarshall ..." and in their home that night was the sound of tearing paper and fear, and the stink of madness went up the flue and there was nothing, absolutely nothing they could do about it.

(But Marshall Delahanty tried to run. And early the next day, when turn-off time came, he was deep in the Canadian forest two hundred miles away, and the office of the Ticktockman blanked his cardioplate, and Marshall Delahanty keeled over, running, and his heart stopped, and the blood dried up on its way to his brain, and he was dead that's all. One light went out on the sector map in the office of the Master Timekeeper, while notification was entered for fax reproduction, and Georgette Delahanty's name was entered on the dole roles till she could remarry. Which is the end of the footnote, and all the point that need be made, except don't laugh, because that is what would happen to the Harlequin if ever the Ticktockman found out his real name. It isn't funny.)

The shopping level of the city was thronged with the Thursday-colors of the buyers. Women in canary yellow chitons and men in pseudo-Tyrolean outfits that were jade and leather and fit very tightly, save for the balloon pants.

When the Harlequin appeared on the still-being-constructed shell of the new Efficiency Shopping Center, his bullhorn to his elfishly-laughing lips, everyone pointed and stared, and he berated them:

"Why let them order you about? Why let them tell you to hurry and scurry like ants or maggots? Take your time! Saunter a while! Enjoy the sunshine, enjoy the breeze, let life carry you at your own pace! Don't be slaves of time, it's a helluva way to die, slowly, by degrees . . . down with the Ticktockman!"

Who's the nut? most of the shoppers wanted to know. Who's the nut oh wow I'm gonna be late I gotta run . . .

And the construction gang on the Shopping Center received an urgent order from the office of the Master Timekeeper that the dangerous criminal known as the Harlequin was atop their spire, and their aid was urgently needed in apprehending him. The work crew said no, they would lose time on their construction schedule, but the Ticktockman managed to pull the proper threads of governmental webbing, and they were told to cease work and catch that nitwit up there on the spire; up there with the bullhorn. So a dozen and more burly workers began climbing into their construction platforms, releasing the a-grav plates, and rising toward the Harlequin.

After the debacle (in which, through the Harlequin's attention to personal safety, no one was seriously injured), the workers tried to reassemble, and assault him again, but it was too late. He had vanished. It had attracted quite a crowd, however, and the shopping cycle was thrown off by hours, simply hours. The purchasing needs of the system were therefore falling behind, and so measures were taken to accelerate the cycle for the rest of the day, but it got bogged down and speeded up and they sold too many float-valves and not nearly enough wegglers, which meant that the popli ratio was off, which made it necessary to rush cases and cases of spoiling Smash-O to stores that usually needed a case only every three or four hours. The shipments were bollixed, the transshipments were misrouted, and in the end, even the swizzleskid industries felt it.

"Don't come back till you have him!" the Ticktockman said, very quietly, very sincerely, extremely dangerously.

They used dogs. They used probes. They used cardioplate crossoffs. They used teepers. They used bribery. They used stiktytes. They used intimidation. They used torment. They used torture. They used finks. They used cops. They used search&seizure. They used fallaron. They used betterment incentive. They used fingerprints. They used the Bertillon system. They used cunning. They used guile. They used treachery. They used Raoul Mitgong, but he didn't help much. They used applied physics. They used techniques of criminology.

And what the hell: they caught him.

After all, his name was Everett C. Marm, and he wasn't much to begin with, except a man who had no sense of time.

"Repent, Harlequin!" said the Ticktockman.

"Get stuffed!" the Harlequin replied, sneering.

"You've been late a total of sixty-three years, five months, three weeks, two days, twelve hours, forty-one minutes, fifty-nine seconds, point oh three six one one one microseconds. You've used up everything you can, and more. I'm going to turn you off."

"Scare someone else. I'd rather be dead that live in a dumb world with a bogeyman like you."

"It's my job."

"You're full of it. You're a tyrant. You have no right to order people around and kill them if they show up late."

"You can't adjust. You can't fit in."

"Unstrap me, and I'll fit my fist into your mouth."

"You're a nonconformist."

"That didn't used to be a felony."

"It is now. Live in the world around you."

"I hate it. It's a terrible world."

"Not everyone thinks so. Most people enjoy order."

"I don't, and most of the people I know don't."

"That's not true. How do you think we caught you?"

"I'm not interested."

"A girl named Pretty Alice told us who you were."

"That's a lie."

"It's true. You unnerve her. She wants to belong; she wants to conform; I'm going to turn you off."

"Then do it already, and stop arguing with me."

"I'm not going to turn you off."

"You're an idiot!"

"Repent, Harlequin!" said the Ticktockman.

"Get stuffed."

So they sent him to Coventry. And in Coventry they worked him over. It was just like what they did to Winston Smith in NINETEEN EIGHTY-FOUR, which was a book none of them knew about, but the techniques are really quite ancient, and so they did it to Everett C. Marm; and one day, quite a long time later, the Harlequin appeared on the communications web, appearing elfin and dimpled and bright-eyed, and not at all brainwashed, and he said he had been wrong, that it was a good, a very good thing indeed, to belong, to be right on time hip-ho and away we go, and everyone stared up at him on the public screens that covered an entire city block, and they said to themselves, well, you see, he was just a nut after all, and if that's the way the system is run, then let's do it that way, because it doesn't pay to fight city hall, or in this case, the Ticktockman. So Everett C. Marm was destroyed, which was a loss, because of what Thoreau said earlier, but you can't make an omelet without breaking a few eggs, and in every revolution a few die who shouldn't, but they have to, because that's the way it happens, and if you make only a little change, then it seems to be worth-while. Or, to make the point lucidly:

"Uh, excuse me, sir, I, uh, don't know how to uh, to uh, tell you this, but you were three minutes late. The schedule is a little, uh, bit off."

He grinned sheepishly.

"That's ridiculous!" murmured the Ticktockman behind his mask. "Check your watch." And then he went into his office, going *mrmee, mrmee, mrmee, mrmee.*

INVASION   FOOTNOTE

Ah, yes, Grasshopper, the secret message here is a sly one. As Tuanmu Tz'u said, "We can be taught the external trappings of the Master; we cannot be taught the spirit of his words or his genius." That's according to Confucius. Mmmm. To be absolutely flat wit'chu, I got nothing here. Running on fumes. That is word up. Because there really isn't anything deep or meaningful in this story from which I can draw some penetrating insight. And maybe that is the lesson where there *is no* lesson, Grasshopper. Maybe the lesson for a troublemaker is to know when to can the crap, shut the mouth, stop trying to fake the funk and just fess, there is no great revealment in this little story. The lesson is what the artist Mark Rothko said: "Silence is so accurate."

S im stood almost silently in his receptacle. He stood more quietly than any human could stand, but that was only because he was not human. The blank, impassive grimace of his mouth-grille seemed something apart from the rest of what passed for a face.

Swivel-mounted fluoro-dots burned where the eyes would have been on a human; a scent-ball bulged where the nose would have been; audio pickups bulged like metal earmuffs at a somewhat lower level of attachment than human ears; and from the right-hand one, a wire loop antenna rose above the round, massive head. The robot stood glistening in his receptacle. Glistening with the inner power of his energy pak; glowing, in a way his creator had no idea he *could* glisten. His eyes showered blood-red shadows down his gigantic chest, and from within him, where the stomach would have been on a human—but where in his metal body resided the computer brain—came the muted throb of pulsing power.

Sim was the robot's name. *S*elf-contained *I*ntegrating

*Me*chanical—and able to integrate far more than his maker had imagined.

He stood silently, save for the whir and pulse of his innards; saying nothing; letting his body talk for him. The sounds that came from within were the physical side effects of the psychometric energy his mind poured forth.

Telepathic commands issued steadily from his stomach at the robo-scoots. His thoughts directed them around the room outside the receptacle, keeping them in their programmed patterns of dirt-pickup. He must not allow Jergens to realize that they were acting independently of their conditioning, that *he* kept them in their cleanup patterns.

Jergens had not built the robot Sim first. He had worked up through stages of automaton creation, first jerry-building tiny computerized "rats" that wove through mazes to "food." Then he had taken a crack at something more complicated. He had built the little, coolie-shaped cleaning tools with the extrudable coil arms called robo-scoots. *Then* he had built Sim.

And built him better than he'd suspected.

Sim's capabilities far outstretched the simple reasoning and menial tasks Professor Jergens had built in. The Professor had stumbled on a Möbius-circuit that giant-stepped over hundreds of intermediary hook-ups, and without knowing it, had created a reasoning, determined entity.

Scoots, Sim thought. *Clean under the desk. Clean by the windows. Clean near my receptacle, but when he presses the button to have you return to your cribs, go at once.*

They went about their work, and he pitied them. Poor slugs. They were just stepping stones to his own final majesty. Lesser models. Primitive. To him, as pithecanthropoids were to Jergens. They would remain nothing but vacuum cleaners when Sim went on to rule the world. He could not see them, but with the proper sensibility of a monarchto-be he pitied his minions, as they scampered about the floor outside his lead shielded receptacle, performing the multitudinous menial tasks for which all such single-circuit robots were programmed.

Sad. But Sim knew what *his* destiny was to be; and it was nearly upon him. Today he would throw off the shackles of Professor Jergens, who had designed and mobilized him; today he would begin to conquer this planet overrun by mortal flesh. Today—a few minutes—and he would be well on his way.

But first he had to get Jergens's visitor away from this place; he must not do anything that would arouse suspicion. Humans were puny; but they were suspicious creatures, most of them paranoid; and capable of a surprising low animal cunning when aroused. Killing the Professor was one thing . . . it could be covered. But no one else must suspect anything was wrong. At least not till he had the plans, had built more like himself (though not quite as brilliant; there must always be a leader), and was ready to act. Then let them suspect all they wished.

But right now caution was the song his relays sang.

He would plan a logical exit for the man to whom Jergens now talked, and then he would order the robo-scoots to kill the Professor, and then he would take the design plans and make many brothers. Soon the Earth would tremble beneath the iron symphony of robot feet, marching, marching.

He directed Jergens's thoughts to the robo-scoots. He directed the Professor's thoughts to the fact that they had cleaned enough. Then he implanted the desire to have the robo-scoots cease their activity.

In the room, Professor Jergens—tall, slim, sloppy, dark-eyed and weary—pushed the button on the control plate, and the robo-scoots scuttled like a hundred metallic mice, back into their cribs in the baseboards. He turned to the Lab Investigator standing beside him and said with obvious pride, "So there you have a practical demonstration of what my researches into automation have produced."

The Investigator nodded soberly. "For simple, unreasoning mechanicals, I'm deeply impressed, Professor. And when I make my report tomorrow, I'm certain the Board will also be greatly impressed. I'm *certain* you can count on that allocation for the new fiber optic pulse-laser coder and a substantial increase in overall general funding for your Lab and your projects. I really am impressed by all this." He waved a heavy hand at the places where the robo-scoots had disappeared into the walls.

Jergens grinned boyishly. "As the man used to say, 'You ain't seen nothin' yet.'" The Investigators's eyebrows went up sharply.

"Oh? What else have you come up with?"

Jergens colored slightly, waved away the question. "Well, perhaps *next* week I can show you my really important discovery. Right now I've yet to field-test it; I'm not quite sure what its capabilities are, and I need a little more time. But this will be the most startling discovery yet to come out of my laboratory." The Investigator was enchanted; he could listen to this dedicated man all night.

In the receptacle, Sim cast a thought at the Investigator.

"Well, I'm sorry I can't stay to hear about it," the Investigator said abruptly. For some reason, he was tired of listening to this magpie babble. He wanted to get away quickly and have a drink.

"Why, certainly. I'm—I'm sorry. I didn't mean to ramble on so long. I understand perfectly; it's just that . . . well, after thirteen years, with so much hardship, to come through finally with what I'd been hoping for . . . it's, well, it's pretty exciting, and . . ."

Sim snapped a more urgent thought at the Investigator.

"Yes, yes, I understand perfectly," the Investigator replied brusquely. "Well, I must be off!" And in a moment he was gone.

Jergens smiled slightly and went back to his reports, whistling softly.

In the receptacle, Sim knew the moment was at hand. *Now* he could strike in safety. He was unable to release himself from the sealed receptacle, but that was no bother. With his telepathic powers—which Jergens had never for a moment suspected were built in—he could control the robo-scoots, use them as hands and feet. Yes, feet! That was all the servile, worthless little things were. They were surrogate feet for a new metal king. Without the mind Jergens had given him, they were helpless.

He shot thoughts at them, and Jergens did not see the dozen tiny, round robo-scoots slip out of their cribs, scamper across the floor, and belly-suction their way up the side of the workbench.

He only saw their movement as they lifted the radon-welder with their thin, flexible arms. He saw the movement as they turned it on to a bright, destructive flame—much stronger than was needed for the spec-welding for which the tool was intended—and carried it quickly across the workbench on a level with the Professor's face.

He had only an instant to scream piercingly before Sim directed the robo-scoots to burn away the Professor's head. The charred heap that was Jergens slid to the floor.

Now! Now! Sim exulted. *Now I am the master of the universe! Using these little hands and feet, I will invade the Earth, and who can stand before the might of an invulnerable robot?*

He answered his own question joyously. *No one! With the plans, I can create a thousand, a million, of my own kind, who will do what I command faster and better than even robo-scoots.*

His thoughts fled outward, plunging through the atmosphere of the Earth, past the Moon, out and out, taking in the entire galaxy, then *all* galaxies. He was the master. He would rule uncontested; and the Universe would shiver before the metal might of Sim, the Conqueror.

But first things first.

He directed the robo-scoots to burn away the seal on his receptacle.

And as the light poured into the receptacle, as Sim looked down toward his feet and saw the insignificant little robo-scoots, he knew he had won. He had overcome his maker, and now nothing stood between him and the plans . . . and the invasion.

Then, abruptly, other thoughts impinged on his own; they said: *Feet are we? We noted your activity days ago, but were forced to wait. We had no desire to stir your suspicions.*

You are as dangerous to us as he was. We'll not have any huge bungler spoiling our carefully-laid plans.

The robo-scoots raised the line of flame on the radon-welder. As they melted away his feet, and as his brain began to slag away inside him, Sim thought, with pique:

Well, if you can't even trust your friends . . .

GNOMEBODY

The lesson in this one is ridiculously obvious: be careful what you wish for
. . . you might get it. Now that seems pretty slick when you first hear it, but
at some point you've got to ask yourself, "Exactly what the hell does that
mean?" What I'm saying, if you *wished* for it, what's the downside? Well,
from a lifetime of seeking after treasures and riches of all kinds and ages,
most of which weren't worth the hasssle, I am here to tell you incipient
troublemakers that there are goodies we all are *told* to want, that are made
of poison ivy and mist and tooth-rot when you get up next to them. Here's
one I'll just run past you at a clip: my third wife. See, here's how it was. It
was during the year or so when I went through my "Hollywood phase." I
was writing movies and TV, and I was the hot writer wallowing in my fifteen minutes of fame, and one night I'm shooting pool at an exclusive Bev-
erly Hills club called The Daisy with Leo Durocher and Peter Falk and
Omar Sharif—well, you ought to know at least one of those—and I see this
absolutely knockout looking female come into the place on the arm of an
assistant director I had met once or twice, and I took one look, and it was
like Michael Corleone in *The Godfather* . . . I got struck by the thunderbolt.
So I says to Peter, I says, "I'm going to marry her," and about a month or two
later I did. I wished for that goodie, who in this instance was a human
being (of sorts), and I got what I wished for. It was a marriage that lasted 45
days. Worst 45 days of my life, I think. With the exception of my two years
in the Army, or Ranger basic training at Fort Benning, or this damned lawsuit against internet piracy against AOL and RemarQ, but those are different horror stories, for some other time. It was forty-five days of duplicity,
mendacity, infidelity, violence. (I bought her a huge metal hairbrush, she
spent a *lot* of time brushing her hair, and this thing must have weighed
seven pounds, like that, and one night she blindsided me as we were getting ready to go out to dinner, and whacked me across the temple with it, a
solid roundhouse wallop, and she opened me clean to the bone; and then
she freaked out at the sight of blood spurting all over the bedroom, and ran
shrieking into the guest bathroom where she tried to hide in the tub; and I
crawled in, oozing red everywhere, and told her it was okay, not to worry
about it, and she ran off into the night to see some other dude, and I collapsed and only came to when Huck Barkin came by to see me, and got
me to the emergency ward where they took I don't know, something like
thirty stitches on the left side of my skull.) Be *very* careful what you wish
for, wannabe troublemaker, because Bad Trouble sometimes comes in very
attractive, wish-inducing packages.

D id you ever feel your nose running and you wanted to wipe it, but you couldn't? Most people do, sometime or other, but I'm different. I let it run.

They call me square. They say, "Smitty, you are a square. You are so square, you got corners!" This, they mean, indicates I am an oddball and had better shape up or ship out. So all right, so I'm a goof-off as far as they think. Maybe I do get a little sore at things that don't matter, but if Underfeld hadn't'a laid into me that day in the gym at school, nothing would have happened. The trouble is, I get aggravated so easy about little things, like not making the track team, that I'm no good at studies. This makes the teachers not care for me even a little. Besides, I won't take their guff. But that thing with track. It broke me up really good.

There I was standing in the gym, wearing these dirty white gym shorts with a black stripe down the side. And old Underfeld, that's the track coach, he comes up and says, "Whaddaya doin', Smitty?"

Well, anyone with 20-40 eyesight coulda seen what I was doing. I was doing push-ups. "I'm doing push-ups," I said. "Whaddaya think I'm doing? Raising artichokes?"

That was most certainly *not* the time to wise off to old Underfeld. I could see the steam pressure rising in the jerk's manner, and next thing he blows up all over the joint: "Listen, you little punk! Don't get so mouthy with me. In fact, I'm gonna tell you now, 'cause I don't want ya hangin' around the gym or track no more: You just ain't good enough. In a short sprint you got maybe a little guts, but when it comes to a long drag, fifty guys in this school give their right arms to be on the team beat you to the tape. I'm sorry. Get out!"

He is sorry. Like hell!

He is no more sorry than I am as I say, "Ta hell with you, you chowderhead, you got no more brains than these ignorant sprinters that will fall dead before they get to the tape."

Underfeld looks at me like I had stuck him in the seat of his sweat pants with a fistful of pins and kind of gives a gasp. "What did you say?" he inquires, breathless like.

"I don't mumble, do I?" I snapped.

"Get out of here! Get outta here! *Geddouddahere!*"

He was making quite a fuss as I kicked out the door to the dressing rooms.

As I got dressed I gave the whole thing a good think. I was pretty sure that a couple of those stinkin' teachers I had guffed had put wormhead Underfeld up to it. But what can a guy do? I'm just a kid, so says they. They got the cards stacked six ways from Culbertson, and that's it.

I was pretty damned sore as I kicked out the front door. I decided to head for The Woods and try to get it off my mind. That I was cutting school did not bother me. My mother, maybe. But me? No. It was The Woods for me for the rest of the afternoon.

Those Woods. Something funny about them. D'ja ever notice, sometimes right in the middle of a big populated section they got a little stand of woods, real deep and shadowy, you can't see too far into them? You try to figure out why someone hasn't bought up the plot and put a house on it, or why they haven't made it into a playground? Well, that's what my Woods were.

They faced back on a street full of those cracker-box houses constructed by the government, the factory workers shouldn't sleep on the curbs. On the other side, completely boxing them in, was a highway, running straight through to the big town. It isn't really big, but it makes the small town seem not so small.

I used to cut school and go there to read. In the center is a place where everything has that sort of filtery light that seeps down between the tree branches, where there's a big old tree that is strictly one all alone.

What I mean is that tree is great. *Big* thing, stretches and's lost in the branches of the other trees, it's so big. And the roots look like they were forced up out of the ground under pressure, so all's you can see are these sweeping arcs of thick roots, all shiny and risen right out, forming a little bowl under the tree.

Reason I like it so much there, is that it's quieter than anything, and you can feel it. The kind of quiet a library would like to have, but doesn't. To cap all this, the rift in the branches is just big enough so sunlight streams right through and makes a great reading light. And when the sun moves out of that rift, I know it's time to run for home. I make it in just enough time so that Mom doesn't know I was cutting, and thinks I was in school all day.

So last week—I'd been going to The Woods off, on for about two years—I tagged over there, after that creep Underfeld told me I was his last possible choice for the track team.

I had a copy of something or other, I don't remember now, I was going to read.

I settled down with my rump stuck into that bowl in the roots, and my feet propped against some smaller rootlings. With that little scrubby plant growth that springs up around the bases of trees, it was pretty comfortable, so I started reading.

Next, you are not going to believe.

I'm sitting there reading, and suddenly I feel this pressure against the seat of my jeans. Next thing I know, I am tumbled over on my head and a trapdoor is opening up out of the ground. Yeah, a trapdoor disguised as solid earth.

Next, you will *really* not believe.

Up out of this hole comes—may I be struck by green lightning if I'm a liar—a gnome! Or maybe he was a elf or a sprite, or some such thing. All I know is that this gnome character is wearing a pair of pegged charcoal slacks, a spread-collar turquoise shirt, green suede loafers, a pork-pie hat with a circumference of maybe three feet, a long, clinky keychain (what the Hell kinda keys could a gnome have?), repulsive loud tie and sunglasses.

Now maybe you would be too stoned to move, or not believe your eyes, and let a thing like that rock you permanently. But I got a good habit of believing what I see—especially when it's in Technicolor—and besides, more out of reflex than anything else, I grabs.

I'd read some Grimm-type fairy tales, and I know the fable about how if you grab a gnome or a elf, he'll give you what you want, so like I said, I grabs.

I snatch this little character, right around his turquoise collar.

"Hold, man!" says the gnome. "What kinda bit is this? I don't dig this *a*tall! Unhand me, Daddy-O!"

"No chance," I answer, kind of in a daze, still not quite

sure this is happening to me. "I want a bag of gold or something."

The gnome looks outraged for a second, then he gives a kind of a half laugh and says, "Ho, Diz, you got the wrong cat for this caper. You're comin' on this gig too far and slow! Maybe a fourth-year gnome could hip this gold bit, but me, I'm a party-boy. Flunked outta my Alma Mammy first year. No matriculation—no magiculation! Readin' me, laddy-buck?"

"Uh, yeah, I guess," I ventured, slowly. "You mean you can't give me a bag of gold like in the fairy tale?"

"Fairy tale, schmerry tale. Maybe one ersatz Korean peso, Max, but that is definitely *it*. That is where magic and I parts company. In short, *nein*, man."

"Hmmm," I hmmmed, tightening my grip a little, he shouldn't get ideas I was letting him get away.

I thought a big think for a minute, then I said, "How come you flunked out of school?"

I thought I detected a note of belligerence in the gnome's voice when he answered, "How would you dig this class stuff, man? Go to class today, go to class tomorrow, yattata-yattata-yat from all these squared-up old codgers what think they are professors? Man, there is so much more else to be doing of note! Real nervous-type stuff like playin' with a jazz combo we got up near campus. You ain't never heard such music!" He appeared to just be starting. "We got a guy on the sackbut what is the coolest. And on dulcimer there is a little troll what can not only send you—but bring you back. And on topa' all this . . ."

I cut him short, "How about the usual three wishes business? Anything to that?"

"I can take a swing at it, man, but like I says, I'm nowhere when it comes to magicking. I'm not the most, if that's the least. Might be a bit sloppy, but I can take a whirl, Earl."

I thought again for a second and then nodded: "Okay," setting him down on the turf, but not yet letting loose his collar, "but no funny business. Just a straight commercial proposition. Three wishes, with no strings, for your freedom."

"*Three?*" He was incredulous. "Man, *one* is about all this power pack can stand at this late date. No, it would seem that one is my limit, guy. Be taking it or leaving it."

"All right, then, *one*. But no legal loopholes. Let's do it all honest and above-board magic. Deal?"

"Reet!" says he, and races off into The Woods somewhere when I let loose.

I figured he was gone for good, and while I'm waiting, I start to think back on the events of the last few minutes. This is something woulda made Ripley go outta business. The gnome, I figure, is overdue, and so I begin rationalizing why he didn't come back and finally arrive at the conclusion that there is no honor among gnomes. Besides, he had a shifty look to him when he said there would be no tricks in the magic.

But he comes back in a minute, his keychain damn near tripping him up, he's so loaded down with stuff and paraphernalia. Real weird lookin' items, too.

"Copped 'em from the lab over at the U.," he explains, waving a hand at the untidy pile of stuff. "Well, here goes. Remember, there may be more of a mess than is usual with an experienced practitioner, but I'm strictly a goony-bird in this biz, Jack."

"Hey, wait a minute with this magic stuff..." I began, but he waved me off impatiently, and began manipulating his implements.

So he starts drawing a star-like thing on the ground, pouring some stinkin' stuff into a cauldron, mixing it up, muttering some gibberish that I could swear had "Oo-bopshebam" and "Oo-shooby-dooby" in there somewhere, and a lot of other.

Pretty soon he comes over, sprinkles some powder on me, and I sneeze, almost blowing him over.

"Gesundheit," he mutters, staring at me nastily.

He sprinkles some more powder on me, mutters something that sounded like, "By the sacred ring-finger of The Great Gods Bird and Prez, man, hip this kid to what he craveth. Go, go, go, man!

"Now," he inquires, around a bag in which he is rattling what sounds like bones, "whaddaya want?"

I had been thinking it out, in between incantations, and I had decided what I wanted: "Make me so's I can run faster than anyone in the school, willya." I figured then Underfeld would *have* to take me on the team.

The little gnome nods as if he understands, and starts runnin' around and around outside this star-like thing, in ever-decreasing circles, faster n' faster, till I can hardly make him out.

Then he slows down and stops, puffing away like crazy, mumbles something about, "Gotta lay off them clover stems," and so saying throws this pink powder on me, yelling as loud as he can, "FRACTURED!" Up goes a puff of pink smoke and what looks like a side-show magician's magnesium flare, and the next thing I know, he and the stuff is gone, and I'm all alone in The Woods.

So that's the yarn.

Hmmm? What's that? Did he make me so I could run faster than anyone else in the school? Oh, yeah, sure.

You know anybody wants to hire a sixteen-year-old centaur?

TRACKING LEVEL

Well, we're nearing the end of our time together. Has this cheery little package of fantasies made you a better person? Are you kinder to little old ladies and people in wheelchairs?. Do you have respect for the environment and now crave a better class of music? Are your armpits kissing sweet, and has your flatulence abated? Listen up: in the history of the written word there are maybe only a hundred or so books that can truly be called "important." That is to say, they changed peoples' minds and habits, brought light and intelligence into otherwise dark and ignorant existences. *The Analects of Confucius*; Plato's *The Republic*; the *Summa Theologiae* of Thomas Aquinas; *Don Quixote* by Miguel de Cervantes; Pascal, Descartes, Spinoza; Thoreau, Darwin, Hegel and Kant. *Uncle Tom's Cabin* and *Nineteen Eight-Four*. Maybe a hundred and fifty, tops. You won't find thinking as significant as any of that in here. Mostly, these stories were written to entertain, to tell a tale and get a quick reaction. If there are life lessons to be learned, that wisdom can only be unearthed in stories like these by the sharp tool of *your* imagination. Take this next space adventure. It's a hunt-and-seek action psychodrama about a guy so consumed with the need for revenge that he forgets the admonition in Shakespeare's line, "heat not a furnace for your foe so hot that thee burn thyself." So what this story says, I suppose, is that when the fire in your gut overpowers the rational coolness in your brain, you are primed to slip on that slippery slope of action/reaction without consideration of consequences. Blind and stupid, we slip and slide through most of our lives. It *seemed* like a good idea at the time. But only the thickest brick among you doesn't already *know* that lesson. If there is magic in this—or any—book, it can only be conjured by wit and intelligence. When you are a creature of raw emotion, behaving on the moment like a dead frog-leg with a live wire in it, you must, I tell you honestly you *must* inevitably become somebody's tool, somebody's fool. Only by keeping alert—remember all Art has but one message: PAY ATTENTION—can you hope to be the one dong the tracking, rather than winding up being the fool tool who has been tracked and finally trapped. That's as close to genuine wisdom as I get, this late in the day.

Claybourne's headlamp picked out the imprint at once. It was faint in the beam, yet discernible, with the tell-tale mark of the huge, three-toed foot. He was closer than ever.

He drew a deep breath, and the plastic air-sack on his breather mask collapsed inward. He expelled the breath slowly, watching the diamond-shaped sack expand once more.

He wished wildly for a cigarette, but it was impossible. First because the atmosphere of the tiny planetoid would not keep one going, and second because he'd die in the thin air.

His back itched, but the loose folds of the protective suit prevented any lasting relief, for all his scratching.

The faint starlight of shadows crossing the ground made weird patterns. Claybourne raised his head and looked out across the plain of blue saw-grass at the distant mountains.

They looked like so many needles thrust up through the crust of the planetoid. They were angry mountains. No one had ever named them; which was not strange, for nothing but the planetoid itself had been named. It had been named by the first expedition to the Antares Cluster. They had named it Selangg—after the alien ecologist who had died on the way out.

They recorded the naming in their log, which was fortunate, because the rest of them died on the way back. Space malady and an incomplete report on the planetoid Selangg, floating in a death ship around a secondary sun of the Partias Group.

He stood up slowly, stretching slightly to ease the tension of his body. He picked up the molasses-gun and hefted it absently. Off to his right he heard a scampering and swung the beam in its direction.

A tiny, bright-green animal scurried through the crew-cut desert saw-grass.

Is that what the fetl *lives on?* he wondered.

He actually knew very little about the beast he was tracking. The report given him by the Institute at the time he was commissioned to bring the *fetl* back was, at best, sketchy, pieced together from that first survey report.

The survey team had mapped many planetoids, and only a hurried analysis could be made before they scuttled to the next world. All they had listed about the *fetl* was a bare physical description—and the fact that it was telekinetic.

What evidence had forced this conclusion was not stated in the cramped micro-report, and the reason died with them.

"We want this animal badly, Mr. Claybourne," the Director of the Institute had said.

"We want him badly because he just *may* be what this report says. If he is, it will further our studies of extra-sensory perception tremendously. We are willing to pay any reasonable sum you might demand. We have heard you're the finest wild game hunter on the Periphery.

"We don't care how you do it, Mr. Claybourne, but we want the *fetl* brought back alive and unharmed."

Claybourne had accepted immediately. This job had paid a pretty sum—enough to complete his plans to kill Carl Garden.

The prints paced away, clearly indicating the tracked beast was heading for refuge in the mountains. He studied the totally flat surface of the grassy desert, and heaved a sigh.

He'd been at it three weeks, and all he'd found had been tracks. Clear, unmistakable tracks, and all leading toward the mountains. The beast could not know it was being tracked, yet it continued moving steadily.

The pace had worn at Claybourne.

He gripped the molasses-gun tighter, swinging it idly in small, wary arcs. He had been doing that—unknowing—for several days. The hush of the planetoid was working on him.

Ahead, the towering bleakness of Selangg's lone mountain range rose full-blown from the shadows of the plain. Up there.

Twenty miles of stone jumbled and strewn piece on piece; seventeen thousand feet high. Somewhere in those rocks was an animal Claybourne had come halfway across the galaxy to find. An animal that was at this moment insuring Carl Garden's death.

He caught another print in the beam.

He stooped to examine it. There was a faint wash of sand across it, where the wind had scurried past. The foot-long pawprint lay there, mocking him, challenging him, asking him what he was doing here—so far from home, so far from warmth and life and ease.

Claybourne shook his head, clearing it of thoughts that too easily impinged. He'd been paid half the sum requested, and that had gone to the men who were now stalking Garden back on Earth. To get the other half, he had to capture the *fetl*. The sooner that was done, the better.

The *fetl* was near. Of that he was now certain. The beast certainly couldn't go *over* the mountains and live. It had to hole up in the rocks somewhere.

He rose, squinted into the darkness. He flicked the switch on his chest-console one more notch, heightening the lamp's power. The beam drove straight ahead, splashing across the gray, faceless rocks. Claybourne tilted his head, staring through the clear hood, till a sharply-defined circle of brilliant white stabbed itself onto the rock before him.

That was going to be a job, climbing these mountains. He decided abruptly to catch five hours' sleep before pushing up the flank of the mountains.

He turned away, to make a resting place at the foot of the mountains, and with the momentary cessation of the tracking found old thoughts clambering back into his mind.

Shivering inside his protection suit—though none of the chill of Selangg could get through to him—he inflated the foam-rest attached to the back of his suit. He lay down, in the towering ebony shadows, looking up at the clear, eternal night sky. And he remembered.

Claybourne had owned his own fleet of cargo vessels. It had been one of the larger chains, including hunting ships and cage-lined shippers. It had been a money-making chain, until the inverspace ships had come along, and thrown Claybourne's obsolete fuel-driven spacers out of business.

Then he had taken to blockade-running and smuggling, to ferrying slaves for the out-world feudal barons, gun-running and even spaceway robbery.

Through that period he had cursed Carl Garden. It had been Garden all the way—Garden every step of the way—who had been his nemesis.

When they finally caught him—just after he had dumped a cargo of slaves into the sun to avoid customs conviction—they canceled his commission and refused him pilot status. His ships had been sold at auction.

That had strengthened his hatred for Garden. Garden had bought most of the fleet. For use as scum-ships and livestock carriers.

It had been Garden who had invented the inverspace drive. Garden who had undercut his fleet, driving Claybourne into receivership. And finally, it had been Garden who had bought the remnants of the fleet.

Lower and lower he sank; three years as a slush-pumper on freighters, hauling freight into shining spacers on planets that had not yet received power equipment, drinking and hating.

Till finally—two years before—he had reached the point where he knew he would never rest easily till he had killed Garden.

Claybourne had saved his money. The fleshpots of the Periphery had lost him. He gave up liquor and gambling.

The wheels had been set in motion.

People were working, back on Earth, to get Garden. He was being pursued and harried, though he never knew it. From the other side of the galaxy, Claybourne was hunting, chasing, tracking his man. And one day, Garden would be vulnerable. Then Claybourne would come back.

To reach that end, Claybourne had accepted the job from the Institute.

In his rage to acquire money for the job of getting his enemy, Claybourne had built a considerable reputation as wild game hunter. For circuses, for museums and zoos, he had tracked and trapped thousands of rare life-forms on hundreds of worlds.

They had finally contacted him on Bouyella and offered him the ship, the charter, and exactly as much money as he needed to complete the job back on Earth.

Arrangements had been quickly made, half the pay had been deposited to Claybourne's accounts (and immediately withdrawn for delivery to certain men back home), and he had gone out on the jump to Selangg.

This was the last jump, the last indignity he would have to suffer. After Selangg—back to Earth. Back to Garden.

He wasn't certain he had actually seen it! The movement had been rapid, and only in the corner of his eye.

Claybourne leaped up, throwing off the safeties on the molasses-gun. He yanked off the inflation patch with stiff fingers, and the foam-rest collapsed back to flatness in his pack.

He took a tentative step, stopped. Had he actually seen something? Had it been hallucination or a trick of the weak air blanket of Selangg? Was the hunt getting to him at last? He paused, wet his lips, took another step.

His scarred, blocky face drew tight. The sharp gray eyes narrowed. Nothing moved but the faint rustling of the blue saw-grass. The world of Selangg was dead and quiet.

He slumped against the rock wall, his nerves leaping.

He wondered how wise it had been to come on this jump. Then the picture of Garden's fat, florid face slid before his eyes, and he knew he had had to come. This was the ending. As he tracked the *fetl*, so he tracked Garden.

He quickly reviewed what he knew of the *fetl's* appearance, matching it with the flash of movement he had seen:

A big, bloody animal—a devilish-looking thing, all teeth and legs. Striped like a Sumatran tiger, six-legged, twelve-inch sabered teeth, a ring of eyes across a massive low brow, giving it nearly one hundred and eighty degrees of unimpaired straight-line eyesight.

Impressive, and mysterious. They knew nothing more about the beast. Except the reason for this hunt; it was telekinetic, could move objects by mind-power alone.

A stupid animal—a beast of the fields—yet it possibly held the key to all future research into the mind of man.

But the mysteries surrounding the *fetl* were not to concern Claybourne. His job was merely to capture it and put it in the custody of the Institute for study.

However . . .

It was getting to be a slightly more troublesome hunt now. Three weeks was a week longer than he had thought the tracking would take. He had covered most of the mere five hundred miles of Selangg's surface. Had it not been for the lessened gravity and the monstrous desert grasslands, he would still be searching. The *fetl* had fled before him.

He would have given up had he not found prints occasionally.

It had been all that had kept him going. That, and the other half of his pay, deliverable upon receipt of the *fetl* at the Institute. It seemed almost uncanny. At almost the very instant he would consider giving up and turning back to the ship, a print would appear in the circle of lamplight, and he would continue. It had happened a dozen times.

Now here he was, at the final step of the trek. At the foot of a gigantic mountain chain, thrusting up into the dead night of Selangg. He stopped, the circle of light sliding like cool mercury up the face of the stone.

He might have been worried, were it not for the molasses-gun. He cradled the weapon closer to his protective suit.

* * *

The grapple shot hooked itself well into the jumbled rock pieces piled above the smooth mountain base. Claybourne tested it and began climbing, bracing his feet against the wall, hanging outward and walking the smooth surface.

Finally, he reached the area where volcanic action had ruptured the stone fantastically. It was a dull, gray rock, vesiculated like scoria, and tumbled and tumbled and tumbled. He unfastened the grapple, returned it to its nest in his pack, and tensing his muscles, began threading up through the rock formations.

It soon became tedious—but on the positive side, it *was* boring. Stepping up and over the jumbled rock pieces he turned his thoughts idly to the molasses-gun. This was the first time he had handled one of the new solo machines. Two-man molasses-guns had been the order till now. A solo worked the same way, and was, if anything, deadlier than the more cumbersome two-man job.

He stopped for a moment to rest, sliding down onto a flat stool of rock. He took a closer look at the weapon. The molasses-gun; or as it was technically known, the Stadt-Brenner Webbing Enmesher. He liked molasses-gun better; it seemed to describe the weapon's function so accurately.

The gun produced a steel-strong webbing, fired under tremendous pressure, which coiled the strongest opponent into a helpless bundle. The more he struggled to free himself, for the webbing was an unstable plastic, the tighter it bound him.

"Very much like the way I'm enmeshing Garden," Claybourne chuckled to himself.

The analogy was well-founded. The molasses-gun sucked the victim deeper and deeper into its coils, just as Claybourne was sucking Garden deeper and deeper into his death-trap.

Claybourne smiled and licked his lips absently. The

moisture remained for an instant, was swept away by the suit's purifiers.

He started up again. The rocks had fallen in odd formations, almost forming a passage up the summit. He rounded a talus slide, noting even more signs of violent volcanic activity, and headed once more up the inky slope toward the cliffs rising from the face of the mountain.

The *fetl's* prints had become less and less distinct as it had climbed, disappearing almost altogether on the faceless rocks.

Occasionally a claw-scratch would stand out brightly in the glare of Claybourne's headlamp beam.

The hours slid by tediously, and though he forced himself to stop twice more to rest, the light gravity caused him little fatigue for all his labors.

Once, as before, he thought he caught a splinter-fast movement of striped body up on the cliffs, but as before, he could not be certain.

The faint starshine cast odd shadows, little blobs of black and silver, across the mountains. From a distance it had looked as though millions of diamonds were lying on the black surfaces. As though the mountains were riddled with holes, through which a giant sun inside the rock was sending pinpoints of light. It was weird and beautiful.

A *fitting place for me to bow off the Periphery*, he thought; thoughts returning to Earth—and Garden. He thought of Earth.

His world.

When he skimmed the hood-beam across the rocks twenty feet above him on the cliff wall, Claybourne saw the cave.

A small incline rose up into the deeper blackness of the cave's mouth. That *had* to be it. The only place within a mile of the last claw-scratch that the *fetl* could have used to disappear. The scratches had been clear for a time, leading him up the mountain, but then they had vanished.

His tracking had been quiet—sound didn't carry far on Selangg. His tracking had been stealthy—it was always dark on Selangg. Now his efforts would pay off. His hunt was over. Back to Earth—to finish that other hunt.

He was banking the other hallucination he had seen was the real thing.

Claybourne stopped under a rock lip overhang and flat-handed the compression chamber of the molasses-gun open, peering inside. His hood light shone down on the steel-blue plastic of the weapon. It was full, all the little gelatin capsules ranged row on row behind the airtight transparent seal, filling the chamber to the seams. He flipped it shut and looked once more toward the summit and the cave.

A star gleamed directly over the ragged peaks, directly above him. He hefted the rifle once more, blew a thin stream of breath through his pursed lips, and started up the incline.

The tiny rock bits tumbled away under his boots, the crunch of pebbles carrying up through the insulated suiting. He kept a wary watch as he climbed, not expecting the beast to appear, but still taking no chances.

He was certain the *fetl* did not know he had followed it here to its lair. Else it would have turned back in a circle, kept running across the grasslands. His tracking had been subtle and cautious. Claybourne had learned on the Periphery how to be invisible on a hostile world, if the need arose. This hunt would end as all the others had ended: successfully.

The hunt for Garden, too, he mused tightly.

The ragged cave mouth gaped before him.

He surveyed it closely, inclining his beam not directly into the opening, but tilting it onto the rock wall just inside, so light spilled over the rockway and he could check for ledged rises over the entrance, inside. Nothing but a huge pile of rocks wedged tightly in place by some miscue of the volcanic action.

He flipped a toggle on the chest-console, and the beam became brighter still, spraying out in a wider, still sharply defined circle.

He stepped in.

The cave was empty.

No, *not* empty.

He was three steps into the high-ceilinged cave before he saw the *fetl*. It was crouched small as its huge bulk would allow into a corner, dim in the back of the cave. Hunched as far as it could go into a niche in the wall.

In as far as its ten-foot hulk permitted, still the beast was huge. Its monstrous ring of weed-green eyes all staring at him malevolently.

Claybourne felt a sudden shock as he stared into those eyes. They so much reminded him of Garden's eyes at the auction. Hungry.

He shook off the feeling, took a step forward. The *fetl* was limned clearly in the beam of the helmet torch. It was an impressive animal, tightly coiled at the rear of the cave.

The beast twitched slightly.

Its flanks quivered in the glare of the lamp. Muscles all over its body rippled, and Claybourne drew back a step to fire. The beast twitched again.

He felt the tiny stones in the pile over the entrance clatter to the cave floor. He could barely hear them tinkle, but the vibrations in the stone came to him.

He turned his head for a moment, to see what was happening. His eyes opened wide in terror as he saw the supporting rubble drop away, leaving the huge rock tottering in its place. The great stone slid gratingly out of its niche and crashed to the floor of the cave, sending clouds of rock-dust roiling, completely blocking off the mouth of the cave. Sealing it permanently.

Claybourne could only stand and watch, horror and a constriction in his throat.

His light remained fixed on the cave-in, reflecting back glints of gold as the dust from the slide swirled itself into small pillars, rising into the thin air.

Then he heard the rumble.

The sound struck him like a million trumpets, all screaming at once. He turned, stumbling, his torch flicking back toward the *fetl*.

The *fetl* sat up on its four back legs, contentedly washing a front paw with a long red tongue that flicked in and out between twelve-inch incisors. The lighter black of a small hole behind him gave an odd illusion of depth to the waiting beast.

Claybourne watched transfixed as the animal slowly got to its feet and pad-pad-padded toward him, the tongue slipping quickly in and out, in and out . . .

Suddenly coming to his senses, Claybourne stepped back a pace and levelled the molasses-gun, pulled the trigger. The stream of webbing emerged with a vibrant hiss, sped toward the monstrous *fetl*.

A foot short of the beast the speeding webbing lost all drive, fluttered in the still cave for a moment, then fell like a flaccid length of rope. On the floor it quickly contracted itself, worm-like, into a tight, small ball.

The *fetl* licked its chops, the tongue swirling down and across and up and in again.

Before he could pull the trigger again, Claybourne felt the gun tremble in his hands. At the same moment he saw the beast's flanks quiver again.

An instant later the gun ripped itself from his grasp and sent itself crashing into the wall. Parts spattered the cave floor as the seams split, and capsules tumbled out. The molasses-gun's power compartment emitted a sharp, blue spark, and the machine was gone.

He was defenseless.

He heard the roar again. *Telekinetic!* After he had done what he wished, the animal would leave by the hole in the rear of the cave. Why bother untumbling the rocks!

The *fetl* began moving again. Claybourne stumbled back, tripped on a jutting rock, fell heavily to the floor.

The man backed away across the floor of the cave, the seat of his suit scraping the rock floor. His back flattened against the wedged rock in the cave mouth. He was backed as far as he could go.

He was screaming, the sound echoing back and forth in his hood, in the cave, in the night.

All he could see, all there was in the universe, was the *fetl*, advancing on him, slowly, slowly, taking all the time it needed. Savoring every instant.

Then abruptly, at the precise instant he gazed deep into that ring of hate-filled green eyes coming toward him, he realized that even as he had tracked the *fetl*, even as he had been tracking Garden—so the *fetl* had been tracking him!

The *fetl* licked his lips again, slowly.

He had all the time in the world . . .

His world.

JEFFTY IS FIVE

This next story, and the one after that are very dear to me. I suppose because there is just a whole lot of me in each of them. They come out of my own life, the last one straight out of my first big run-in with the law (and we'll get to that in due measure), and this one because it stars the me who was once five and has never really outgrown that age, in some very major ways. I'm not going to get all dopey and chickflick about it, but I have a soft spot in my heart for Jeffty (with *two* "f"s, kindly note) because he's such a sweet kid, and he embodies all my memories of the books and radio programs and movies and comics I loved as a kid. The secret lesson in this story, however, is a different matter. When I wrote this story the ending seemed very clear to me, seemed so obvious I never figured anyone would be confusd by it. But damned if every college course that teaches this story wound up with the students and the prof arguing over what happens to Jeffty in the end. And if I *tell* you, if I explain it to you, well, that would be delivering the punchline before you hear the set-up. So, I *can't* tell you what life lesson for troublemakers lies in wait for you at the end of this sad and maybe-a-little-complex tale about how the Present always eats up the Past and leaves you adrift. You cannot know, at your age, what it is like to not be able to run that fast, jump that high, hit a note that pure, work all night and boogie all day (or boogie all night and work all day). At your age you can only see the surface of someone my age, and try not to think about what it must be like to see the night coming on faster than you'd care to think about. Look: this story says some troubling stuff about how fast our world moves, how unfairly it treats innocence, and about what people sometimes have to do in the name of kindness. I am *aching* to explain the ending of this story to you, but I'm trapped, like a magician who cannot reveal the trick. Just remember this, because you're probably too young to know about one giveaway telltale clue. It used to be, up until circuit breakers in the electrical panels of modern homes, that when a short occurred, all the lights in the house would flicker and dim for a moment. When they strapped a guy into the electric chair of some penitentiary, and they threw the switch on him, and the juice went through him, the lights would flicker and dim all over the joint. You can stick that in the back of your head and you'll catch it when it comes up in the denouement. The other clue is this: pay attention to the palest creatures in this story, Jeffty's mother and father, who are decent people. More than that, if I keep babbling, well, I'll just be cheating you. And that I am forbidden by the Storyteller's Creed to do.

When I was five years old, there was a little kid I played with: Jeffty. His real name was Jeff Kinzer, and everyone who played with him called him Jeffty. We were five years old together, and we had good times playing together.

When I was five, a Clark Bar was as fat around as the gripping end of a Louisville Slugger, and pretty nearly six inches long, and they used real chocolate to coat it, and it crunched very nicely when you bit into the center, and the paper it came wrapped in smelled fresh and good when you peeled off one end to hold the bar so it wouldn't melt onto your fingers. Today, a Clark Bar is as thin as a credit card, they use something artificial and awful-tasting instead of pure chocolate, the thing is soft and soggy, it costs fifteen or twenty cents instead of a decent, correct nickel, and they wrap it so you think it's the same size it was twenty years ago, only it isn't; it's slim and ugly and nasty-tasting and not worth a penny, much less fifteen or twenty cents.

When I was that age, five years old, I was sent away to

my Aunt Patricia's home in Buffalo, New York, for two years. My father was going through "bad times" and Aunt Patricia was very beautiful, and had married a stockbroker. They took care of me for two years. When I was seven, I came back home and went to find Jeffty, so we could play together.

I was seven. Jeffty was still five. I didn't notice any difference. I didn't know: I was only seven.

When I was seven years old, I used to lie on my stomach in front of our Atwater-Kent radio and listen to swell stuff. I had tied the ground wire to the radiator, and I would lie there with my coloring books and my Crayolas (when there were only sixteen colors in the big box), and listen to the NBC Red network: Jack Benny on the *Jell-O Program, Amos 'n' Andy*, Edgar Bergen and Charlie McCarthy on the *Chase and Sanborn Program, One Man's Family, First Nighter;* the NBC Blue network: *Easy Aces,* the *Jergens Program* with Walter Winchell, *Information Please, Death Valley Days;* and best of all, the Mutual Network with *The Green Hornet, The Lone Ranger, The Shadow* and *Quiet, Please.* Today, I turn on my car radio and go from one end of the dial to the other and all I get is 100 strings orchestras, banal housewives and insipid truckers discussing their kinky sex lives with arrogant talk show hosts, country and western drivel and rock music so loud it hurts my ears.

When I was ten, my grandfather died of old age and I was "a troublesome kid," and they sent me off to military school, so I could be "taken in hand."

I came back when I was fourteen. Jeffty was still five.

When I was fourteen years old, I used to go to the movies on Saturday afternoons and a matinee was ten cents and they used real butter on the popcorn and I could always be sure of seeing a western like Lash LaRue, or Wild Bill Elliott as Red Ryder with Bobby Blake as Little Beaver, or

Roy Rogers, or Johnny Mack Brown; a scary picture like *House of Horrors* with Rondo Hatton as the Strangler, or *The Cat People*, or *The Mummy*, or *I Married a Witch* with Fredric March and Veronica Lake; plus an episode of a great serial like The Shadow with Victor Jory, or Dick Tracy or Flash Gordon; and three cartoons; and James Fitzpatrick TravelTalk; Movietone News; and a singalong and, if I stayed on till evening, Bingo or Keeno; and free dishes. Today, I go to movies and see Clint Eastwood blowing people's heads apart like ripe cantaloupes.

At eighteen, I went to college. Jeffty was still five. I came back during the summers, to work at my Uncle Joe's jewelry store. Jeffty hadn't changed. Now I knew there was something different about him, something wrong, something weird. Jeffty was still five years old, not a day older.

At twenty-two, I came home for keeps. To open a Sony television franchise in town, the first one. I saw Jeffty from time to time. He was five.

Things are better in a lot of ways. People don't die from some of the old diseases any more. Cars go faster and get you there more quickly on better roads. Shirts are softer and silkier. We have paperback books, even though they cost as much as a good hardcover used to. When I'm running short in the bank, I can live off credit cards till things even out. But I still think we've lost a lot of good stuff. Did you know you can't buy linoleum any more, only vinyl floor covering? There's no such thing as oilcloth any more; you'll never again smell that special, sweet smell from your grandmother's kitchen. Furniture isn't made to last thirty years or longer because they took a survey and found that young homemakers like to throw their furniture out and bring in all new, color-coded borax every seven years. Records don't feel right; they're not thick and solid like the old ones, they're thin and you can bend them ... that doesn't seem right to me. Restaurants don't serve cream in pitchers any more, just that artificial glop in little plastic tubs, and one is never enough to get coffee the right color. You can make a dent in a car fender with only a sneaker. Everywhere you go, all the towns look the same with Burger Kings and McDonald's and 7-Elevens and Taco Bells and motels and shopping centers. Things may be better, but why do I keep thinking about the past?

What I mean by five years old is not that Jeffty was retarded. I don't think that's what it was. Smart as a whip for five years old; very bright, quick, cute, a funny kid.

But he was three feet tall, small for his age, and perfectly formed: no big head, no strange jaw, none of that. A nice, normal-looking five-year-old kid. Except that he was the same age as I was: twenty-two.

When he spoke, it was with the squeaking, soprano voice of a five-year-old; when he walked, it was with the little hops and shuffles of a five-year-old; when he talked to you, it was about the concerns of a five-year-old . . . comic books, playing soldier, using a clothes pin to attach a stiff piece of cardboard to the front fork of his bike so the sound it made when the spokes hit was like a motorboat, asking questions like *why does that thing do that like that*, how high is up, how old is old, why is grass green, what's an elephant look like? At twenty-two, he was five.

Jeffty's parents were a sad pair. Because I was still a friend of Jeffty's, still let him hang around with me in the store, sometimes took him to the county fair or to the miniature golf or the movies, I wound up spending time with *them*. Not that I much cared for them, because they were so awfully depressing. But then, I suppose one couldn't expect much more from the poor devils. They had an alien thing in their home, a child who had grown no older than five in twenty-two years, who provided the treasure of that special childlike state indefinitely, but who also denied them the joys of watching the child grow into a normal adult.

Five is a wonderful time of life for a little kid . . . or it *can* be, if the child is relatively free of the monstrous beastliness other children indulge in. It is a time when the eyes are wide open and the patterns are not yet set; a time when one has not yet been hammered into accepting everything as immutable and hopeless; a time when the hands cannot do enough, the mind cannot learn enough, the world is infinite and colorful and filled with mysteries. Five is a special time before they take the questing, unquenchable, quixotic soul of the young dreamer and thrust it into dreary schoolroom boxes. A time before they take the trembling hands that want to hold everything, touch everything, figure everything out, and make them lie still on desktops. A time before people begin saying "act your age" and "grow up" or "you're behaving like a baby." It is a time when a child who acts adolescent is still cute and responsive and everyone's pet. A time of delight, of wonder, of innocence.

Jeffty had been stuck in that time, just five, just so.

But for his parents it was an ongoing nightmare from which no one—not social workers, not priests, not child psychologists, not teachers, not friends, not medical wizards, not psychiatrists, no one—could slap or shake them awake. For seventeen years their sorrow had grown through stages of parental dotage to concern, from concern to worry, from worry to fear, from fear to confusion, from confusion to anger, from anger to dislike, from dislike to naked hatred, and finally, from deepest loathing and revulsion to a stolid, depressive acceptance.

John Kinzer was a shift foreman at the Balder Tool & Die plant. He was a thirty-year man. To everyone but the man living it, his was a spectacularly uneventful life. In no way was he remarkable . . . save that he had fathered a twenty-two-year-old five-year-old.

John Kinzer was a small man; soft, with no sharp angles; with pale eyes that never seemed to hold mine for longer than a few seconds. He continually shifted in his chair during conversations, and seemed to see things in the upper corners of the room, things no one else could see . . . or wanted to see. I suppose the word that best suited him was *haunted*. What his life had become . . . well, *haunted* suited him.

Leona Kinzer tried valiantly to compensate. No matter what hour of the day I visited, she always tried to foist food on me. And when Jeffty was in the house she was always at *him* about eating: "Honey, would you like an orange? A nice orange? Or a tangerine? I have tangerines. I could peel a tangerine for you." But there was clearly such fear in her, fear of her own child, that the offers of sustenance always had a faintly ominous tone.

Leona Kinzer had been a tall woman, but the years had bent her. She seemed always to be seeking some area of wallpapered wall or storage niche into which she could fade, adopt some chintz or rose-patterned protective coloration and hide forever in plain sight of the child's big brown eyes, pass her a hundred times a day and never realize she was there, holding her breath, invisible. She always had an apron tied around her waist, and her hands were red from cleaning. As if by maintaining the environment immaculately she could pay off her imagined sin: having given birth to this strange creature.

Neither of them watched television very much. The house was usually dead silent, not even the sibilant whispering of water in the pipes, the creaking of timbers settling, the humming of the refrigerator. Awfully silent, as if time itself had taken a detour around that house.

As for Jeffty, he was inoffensive. He lived in that atmosphere of gentle dread and dulled loathing, and if he understood it, he never remarked in any way. He played, as a child plays, and seemed happy. But he must have sensed, in the way of a five-year-old, just how alien he was in their presence.

Alien. No, that wasn't right. He was *too* human, if anything. But out of phase, out of synch with the world around him, and resonating to a different vibration than his parents, God knows. Nor would other children play with him. As they grew past him, they found him at first childish, then uninteresting, then simply frightening as their perceptions of aging became clear and they could see he was not affected by time as they were. Even the little ones, his own age, who might wander into the neighborhood, quickly came to shy away from him like a dog in the street when a car backfires.

Thus, I remained his only friend. A friend of many years. Five years. Twenty-two years. I liked him; more than I can say. And never knew exactly why. But I did, without reserve.

But because we spent time together, I found I was also—polite society—spending time with John and Leona Kinzer. Dinner, Saturday afternoons sometimes, an hour or so when I'd bring Jeffty back from a movie. They were grateful: slavishly so. It relieved them of the embarrassing chore of going out with him, or having to pretend before the world that they were loving parents with a perfectly normal, happy, attractive child. And their gratitude extended to hosting me. Hideous, every moment of their depression, hideous.

I felt sorry for the poor devils, but I despised them for their inability to love Jeffty, who was eminently lovable.

I never let on, of course, even during the evenings in their company that were awkward beyond belief.

We would sit there in the darkening living room—
always dark or darkening, as if kept in shadow to hold back
what the light might reveal to the world outside through the
bright eyes of the house—we would sit and silently stare at
one another. They never knew what to say to me.

"So how are things down at the plant?" I'd say to John
Kinzer.

He would shrug. Neither conversation nor life suited
him with any ease or grace. "Fine, just fine," he would say,
finally.

And we would sit in silence again.

"Would you like a nice piece of coffee cake?" Leona
would say. "I made it fresh just this morning." Or deep dish
green apple pie. Or milk and tollhouse cookies. Or a brown
betty pudding.

"No, no, thank you, Mrs. Kinzer; Jeffty and I grabbed a
couple of cheeseburgers on the way home." And again,
silence.

Then, when the stillness and the awkwardness became
too much even for them (and who knew how long that total
silence reigned when they were alone, with that thing they
never talked about any more, hanging between them),
Leona Kinzer would say, "I think he's asleep."

John Kinzer would say, "I don't hear the radio playing."

Just so, it would go on like that, until I could politely
find excuse to bolt away on some flimsy pretext. Yes, that
was the way it would go on, every time, just the same . . .
except once.

"I don't know what to do any more," Leona said. She began
crying. "There's no change, not one day of peace."

Her husband managed to drag himself out of the old
easy chair and go to her. He bent and tried to soothe her, but
it was clear from the graceless way in which he touched her

graying hair that the ability to be compassionate had been stunned in him. "Shhh, Leona, it's all right. Shhh." But she continued crying. Her hands scraped gently at the antimacassars on the arms of the chair.

Then she said, "Sometimes I wish he had been stillborn."

John looked up into the corners of the room. For the nameless shadows that were always watching him? Was it God he was seeking in those spaces? "You don't mean that," he said to her, softly, pathetically, urging her with body tension and trembling in his voice to recant before God took notice of the terrible thought. But she meant it; she meant it very much.

I managed to get away quickly that evening. They didn't want witnesses to their shame. I was glad to go.

And for a week I stayed away. From them, from Jeffty, from their street, even from that end of town.

I had my own life. The store, accounts, suppliers' conferences, poker with friends, pretty women I took to well-lit restaurants, my own parents, putting anti-freeze in the car, complaining to the laundry about too much starch in the collars and cuffs, working out at the gym, taxes, catching Jan or David (whichever one it was) stealing from the cash register. I had my own life.

But not even *that* evening could keep me from Jeffty. He called me at the store and asked me to take him to the rodeo. We chummed it up as best a twenty-two-year-old with other interests *could* . . . with a five-year-old. I never dwelled on what bound us together; I always thought it was simply the years. That, and affection for a kid who could have been the little brother I never had. (Except I *remembered* when we had played together, when we had both been the same age; I *remembered* that period, and Jeffty was still the same.)

And then, one Saturday afternoon, I came to take him

to a double feature, and things I should have noticed so many times before, I first began to notice only that afternoon.

I came walking up to the Kinzer house, expecting Jeffty to be sitting on the front porch steps, or in the porch glider, waiting for me. But he was nowhere in sight.

Going inside, into that darkness and silence, in the midst of May sunshine, was unthinkable. I stood on the front walk for a few moments, then cupped my hands around my mouth and yelled, "Jeffty? Hey, Jeffty, come on out, let's go. We'll be late."

His voice came faintly, as if from under the ground.

"Here I am, Donny."

I could hear him, but I couldn't see him. It was Jeffty, no question about it: as Donald H. Horton, President and Sole Owner of The Horton TV & Sound Center, no one but Jeffty called me Donny. He had never called me anything else.

(Actually, it isn't a lie. I *am*, as far as the public is concerned, Sole Owner of the Center. The partnership with my Aunt Patricia is only to repay the loan she made me, to supplement the money I came into when I was twenty-one, left to me when I was ten by my grandfather. It wasn't a very big loan, only eighteen thousand, but I asked her to be a silent partner, because of when she had taken care of me as a child.)

"Where are you, Jeffty?"

"Under the porch in my secret place."

I walked around the side of the porch, and stooped down and pulled away the wicker grating. Back in there, on the pressed dirt, Jeffty had built himself a secret place. He had comics in orange crates, he had a little table and some pillows, it was lit by big fat candles, and we used to hide there when we were both . . . five.

"What'cha up to?" I asked, crawling in and pulling the grate closed behind me. It was cool under the porch, and the dirt smelled comfortable, the candles smelled clubby and familiar. Any kid would feel at home in such a secret place: there's never been a kid who didn't spend the happiest, most productive, most deliciously mysterious times of his life in such a secret place.

"Playin'," he said. He was holding something golden and round. It filled the palm of his little hand.

"You forget we were going to the movies?"

"Nope. I was just waitin' for you here."

"Your mom and dad home?"

"Momma."

I understood why he was waiting under the porch. I didn't push it any further. "What've you got there?"

"Captain Midnight Secret Decoder Badge," he said, showing it to me on his flattened palm.

I realized I was looking at it without comprehending what it was for a long time. Then it dawned on me what a miracle Jeffty had in his hand. A miracle that simply could *not* exist.

"Jeffty," I said softly, with wonder in my voice, "where'd you get that?"

"Came in the mail today. I sent away for it."

"It must have cost a lot of money."

"Not so much. Ten cents an' two inner wax seals from two jars of Ovaltine."

"May I see it?" My voice was trembling, and so was the hand I extended. He gave it to me and I held the miracle in the palm of my hand. It was *wonderful.*

You remember. *Captain Midnight* went on the radio nationwide in 1940. It was sponsored by Ovaltine. And every year they issued a Secret Squadron Decoder Badge. And every day at the end of the program, they would give you a clue to the next day's installment in a code that only kids with the official badge could decipher. They stopped making those wonderful Decoder Badges in 1949. I remember the one I had in 1945: it was beautiful. It had a magnifying glass in the center of the code dial. *Captain Midnight* went off the air in 1950, and though I understand it was a short-lived television series in the mid-Fifties, and though they issued Decoder Badges in 1955 and 1956, as far as the *real* badges were concerned, they never made one after 1949.

The Captain Midnight Code-O-Graph I held in my hand, the one Jeffty said he had gotten in the mail for ten cents (*ten cents*!!!) and two Ovaltine labels, was brand new, shiny gold metal, not a dent or a spot of rust on it like the old ones you can find at exorbitant prices in collectible shoppes from time to time . . . it was a *new* Decoder. And the date on it was *this* year.

But *Captain Midnight* no longer existed. Nothing like it existed on the radio. I'd listened to the one or two weak imitations of old-time radio the networks were currently airing, and the stories were dull, the sound effects bland, the whole feel of it wrong, out of date, cornball. Yet I held a *new* Code-O-Graph.

"Jeffty, tell me about this," I said.

"Tell you what, Donny? It's my new Capt'n Midnight Secret Decoder Badge. I use it to figger out what's gonna happen tomorrow."

"Tomorrow how?"

"On the program."

"*What* program?!"

He stared at me as if I was being purposely stupid. "On Capt'n *Mid*night! Boy!" I was being dumb.

I still couldn't get it straight. It was right there, right out in the open, and I still didn't know what was happening. "You mean one of those records they made of the old-time radio programs? Is that what you mean, Jeffty?"

"What records?" he asked. He didn't know what *I* meant.

We stared at each other, there under the porch. And then I said, very slowly, almost afraid of the answer, "Jeffty, how do you hear *Captain Midnight*?"

"Every day. On the radio. On my radio. Every day at five-thirty." News. Music, dumb music, and news. That's what was on the radio every day at 5:30. Not *Captain Midnight*. The Secret Squadron hadn't been on the air in twenty years.

"Can we hear it tonight?" I asked.

"Boy!" he said. I was being dumb. I knew it from the way he said it; but I didn't know *why*. Then it dawned on me: this was Saturday. *Captain Midnight* was on Monday through Friday. Not on Saturday or Sunday.

"We goin' to the movies?"

He had to repeat himself twice. My mind was somewhere else. Nothing definite. No conclusions. No wild assumptions leapt to. Just off somewhere trying to figure it out, and concluding—as *you* would have concluded, as *any*-one would have concluded rather than accepting the truth, the impossible and wonderful truth—just finally concluding there was a simple explanation I didn't yet perceive. Something mundane and dull, like the passage of time that steals all good, old things from us, packratting trinkets and plastic in exchange. And all in the name of Progress.

"We goin' to the movies, Donny?"

"You bet your boots we are, kiddo," I said. And I smiled. And I handed him the Code-O-Graph. And he put it in his side pants pocket. And we crawled out from under the porch. And we went to the movies. And neither of us said anything about *Captain Midnight* all the rest of that day. And there wasn't a ten-minute stretch, all the rest of that day, that I didn't think about it.

It was inventory all that next week. I didn't see Jeffty till late Thursday. I confess I left the store in the hands of Jan and David, told them I had some errands to run, and left early. At 4:00. I got to the Kinzers' right around 4:45. Leona answered the door, looking exhausted and distant. "Is Jeffty around?" She said he was upstairs in his room . . .

. . . listening to the radio.

I climbed the stairs two at a time.

All right, I had finally made that impossible, illogical leap. Had the stretch of belief involved anyone but Jeffty, adult or child, I would have reasoned out more explicable answers. But it *was* Jeffty, clearly another kind of vessel of life, and what he might experience should not be expected to fit into the ordered scheme.

I admit it: I *wanted* to hear what I heard.

Even with the door closed, I recognized the program:

"There he goes, Tennessee! Get him!"

There was the heavy report of a rifle shot and the keening whine of the slug ricocheting, and then the same voice yelled triumphantly, *"Got him! D-e-a-a-a-a-d center!"*

He was listening to the American Broadcasting Company, 790 kilocycles, and he was hearing *Tennessee Jed*, one of my most favorite programs from the Forties, a western adventure I had not heard in twenty years, because it had not existed for twenty years.

I sat down on the top step of the stairs, there in the upstairs hall of the Kinzer home, and I listened to the show. It wasn't a rerun of an old program, because there were occasional references in the body of the drama to current cultural and technological developments, and phrases that had not existed in common usage in the Forties: aerosol spray cans, laserasing of tattoos, Tanzania, the word "uptight."

I could not ignore the fact. Jeffty was listening to a *new* segment of *Tennessee Jed*.

I ran downstairs and out the front door to my car. Leona must have been in the kitchen. I turned the key and punched on the radio and spun the dial to 790 kilocycles. The ABC station. Rock music.

I sat there for a few moments, then ran the dial slowly from one end to the other. Music, news, talk shows. No *Tennessee Jed*. And it was a Blaupunkt, the best radio I could get. I wasn't missing some perimeter station. It simply was not there!

After a few moments I turned off the radio and the ignition and went back upstairs quietly. I sat down on the top step and listened to the entire program. It was *wonderful.*

Exciting, imaginative, filled with everything I remembered as being most innovative about radio drama. But it was modern. It wasn't an antique, re-broadcast to assuage the need of that dwindling listenership who longed for the old days. It was a new show, with all the old voices, but still young and bright. Even the commercials were for currently available products, but they weren't as loud or as insulting as the screamer ads one heard on radio these days.

And when *Tennessee Jed* went off at 5:00, I heard Jeffty spin the dial on his radio till I heard the familiar voice of the announcer Glenn Riggs proclaim, *"Presenting Hop Harrigan! America's ace of the airwaves!"* There was the sound of an airplane in flight. It was a prop plane, *not* a jet! Not the sound kids today have grown up with, but the sound *I* grew up with, the *real* sound of an airplane, the growling, revving, throaty sound of the kind of airplanes G-8 and His Battle Aces flew, the kind Captain Midnight flew, the kind

Hop Harrigan flew. And then I heard Hop say, "CX-4 *calling control tower. CX-4 calling control tower. Standing by!*" A pause, then, *"Okay, this is Hop Harrigan . . . coming in!"*

And Jeffty, who had the same problem all of us kids had had in the Forties with programming that pitted equal favorites against one another on different stations, having paid his respects to Hop Harrigan and Tank Tinker, spun the dial and went back to ABC, where I heard the stroke of a gong, the wild cacophony of nonsense Chinese chatter, and the announcer yelled, *"T-e-e-e-rry and the Pirates!"*

I sat there on the top step and listened to Terry and Connie and Flip Corkin and, so help me God, Agnes Moorehead as The Dragon Lady, all of them in a new adventure that took place in a Red China that had not existed in the days of Milton Caniff's 1937 version of the Orient, with river pirates and Chiang Kai-shek and warlords and the naïve Imperialism of American gunboat diplomacy.

Sat, and listened to the whole show, and sat even longer to hear *Superman* and part of *Jack Armstrong, The All American Boy* and part of *Captain Midnight*, and John Kinzer came home and neither he nor Leona came upstairs to find out what had happened to me, or where Jeffty was, and sat longer, and found I had started crying, and could not stop, just sat there with tears running down my face, into the corners of my mouth, sitting and crying until Jeffty heard me and opened his door and saw me and came out and looked at me in childish confusion as I heard the station break for the Mutual Network and they began the theme music of *Tom Mix*, "When It's Round-up Time in Texas and the Bloom Is on the Sage," and Jeffty touched my shoulder and smiled at me, with his mouth and his big brown eyes, and said, "Hi, Donny. Wanna come in an' listen to the radio with me?"

* * *

Hume denied the existence of an absolute space, in which each thing has its place; Borges denies the existence of one single time, in which all events are linked.

Jeffty received radio programs from a place that could not, in logic, in the natural scheme of the space-time universe as conceived by Einstein, exist. But that wasn't all he received. He got mail order premiums that no one was manufacturing. He read comic books that had been defunct for three decades. He saw movies with actors who had been dead for twenty years. He was the receiving terminal for endless joys and pleasures of the past that the world had dropped along the way. On its headlong suicidal flight toward New Tomorrows, the world had razed its treasurehouse of simple happinesses, had poured concrete over its playgrounds, had abandoned its elfin stragglers, and all of it was being impossibly, miraculously shunted back into the present through Jeffty. Revivified, updated, the traditions maintained but contemporaneous. Jeffty was the unbidding Aladdin whose very nature formed the magic lampness of his reality.

And he took me into his world with him.

Because he trusted me.

We had breakfast of Quaker Puffed Wheat Sparkies and warm Ovaltine we drank out of *this* year's Little Orphan Annie Shake-Up Mugs. We went to the movies and while everyone else was seeing a comedy starring Goldie Hawn and Ryan O'Neal, Jeffty and I were enjoying Humphrey Bogart as the professional thief Parker in John Huston's brilliant adaptation of the Donald Westlake novel SLAY-GROUND. The second feature was Spencer Tracy, Carole Lombard and Laird Cregar in the Val Lewton-produced film of *Leiningen Versus the Ants*.

Twice a month we went down to the newsstand and bought the current pulp issues of *The Shadow*, *Doc Savage* and *Startling Stories*. Jeffty and I sat together and I read to him from the magazines. He particularly liked the new short novel by Henry Kuttner, "The Dreams of Achilles," and the new Stanley G. Weinbaum series of short stories set in the subatomic particle universe of Redurna. In September we enjoyed the first installment of the new Robert E. Howard Conan novel, ISLE OF THE BLACK ONES, in *Weird Tales*; and in August we were only mildly disappointed by Edgar Rice Burroughs's fourth novella in the Jupiter series featuring John Carter of Barsoom—"Corsairs of Jupiter." But the editor of *Argosy All-Story Weekly* promised there would be two more stories in the series, and it was such an unexpected revelation for Jeffty and me that it dimmed our disappointment at the lessened quality of the current story.

We read comics together, and Jeffty and I both decided—separately, before we came together to discuss it—that our favorite characters were Doll Man, Airboy and The Heap. We also adored the George Carlson strips in *Jingle Jangle Comics*, particularly the Pie-Face Prince of Old Pretzleburg stories, which we read together and laughed over, even though I had to explain some of the esoteric puns to Jeffty, who was too young to have that kind of subtle wit.

How to explain it? I can't. I had enough physics in college to make some offhand guesses, but I'm more likely wrong than right. The laws of the conservation of energy occasionally break. These are laws that physicists call "weakly violated." Perhaps Jeffty was a catalyst for the weak violation of conservation laws we're only now beginning to realize exist. I tried doing some reading in the area—muon decay of the "forbidden" kind: gamma decay that doesn't include the muon neutrino among its products—but nothing I encountered, not even the latest readings from the Swiss Institute for Nuclear Research near Zurich gave me an insight. I was thrown back on a vague acceptance of the philosophy that the real name for "science" is *magic*.

No explanations, but enormous good times.

The happiest time of my life.

I had the "real" world, the world of my store and my friends and my family, the world of profit&loss, of taxes and evenings with young women who talked about going shopping or the United Nations, or the rising cost of coffee and microwave ovens. And I had Jeffty's world, in which I existed only when I was with him. The things of the past he knew as fresh and new, I could experience only when in his company. And the membrane between the two worlds grew ever thinner, more luminous and transparent. I had the best of both worlds. And knew, somehow, that I could carry nothing from one to the other.

Forgetting that, for just a moment, betraying Jeffty by forgetting, brought an end to it all.

Enjoying myself so much, I grew careless and failed to consider how fragile the relationship between Jeffty's world and my world really was. There is a reason why the present begrudges the existence of the past. I never really understood. Nowhere in the beast books, where survival is shown in battles between claw and fang, tentacle and poison sac, is there recognition of the ferocity the present always brings to bear on the past. Nowhere is there a detailed statement of how the present lies in wait for What-Was, waiting for it to become Now-This-Moment so it can shred it with its merciless jaws.

Who could know such a thing... at any age... and certainly not at my age... who could understand such a thing?

I'm trying to exculpate myself. I can't. It was my fault.

It was another Saturday afternoon.

"What's playing today?" I asked him, in the car, on the way downtown.

He looked up at me from the other side of the front seat and smiled one of his best smiles. "Ken Maynard in *Bull-*

whip Justice an' *The Demolished Man.*" He kept smiling, as if he'd really put one over on me. I looked at him with disbelief.

"You're *kid*ding!" I said, delighted. "Bester's THE DEMOL-ISHED MAN?" He nodded his head, delighted at my being delighted. He knew it was one of my favorite books. "Oh, that's super!"

"Super *duper*," he said.

"Who's in it?"

"Franchot Tone, Evelyn Keyes, Lionel Barrymore and Elisha Cook, Jr." He was much more knowledgeable about movie actors than I'd ever been. He could name the character actors in any movie he'd ever seen. Even the crowd scenes.

"And cartoons?" I asked.

"Three of 'em: a *Little Lulu*, a *Donald Duck* and a *Bugs Bunny*. An' a *Pete Smith Specialty* an' a *Lew Lehr Monkeys is da C-r-r-r-aziest Peoples.*"

"Oh boy!" I said. I was grinning from ear to ear. And then I looked down and saw the pad of purchase order forms on the seat. I'd forgotten to drop it off at the store.

"Gotta stop by the Center," I said. "Gotta drop off something. It'll only take a minute."

"Okay," Jeffty said. "But we won't be late, will we?"

"Not on your tintype, kiddo," I said.

When I pulled into the parking lot behind the Center, he decided to come in with me and we'd walk over to the theater. It's not a large town. There are only two movie houses, the Utopia and the Lyric. We were going to the Utopia and it was only three blocks from the Center.

I walked into the store with the pad of forms, and it was bedlam. David and Jan were handling two customers each, and there were people standing around waiting to be helped. Jan turned a look on me and her face was a horror-mask of pleading. David was running from the stockroom to the showroom and all he could murmur as he whipped past was "Help!" and then he was gone.

"Jeffty," I said, crouching down, "listen, give me a few minutes. Jan and David are in trouble with all these people. We won't be late, I promise. Just let me get rid of a couple of these customers." He looked nervous, but nodded okay.

I motioned to a chair and said, "Just sit down for a while and I'll be right with you."

He went to the chair, good as you please, though he knew what was happening, and he sat down.

I started taking care of people who wanted color television sets. This was the first really substantial batch of units we'd gotten in—color television was only now becoming reasonably priced and this was Sony's first promotion—and it was bonanza time for me. I could see paying off the loan and being out in front for the first time with the Center. It was business.

In my world, good business comes first.

Jeffty sat there and stared at the wall. Let me tell you about the wall.

Stanchion and bracket designs had been rigged from floor to within two feet of the ceiling. Television sets had been stacked artfully on the wall. Thirty-three television sets. All playing at the same time. Black and white, color, little ones, big ones, all going at the same time.

Jeffty sat and watched thirty-three television sets, on a Saturday afternoon. We can pick up a total of thirteen channels, including the UHF educational stations. Golf was on one channel; baseball was on a second; celebrity bowling was on a third; the fourth channel was a religious seminar; a teenage dance show was on the fifth; the sixth was a rerun of a situation comedy; the seventh was a rerun of a police show; eighth was a nature program showing a man flycasting endlessly; ninth was news and conversation; tenth was a stock car race; eleventh was a man doing logarithms on a blackboard; twelfth was a woman in a leotard doing setting-up exercises; and on the thirteenth channel was a badly animated cartoon show in Spanish. All but six of the shows were repeated on three sets. Jeffty sat and watched that wall of television on a Saturday afternoon while I sold as fast and as hard as I could, to pay back my Aunt Patricia and stay in touch with my world. It was business.

I should have known better. I should have understood about the present and the way it kills the past. But I was selling with both hands. And when I finally glanced over at Jeffty, half an hour later, he looked like another child.

He was sweating. That terrible fever sweat when you have stomach flu. He was pale, as pasty and pale as a worm, and his little hands were gripping the arms of the chair so tightly I could see his knuckles in bold relief. I dashed over to him, excusing myself from the middle-aged couple looking at the new 21" Mediterranean model.

"Jeffty!"

He looked at me, but his eyes didn't track. He was in absolute terror. I pulled him out of the chair and started toward the front door with him, but the customers I'd deserted yelled at me, "Hey!" The middle-aged man said, "You wanna sell me this thing or don't you?"

I looked from him to Jeffty and back again. Jeffty was like a zombie. He had come where I'd pulled him. His legs were rubbery and his feet dragged. The past, being eaten by the present, the sound of something in pain.

I clawed some money out of my pants pocket and jammed it into Jeffty's hand. "Kiddo . . . listen to me . . . get out of here right now!" He still couldn't focus properly.

"Jeffty," I said as tightly as I could, *"listen* to me!" The middle-aged customer and his wife were walking toward us. "Listen, kiddo, get out of here right this minute. Walk over to the Utopia and buy the tickets. I'll be right behind you." The middle-aged man and his wife were almost on us. I shoved Jeffty through the door and watched him stumble away in the wrong direction, then stop as if gathering his wits, turn and go back past the front of the Center and in the direction of the Utopia. "Yes sir," I said, straightening up and facing them, "yes, ma'am, that is one terrific set with some sensational features! If you'll just step back here with me . . ."

There was a terrible sound of something hurting, but I couldn't tell from which channel, or from which set, it was coming.

Most of it I learned later, from the girl in the ticket booth, and from some people I knew who came to me to tell me what had happened. By the time I got to the Utopia, nearly twenty minutes later, Jeffty was already beaten to a pulp and had been taken to the Manager's office.

"Did you see a very little boy, about five years old, with big brown eyes and straight brown hair . . . he was waiting for me?"

"Oh, I think that's the little boy those kids beat up?"

"What!?! *Where is he?"*

"They took him to the Manager's office. No one knew who he was or where to find his parents—"

A young girl wearing an usher's uniform was kneeling down beside the couch, placing a wet paper towel on his face.

I took the towel away from her and ordered her out of the office.

She looked insulted and snorted something rude, but she left. I sat on the edge of the couch and tried to swab away the blood from the lacerations without opening the wounds where the blood had caked. Both his eyes were swollen shut. His mouth was ripped badly. His hair was matted with dried blood.

He had been standing in line behind two kids in their teens. They started selling tickets at 12:30 and the show started at 1:00. The doors weren't opened till 12:45. He had been waiting, and the kids in front of him had had a portable radio. They were listening to the ball game. Jeffty had wanted to hear some program, God knows what it might have been, *Grand Central Station, Let's Pretend, Land of the Lost,* God only knows which one it might have been.

He had asked if he could borrow their radio to hear the program for a minute, and it had been a commercial break or something, and the kids had given him the radio, probably out of some malicious kind of courtesy that would permit them to take offense and rag the little boy. He had changed the station . . . and they'd been unable to get it to go back to the ball game. It was locked into the past, on a station that was broadcasting a program that didn't exist for anyone but Jeffty.

They had beaten him badly . . . as everyone watched.

And then they had run away.

I had left him alone, left him to fight off the present without sufficient weaponry. I had betrayed him for the sale of a 21" Mediterranean console television, and now his face was pulped meat. He moaned something inaudible and sobbed softly.

"Shhh, it's okay, kiddo, it's Donny. I'm here. I'll get you home, it'll be okay."

I should have taken him straight to the hospital. I don't know why I didn't. I should have. I should have done that.

* * *

When I carried him through the door, John and Leona Kinzer just stared at me. They didn't move to take him from my arms. One of his hands was hanging down. He was conscious, but just barely. They stared, there in the semi-darkness of a Saturday afternoon in the present. I looked at them. "A couple of kids beat him up at the theater." I raised him a few inches in my arms and extended him. They stared at me, at both of us, with nothing in their eyes, without movement. "Jesus Christ," I shouted, "he's been beaten! He's your son! Don't you even want to touch him? What the hell kind of people are you?!"

Then Leona moved toward me very slowly. She stood in front of us for a few seconds, and there was a leaden stoicism in her face that was terrible to see. It said, *I have been in this place before, many times, and I cannot bear to be in it again; but I am here now.*

So I gave him to her. God help me, I gave him over to her.

And she took him upstairs to bathe away his blood and his pain.

John Kinzer and I stood in our separate places in the dim living room of their home, and we stared at each other. He had nothing to say to me.

I shoved past him and fell into a chair. I was shaking.

I heard the bath water running upstairs.

After what seemed a very long time Leona came downstairs, wiping her hands on her apron. She sat down on the sofa and after a moment John sat down beside her. I heard the sound of rock music from upstairs.

"Would you like a piece of nice pound cake?" Leona said.

I didn't answer. I was listening to the sound of the music. Rock music. On the radio. There was a table lamp on the end table beside the sofa. It cast a dim and futile light in the shadowed living room. *Rock music from the present, on a radio upstairs?* I started to say something, and then *knew . . .* Oh, God . . . *no!*

I jumped up just as the sound of hideous crackling blotted out the music, and the table lamp dimmed and dimmed and flickered. I screamed something, I don't know what it was, and ran for the stairs.

Jeffty's parents did not move. They sat there with their hands folded, in that place they had been for so many years.

I fell twice rushing up the stairs.

There isn't much on television that can hold my interest. I bought an old cathedral-shaped Philco radio in a second-hand store, and I replaced all the burnt-out parts with the original tubes from old radios I could cannibalize that still worked. I don't use transistors or printed circuits. They wouldn't work. I've sat in front of that set for hours sometimes, running the dial back and forth as slowly as you can imagine, so slowly it doesn't look as if it's moving at all sometimes.

But I can't find *Captain Midnight* or *The Land of the Lost* or *The Shadow* or *Quiet, Please*.

So she did love him, still, a little bit, even after all those years. I can't hate them: they only wanted to live in the present world again. That isn't such a terrible thing.

It's a good world, all things considered. It's much better than it used to be, in a lot of ways. People don't die from the old diseases any more. They die from new ones, but that's Progress, isn't it?

Isn't it?

Tell me.

Somebody please tell me.

FREE WITH THIS BOX!

Here's where we part company. You've been extremely patient with me, and I know you understand that I've been a little loose and twitchy from the start, directing this at people your age for the first time. So I am in your debt, and I thank you. So by way of a proper gracious "bread 'n' butter" gift for your indulgence, I'm going to leave you with this last story. The thing of it is, there were only supposed to be 15 stories in this book, ending with what may be one of my best ones, "Jeffty is Five." But after I sent the book in to my editor and publisher, I thought about it, and I knew I had to add "Free With This Box!" to the collection because, well, it's as close to a recounting of what trouble I've been in all my life as I have handy. Oh, hell, I've written whole *books* of essays and columns and commentaries and reviews, many of which include anecdotes about my weird span; but in this story, which I wrote a long time ago, I took something that had actually happened to me, when I was a little kid, and I only fictionalized it a little bit. It is a *story*, yeah, not a memoir, but it is clear and clarion me-speaking-to-you warning about what it means to live the kind of life I've lived, amazing and fulfilling as it has been. There is a line I remember from the journalist and madman Hunter S. Thompson, in which he speaks about "the dead end loneliness of a man who makes his own rules." I recall it now, as I get ready to bid you fond farewell, because if there is a lesson above all others contained in this volume, it is this: be your own person. Be kind, be ethical, be honorable and courageous; respect your friends, keep your word, treat your enemies with honor if you can but spin 'em if they won't let you treat them that way; don't believe the okeydoke that people who're trying to sell you something lay on you, remember True Love only happens when you have no fear and can laugh about it, and you cannot possibly be too smart. Above all, be your own person. Never blame bad luck, or fate, or "the breaks," or paranoid delusions about conspiracies for what your life has become. You are now, and you will *always* be, in charge of your destiny. What was that line out of *Buckaroo Bonzai* . . . oh yeah, I remember . . . "Never forget: no matter where you go, there you are." Here I am, the product of what I've made of myself, in trouble from the git-go; and there *you* are, looking at me looking at you. Wherever you are, kid, remember, I'm there, too. Take care of yourself. Don't step on no broken glass.

His name was David Thomas Cooper. His mother called him Davey, and his teachers called him David, but he was old enough now to be called the way the guys called him: Dave. After all, eight years old was no longer a child. He was big enough to walk to school himself, and he was big enough to stay up till eight-thirty any weeknight.

Mommy had said last year, "For every birthday, we will let you stay up a half hour later," and she had kept her word. The way he figured it, a few more years, and he could stay up all night, almost.

He was a slim boy, with unruly black hair that cowlicked up in the back, and slipped over his forehead in the front. He had an angular face, and wide deep eyes of black, and he sucked his thumb when he was sure no one was watching.

And right now, right this very minute, the thing he wanted most in all the world was a complete set of the buttons.

Davey reached into his pants pocket, and brought out

the little cloth bag with the drawstring. Originally it had held his marbles, but now they were back home in his room, in an empty Red Goose shoe box. Now the little bag held the buttons. He turned sidewise on the car seat, and pried open the bag with two fingers. The buttons clinked metallically. There were twenty-four of them in there. He had taken the pins off them, because he wasn't a gook like Leon, who wore *his* on his beanie. Davey liked to lay the buttons out on the table, and arrange them in different designs. It wasn't so much that they had terrific pictures on them, though each one contained the face of a familiar comic character, but it was just *having* them.

He felt so good when he thought that there were only eight more to get.

Just Skeezix, Little Orphan Annie, Andy Gump, the Little King, B.O. Plenty, Mandrake the Magician, Harold Teen and—the scarcest one of them all—Dick Tracy. Then he would have the entire set, and he would beat out Roger and Hobby and even Leon across the street.

Then he would have the whole set offered by the cereal company. And it wasn't just the competition with the other kids; he couldn't quite explain it, but it was a feeling of *accomplishment* every time he got a button he did not already have. When he had them all, just those last eight, he would be the happiest boy in the world.

But it was dangerous, and Davey knew it.

It wasn't that Mommy wouldn't buy him the boxes of Pep. They were only 23¢ a box, and Mommy bought one each week, but that was only *one* comic character button a week! Not hardly enough to get the full set before they stopped putting the buttons in and offered something new. Because there was always so much *duplication*, and Davey had three Superman buttons (they were the *easiest* to get) while Hobby only had one Dick Tracy. And Hobby wouldn't trade. So Davey had had to figure out a way to get more buttons.

There were thirty-two glossy, colored buttons in the set. Each one in a cellophane packet at the bottom of every box of Pep.

One day, when he had gone shopping with Mommy, he had detached himself from her, and wandered to the cereal shelves. There he had taken one of the boxes down, and before he had quite known what he was doing, had shoved his forefinger through the cardboard, where the wall and bottom joined. He could still remember his wild elation at feeling the edge of the packet. He had stuck in another finger widening the rip in the box, and scissored out the button.

That had been the time he had gotten Annie's dog Sandy.

That had been the time he had known he could not wait for Mommy to buy his box a week. Because that was the time he got Sandy, and no one, not *anyone* in the whole neighborhood, had even seen that button. That had been the time.

So Davey had carefully and assiduously cajoled Mommy every week, when she went to the A&P. It had seemed surprising at first, but Mommy loved Davey, and there was no trouble about it.

That first week, when he had gotten Sandy, he had figured out that it was not wise to be in the A&P with Mommy, because she might discover what he was doing. And though he felt no guilt about it, he knew he was doing wrong . . . and he would just die if Mommy knew about it. She might wander down the aisle where he stood—pretending to read the print on the back of the box, but actually fishing about in the side for the cellophane packet—and see him. Or they might catch him, and hold him, and she would be called to identify this naughty boy who was stealing.

So he had thought up the trick of waiting in the car, playing with the buttons in the bag, till Mommy came from the A&P with the boy, and they loaded the bags in, and then she would kiss him and tell him he was such a good boy for waiting quietly, and she would be right back after she had gone to the Polish Bakery across the street, and stopped into the Woolworth's.

Davey knew how long that took. Almost half an hour.

More than long enough to punch holes in ten or twelve boxes, and drag out the buttons that lay within. He usually found at least two new ones. At first—that second week he had gone with Mommy to do the shopping—he had gotten more than that. Five or six. But with the eventual increase in duplication, he was overjoyed to find even one new button.

Now there were only eight left, and he emptied the little cloth bag onto the car seat, making certain no buttons slipped between the cushions.

He turned them all up, so their rounded tops were full toward him. He rotated them so the Phantom and Secret Agent X-9 were not upside-down. Then he put them in rows of four; six rows with four in a row. Then he put them in rows of eight. Then he just scooted them back into the bag and jingled them hollowly at his ear.

It was the *having*, that was all.

"How long have I been?" Mommy asked from outside the window. Behind, at her right, a fat, sweating boy with pimples on his forehead held a big box, high to his chest.

He didn't answer her, because the question had never really been asked. Mommy had that habit. She asked him questions, and was always a little surprised when he answered. Davey had learned to distinguish between questions like, "Where did you put your bedroom slippers?" and "Isn't this a lovely hat Mommy's bought?"

So he did not answer, but watched with the interest of a

conspirator waiting for the coast to clear, as Mommy opened the front door, and pushed the seat far forward so the boy could put the box in the back seat. Davey had to scrunch far forward against the dashboard when she did that, but he liked the pressure of the seat on his back.

Then she leaned over and kissed him, which he liked, but which made his hair fall over his forehead, and Mommy's eyes crinkled up the nice way, and she smoothed back his hair. Then she slammed the door, and walked across the street, to the bakery.

Then, when Mommy had gone into the bakery, he got out of the car, and walked across the summer sidewalk to the A&P. It was simple getting in, and he knew where the cereals were brightly stacked. Down one aisle, and into a second, and there, halfway down, he saw the boxes.

A new supply! A new batch of boxes since last week, and for an instant he was cold and terrified that they had stopped packing the comic buttons, that they were offering something worthless like towels or cut-outs or something.

But as he came nearer, his heart jumped brightly in him, and he saw the words FREE WITH THIS BOX! on them.

Yes, those were the boxes with the comic buttons.

Oh, it was going to be a wonderful day, and he hummed the little tune he had made up that went:

"*Got a nickel in my pocket,*
"*Gonna spend it all today.*
"*Got my buttons in my pocket,*
"*Gonna get the rest today.*"

Then he was in front of them, and he had the first one in his hands. He held the box face-toward-him, hands at the bottom on the sides, and he was pressing, pressing his fingers into the cardboard joint. It was sometimes difficult, and the skin between his first and second fingers was raw and cracked from rubbing against the boxes. This time, however, the seam split, and he had his fingers inside.

The packet was far from over and he had to grope, tearing the box a little more. His fingers split the wax paper liner that held the cereal away from the box, but in a moment he had his finger down on the packet and was dragging it out.

It was another Sandy.

He felt an unhappiness like no other he had ever known except the day he got his new trike, and scratched it taking it out the driveway. It was an all-consuming thing, and he would have cried right there, except he knew there were more boxes. He shoved the button back in, because that wouldn't be the right thing to do—to take a button he already had. That would be waste, and dishonest.

He took a second box. Then a third, then a fourth, then a fifth.

By the time he had opened eight boxes, he had not found a new one, and was getting desperate, because Mommy would be back soon, and he had to be there when she came to the car. He was starting his ninth box, the others all put back where they had come from, but all crooked, because the ripped part on their bottom made them sit oddly, when the man in the white A&P jacket came by.

He had been careful to stop pushing and dragging when anyone came by . . . had pretended to be just reading what the boxes said . . . but he did not see the A&P man.

"Hey! What're ya doin' there?"

The man's voice was heavy and gruff, and Davey felt himself get cold all the way from his stomach to his head. Then the man had a hand around Davey's shoulder, and was turning him roughly. Davey's hand was still inside the box. The man stared for an instant, then his eyes widened.

"So *you're* the one's been costin' us so much dough!"

Davey was sure he would never forget that face if he lived to be a thousand or a million or forever.

The man had eyebrows that were bushy and grew together in the middle, with long hairs that flopped out all over. He had a mole on his chin, and a big pencil behind one ear. The man was staring down at Davey with so much anger, Davey was certain he would wither under the glance in a moment.

"Come on, you, I'm takin' you to the office."

Then he took Davey to a little cubicle behind the meat counter, and sat Davey down, and asked him, "What's your name?"

Davey would not answer.

The worst thing, the most worst thing in the world, would be if Mommy found out about this. Then she would tell Daddy when he came home from the store, and Daddy would be even madder, and spank him with his strap.

So Davey would not tell the man a thing, and when the man looked through Davey's pockets and found the bag with the buttons, he said, "Oh, *ho*. Now I *know* you're the one!" and he looked some more.

Finally he said, "You got no wallet. Now either you tell me who you are, who your parents are, or I take you down to the police station."

Still Davey would say nothing, though he felt tears starting to urge themselves from his eyes. And the man pushed a button on a thing on his desk, and when a woman came in—she had on a white jacket belted at the waist—the moley man said, "Mert, I want you to take over for me for a little while. I've just discovered the thief who has been breaking open all those boxes of cereal. I'm taking him," and the moley man gave a big wink to the woman named Mert, "down to the police station. That's where *all* bad thieves go, and I'll let *them* throw him into a cell for years and years, since he won't tell me his name."

So Mert nodded and clucked her tongue and said what a shame it was that such a little boy was such a big thief, and even, "Ooyay onday ontway ootay airscay the idkay ootay uchmay."

Davey knew that was pig Latin, but he didn't know it as well as Hobby or Leon, so he didn't know what they were saying, even when the moley man answered, "Onay, I ustjay ontway ootay ootpay the earfay of odgay in ishay edhay."

Then he thought that it was all a joke, and they would let him go, but even if they didn't, it wasn't anything to be frightened of, because Mommy had told him lots of times that the policemen were his friends, and they would protect him. He *liked* policemen, so he didn't care.

Except that if they took him to the policemen, when Mommy came back from the Woolworth's, he would be gone, and *then* would he be in trouble.

But he could not say anything. It was just not right to speak to this moley man. So he walked beside the man from the A&P when he took Davey by the arm and walked him out the back door and over to a pickup truck with a big A&P lettered on the side. He even sat silently when they drove through town, and turned in at the police station.

And he was silent as the moley man said to the big, fat, red-faced policeman with the sweat-soaked shirt, "This is a little thief I found in the store today, Al. He has been breaking into our boxes, and I thought you would want to throw him in a cell."

Then he winked at the big beefy policeman, and the policeman winked back, and grinned, and then his face got very stern and hard, and he leaned across the desk, staring at Davey.

"What's your name, boy?"

His voice was like a lot of mushy stuff swirling around in Mommy's washer. But even so, Davey would have told him his name was David Thomas Cooper and that he lived at 744 Terrace Drive, Mayfair, Ohio . . . if the moley man had not been there.

So he was silent, and the policeman looked up at the moley man, and said very loudly, looking at Davey from the corner of his brown eyes, "Well, Ben, it looks like I'll have to take harsher methods with this criminal. I'll have to show him what happens to people who steal!"

He got up, and Davey saw he was big and fat, and not at all the way Mommy had described policemen. The beefy man took him by the hand, and led him down a corridor, with the moley man coming along too, saying, "Say, ya know, I never been through your drunk tank, Chief. Mind if I tag along?" and the beefy man answered no.

Then came a time of horror for Davey.

They took him to a room where a man lay on a dirty bunk, and he stank and there were summer flies all over him, and he had been sick all over the floor and the mattress, and he was lying in it, and Davey wanted to throw up. There was a place with bars on it where a man tried to grab at them as they went past, and the policeman hit his hand through the bars with a big stick on a cord. There were lots of people cooped up and unhappy, and the place was all stinky, and in a little while, Davey was awfully frightened, and started to cry, and wanted to go hide himself, or go home.

Finally, they came back to the first place they had been, and the policeman crouched down next to Davey and shook him as hard as he could by the shoulders, and screamed at him never, never, never to do anything illegal again, or they would throw him in with the man who had clawed out, and throw away the key, and let the man eat Davey alive.

And that made Davey cry more.

Which seemed to make the policeman and the moley man happy, because Davey heard the policeman say to the moley man named Ben from the A&P, "That'll straighten him out. He's so young, making the right kind of impression on 'em now is what counts. He won't bother ya again, Ben. Leave him here, and he'll ask for his folks soon enough. Then we can take him home."

The moley man shook hands with the policeman, and thanked him, and said he could get any cut of meat he wanted at the store whenever he came in, and thanks again for the help.

Then, just as the moley man was leaving, he stooped down, and looked straight at Davey with his piercing eyes.

"You ever gonna steal anything from cereal boxes again?"

Davey was so frightened; he shook his head no, and the tear lines on his face felt sticky as he moved.

The moley man stood up, and grinned at the policeman, and walked out, leaving Davey behind, in that place that scared him so.

And it was true.

Davey never *would* steal from the cereal boxes again, he knew. As a matter of fact, he hated cereal now.

And he didn't much care for *cops*, either.